CW00867441

'With My Little Eye'

Jacky Strong.

ISBN 978-1-4716-0867-4

Table of Contents

BBC news.....Unemployment has reached over one million for the first time since the nineteen thirties. The Prime Minister Mr Edward Heath spoke in Parliament and said..............

We started training.

"Come on move, get fell in." We rumbled out of the quarters, a big four storey building. It had been built by the Germans in the run up to the Second World War and now the British Army occupied the barracks. It was January 1972, there was a biting wind sweeping across the parade ground. We lined up in three ranks and the N.C.O.s made sure we were standing up straight.

Major Ellis (DSO) came down the steps. He normally did not come out for daily parades, so something was up. He was followed by his side kick Captain John Cook, he always walked a quarter of a step behind Ellis like a well trained dog.

Sergeant Major Bill Stone brought us to attention, turned and saluted Ellis, then with a stamp of his feet marched to his place on the parade. Ellis, with his weedy voice gave us the command to stand at ease.

"We've just received the orders from Brigade Head Quarters," he paused and just had a quick look at his notes to make sure of the dates. "We are going to Northern Ireland on the 24th March. It's for a tour of 4 months and we will be serving as an infantry unit."

There was a hubbub ran through the ranks, each man with his own excitement or dread, each man with his own agenda.

"Quiet." Stone brought some order back to the parade.

Ellis continued, "We will be based in Belfast and will start training with immediate effect." He looked over to Stone. "Let the men fall out Sergeant Major." He saluted Stone, Cook following suit. Then both of them disappeared into the warm.

Stone returned the salute and turned to the parade.

"PARADE, PARADE, SHUN." We all moved to his time "PARADE, DISSSSS...MISS." A sharp turn to the left, a stamping of feet and we broke off.

We all gathered round in groups and I was drawn to my section. Our troop consisted of four sections of ten men with a Corporal and a Lance Corporal, but as normal most of the sections were undermanned. We also had a Troop officer and a Sergeant.

Jock was the first to speak. "Will we lose our overseas allowance?"

I burst out laughing. "Trust you to think of that." Jock was a typical Glaswegian. Eddie Wright, our section leader, a married man with two kids, must have been dreading this call up. "Shut up and listen, you sweaty little Scot. We need to wake our ideas up, especially you." He scowled at Jock.

"I'm not going if it means a pay cut." The Scot kept his line.

"You won't lose your overseas, because you're still based in Germany, and you don't have a choice." Eddie wanted time to think. "Look everyone go to the NAAFI get a cup of tea and be down the MT park for." He looked at his watch "...ten thirty."

I looked around the square, men were milling around and generally talking excitedly. There seemed to be two camps, married men, who were worried and the single men who would get some excitement after years of training. We ambled over to the canteen, glad to get out of the cold.

Gaff Gaffy a short stocky man, a pragmatic Yorkshire-man always good tempered, always seeing the funny side of life, poked me in the ribs. "Get them seats over there, I'll get the teas in." He held out his hand for the money, he wasn't that generous. I gave him a few coins.

"Get me a jam doughnut as well." I made my way over to one of the few empty tables. There was an amazing amount of excitement running through the hall. As I sat down I saw Tom Edwards just leaving the front of the queue. He saw me and made his way through the crowd. He sat down with his two cups of tea laced with sugar and a plate of buns. He had a massive appetite, but he didn't have a pinch of fat on him. He played for the regimental football and rugby teams and in his spare time would swim up and down the baths.

"Well I joined up to shoot someone, so now I'll get me chance."

I knew he made statements like this all the time, so wasn't surprised. I had stopped taking the bait a long time ago. He also was heading for the world record for marrying. He was only twenty and had been married twice, divorced twice. He said he didn't think one night stands were fair on the girls. I'd replied, "Why not just get engaged for the night?"

"Are you looking forward to the tour?" I probed.

"Hell yes, the tarts are very pretty there, and they fuck for buttons." He kept his mouth full all the time; he filled his mouth up again, "...and we'll get a medal."

"You're not going for more wedding cake are you?" I loved the subject of his marriages.

Gaff arrived with his hands full of cups and plates.

"Shift your arse." Tom as usual was taking up most of the table. He pulled back a bit and finished off his buns and washed them down with the last of his tea. He leaned back in his seat and lit a cigarette, and keeping in character, blew smoke in my face while I quietly munched on my doughnut.

"Eddie seems pissed off about Belfast." Gaff said.

"Well you'd miss nookie every night and your own bed." Tom's misconception of marriage showing itself again.

I finished off my doughnut and open my cigarette packet. "Well, I think I'm going to enjoy this tour." I watched them for their reaction.

"Yep, better than sitting around here waiting for the Russkies to come." Gaff was in the same camp as me. We had been building bridges and blowing them up for two years all together and we were ready for a change. We wanted to be back to where the women spoke English. A change was as good as a rest.

Simon Rutter came over to our table and sat down. Nobody ever called him Simon; in true army fashion we called him Wally after something that happened to him in training camp. He was a slight man, happy go lucky and with an easy laugh.

10

"We start training on Monday," he said and started to eat his bun.

"Well it'll be better than building bridges at midnight." Gaff replied.

I went into one of those mini daydreams. Nobody knew I had been brought up in Belfast. It never occurred to me to tell anyone; my accent was Liverpudlian. I started to think of the streets I had been brought up in, remembering people who I had known. Would they recognize me? Would I be on my old patch?

At that moment, there was a scraping of chairs on the concrete floor as men started to make their way back to their units. Gaff slapped me on the back of my head with the back of his hand.

"Come on hero." I came to and followed the rest.

There was a biting wind as we made our way back to the motor transport sheds and we grabbed a last fag as we entered. Normally we would have been cleaning the APC, or checking our kit and making sure that everything that should be sharp was sharp, or making sure that everything that should be clean was clean. We did the basic maintenance on the APC ourselves, changing oil, greasing up the tracks and making sure the air filters were working, and most of all painting the damned thing. But that day was different. We piled into the back and closed the door. We left the top open.

Eddie had composed himself, he had a fag hanging out of his lip.

He nodded at Jock, "Get a brew going." But we all mucked in; that's the way it was in such a small space. The pump stove was produced and lit, someone found a kettle and we all had our mugs, teabags and dried milk ready, next to the driver's seat; our only spoon was hidden in the top shelf next to the first aid kit and the gas-masks.

"Where's the fucking sugar?" We all looked blank, we all knew that we had run out. We all took sugar, we all took loads of sugar. Everyone looked at me. When anything was needed it was my job to steal it. I don't know how it started, but I once had to find a camouflage net and the engine to an assault boat one hour before handover. Ever after that, even the officers would make a list and expect me to replace all sorts of missing things. Everyone turned to me.

"Boil the water and give me a minute." I disappeared out of the back door of the wagon. The cookhouse was a three minute walk away, but I didn't want to miss the sentiment in the wagon so I ran. I went in through the back door of the cookhouse, straight past the dishwashing staff and into the main kitchen and bumped into Sergeant Todd in his full whites and a very tall cook's hat, telling me he was top dog.

"Excuse me Sergeant, I've been sent by Sergeant Major Stone." I put my humble face on. "He's asked if he could have some sugar, his office has run out." He looked around the cookhouse, everyone was busy preparing the lunch for the regiment. He led me through to the dry storeroom and filled a brown paper bag with sugar and as an afterthought, gave me a massive tin of coffee. I looked at him, we both knew this was wrong, but I was in too deep now, so took the tin.

"Tell him I'll see him at the mess tonight." I thought shit no, now I've torn it, they're buddies. "He needs to play bridge better than last week."

"I'll tell him." I said weakly and made my way back to the wagon. The back of the wagon was nice and warm and there were yelps of joy when they saw the tin of coffee. I kept my mouth shut about how I had come by it.

"All engineering training is out of the window." Eddie was filling us in while we carried on making coffee and generally making a mess. "I've had a quick look at the training schedule and it looks good." We sniggered, we had heard it all before.

Eddie went on, "We start on Monday, fitness, yellow card, riot control, intelligence, weapon training and ....." He droned on listing all the training we would be doing over the next few months, we carried on making coffee and smoking and only half listening to him.

Meanwhile, in his office, Major Ellis was being handed a memo by the duty clerk,

Memo; Ref order 113211.

To Major E. Ellis,

7 Squadron,

1174 Engineer Regiment,

Dear Sir,

> *Due to the shortage of Intelligence personnel at this point in time, and the on-going problems in Northern Ireland, we need 3 personnel to assist during this tour. These personnel will be required for the full tour. They must have 2 years' experience. We look forward to your help in this matter.*

Yours respectfully,

Lt-Col G. Allen.

Ellis looked at the memo and wondered why, when a unit was preparing for their first action in years, they would take away much needed personnel for intelligence duties. He walked to the door, "Thomas." He shouted down the corridor. The clerk came on the double.

"Sir." Thomas stood at the door.

Ellis looked up from the memo, "Get me the sergeant major." He went back and re-read the memo. Bill Stone wandered down the corridor to Ellis's office. "Close the door please Sergeant Major." He handed the memo to Stone, and after reading it, Stone looked at Ellis.

"Can we stop this?"

"I don't think so sir."

Stone knew it was tight for manpower. His mind went into overdrive, mentally selecting the worst, wackiest and least able.

"I want you to select the men who we send and I'll also make sure that we have an influx of men from the next intake coming out of basic training." Stone stood up, he was already making a list in his head.

"Just leave it with me sir." He made his way back to his office. Now his mind was on the bridge game tonight; there was plenty of time to choose who to get rid of.

In the wagon, smoke thick in the air, we were starting to warm to the idea of Belfast and were speculating.

"Bet I'm first to shoot one of the bastards." Jock always liked to reduce it down to violence.

Gaff lifted his leg and let out a noisy fart. "Piss off, you couldn't hit a barn door with a banjo." He took a deep breath to take in the aroma.

"Open the back door for fuck sake." Smoke and foul air leaked out of the back of the A.P.C. but we stayed inside. We were used to this sort of thing. We carried on musing about what we were going to do on the tour.

That evening, Todd stood at the sergeants' mess bar drinking with Sergeant Stone. After the initial chat about the posting to Northern Ireland, he remembered his gift to Stone. "Did you get the coffee?" Todd looked at Stone for some sort of recognition for the favour. Stone paid the barman and turned to Todd with a questioning look on his face.

"What coffee?" They walked to the tables and took a seat.

"The coffee and sugar, I sent them over with your runner, the ugly little twat you sent in this morning for sugar." Stone thought about this.

"I don't send for sugar, the clerk runs that sort of thing." He took a long pull on his pint.

"Well that little twat Deery, the cocky sod came in this morning and asked for sugar for your office. And I gave him a big tin of coffee too." Stone could feel his face flush; he did not like Deery, just something about him.

"Leave it with me." It was at this point Deery went to the top of the list. Stone decided he needed to get rid of shirkers like Deery. Their minds turned to the night's bridge tactics.

The next morning Stone went into Ellis's office.

"Good morning Sir." He laid down the list of men who he wanted out before they had live rounds up the spout, before those little mistakes could cost lives, before the action started. Ellis glanced at the list, all the usual suspects were on the list.

"Thank you Sergeant Major." Ellis put the list to one side and leaned back in his chair and put his hands behind his head.

"How did the bridge go?" He played for the officers' mess, and liked to keep abreast of what was happening in the enemy camp.

Memo ;Ref order 113211

To Lt-Col. G. Allen

MI 3rd Battalion.

Johnson's Barracks.

26 Jan 1972

Dear Sir,
After due consideration of your position, and with the man power at our command, we have selected 3 men whom we consider to be best suited to the task. These personnel will be sent to your Depot on Monday 13 March.

The men will be expected back to the Regiment immediately after tour. We hope this meets with your satisfaction.

Maj. T. E. Ellis. DSM.

We carried on training. Out on the firing ranges, we got to use some of the more unusual weapons. Each man was given the chance to fire a Carl Gustav 84mm and throw hand grenades. We needed this experience mainly because we were an engineering unit and had not been trained in anything but the rifle and pistols. In the class room we did memory training, history of Northern Ireland, riot training, politics, yellow card and intelligence. But the main thing was team building and fitness. They ran us ragged, pushing us to the very end of our tether.

After our final day's training, we piled out of the wagon, wet through, our weapons covered in dirt and needing to be cleaned before being handed in to the armoury. Normally at the end of each day, everyone would have a quick glance at the orders posted on the notice board, but not this evening.

"What have you been up to?" Wally Rutter stuck his head in my room to give me the bad news. I could tell by his voice that it was not good news for me and he was enjoying it. "What's up?"

He smiled, "You have to report to Cook's office at six tonight, you and that fat lad in 3 Troop and a couple more." He closed the door and was gone. My rifle was stripped down on the floor for cleaning. I looked at my watch, 16.52, shit. Tea was at 17.15 and I was starving, I carried on pulling the four by two through the barrel, it had to be shining before they would accept it back into the armoury. Gaff came in and threw his rifle on his bed.

"Have you read orders?" He started to take off his wet boots.

"No but Wally's just told me I have to report to Cook's office at six." I carried on oiling the rifle.

"Yep and the other two, bit of a motley crew if you ask me, what've you done wrong?" We both knew it was not a promotion.

At the armoury, I stood in the queue to hand my weapon in. Each weapon was inspected very carefully.

"Fuck off and get it cleaned properly cunt, this Gat is manky." There were two NCOs and the armourer inspecting and they were not taking anything that did not shine. The soldier wandered off dejected.

I crossed my fingers as I handed my gun over. It was quickly stripped down and a critical eye expertly inspected.

"That's fine." He started to make the rifle up. "Do you know you're in the office tonight?"

"Yes, any idea what's it about?" I knew he wouldn't say, but it was worth a try.

"I think he wants you to baby-sit his daughter, she's only seventeen." He winked at me, the other men around laughed, I headed for the canteen.

I rushed back from a hurried meal; I was still in my combat gear, still covered in muck, but time was running out and I went straight to Cook's door. The other men were already there and I did not like what I saw. If you could hand pick two of the most useless turkeys from the Squadron this would be the two and I was the third. I fell in at the end of the line standing at ease, ready. I was running things through my head, preparing excuses. Suddenly the door opened and the clerk came out of Cook's office.

"Listen in to my word of command." We were being marched in. I would have expected just to be told to walk in, but no.

The clerk's voice was thin but carried the length of the hall. "Attention." We snapped to attention. "Left turn, quick march." We filed into the office, marking time until the clerk gave the order to halt, on the wrong foot so we lost our time and we looked like a bunch of new recruits.

Cook looked up from the memo. "Well men, we have had a request from Military Intelligence for three men to work for them during the tour of Northern Ireland and although we are very short handed at the moment, we have to follow orders." He looked at our faces to see the effect of this news. "And we have picked you three, because we feel you meet the requirements." He looked again at the document. "You must report to 3rd battalion on Monday morning 08:00. You will need to take all your army kit and all the civvies you think you'll need for the full four months. Your mail address will still be the same." He thought for a while. "I want you back safe and ready for work at the end of the tour, so be careful." He looked at the clerk. "Dismiss the men please." The clerk marched us out telling us that the transport would pick us up at seven thirty on the Monday. We turned to our right and broke off.

None of us said anything until we were outside; it was cold, the wind was cutting but we stood and chatted for a while. I lit a cigarette.

"Whoa, wait till I tell my Mum." The chubby lad was beaming; the others seemed pleased as well.

"What do you think we'll be doing?" The tall gangly lance corporal asked, as if we knew the answer.

"Well someone has to clean the bogs out." I said. This brought them down with a bump.

"I'm a radio op," the fat boy asserted. "I'm damned if I'm doing that"

"I'm a bridge builder and mine warfare man myself." I said quietly. The radio op course was only six weeks and we all did a bit of that. "No, we'll be doing dogsbody stuff." I was not hopeful it would be James Bond stuff.

"See you on Monday." I left them there speculating, and went up to my room.

Gaff was sitting on my bed. I went over and sat on the bedside locker. He passed me a cigarette. "Well?"

"I'm being sent to Intelligence." I waited till he thought about this for a while and slowly a smile came across his face.

"You can't even do the Sun crossword. God they must be desperate."

"Well I don't think they want Einstein, we'll just be filling in. Anyway I'll find out next week. I have to be there on Monday; we go out on the same day as you."

"Do you fancy a pint?" I nodded. "I'll get a quick shower and then we can go to the club."

We played table football all night and bowled back to our room nicely mellow. I fell asleep quickly.

The transport rolled up spot on time, a three tonner. I had only just arrived from breakfast and making sure everything was locked up in my room. We clambered aboard and I saw Gaff and Jock, on their way to breakfast, they waved me off. I had a feeling of impending doom and lit a cigarette.

We piled out at 3rd battalion headquarters and were met by a sergeant who broke the news that because they were shipping in over fifty temps, we had to bunk in the gym. We struggled over there and found rows of camping beds, each one with a bedside locker, a floor mat, and pillow with no pillow case and two woolly blankets. In the drawer was an ashtray.

"The bogs and showers are over there." The sergeant pointed over to the end of the gym. He looked at his watch. "You have forty minutes to get over to classroom two." He pointed at the building we had just come from, and then marched off.

"It's a regular home from home." The chubby lad said sitting down on his new bed. It tipped over. I waited until he'd righted himself.

I stuck my hand out, "Billy Deery, I've seen you around." He shook my hand.

"Brian Fodden." He nodded over to the lanky corporal. "He's Paul, Paul Walker." I nodded.

"Do you think the cookhouse is still doing breakfast?" Brian had missed breakfast that morning.

Paul was busy making himself at home, putting things into his bedside locker and placing his case and kitbag neatly behind the top of his bed, like some sort of head board. "Do you know where the canteen is?"

"I just follow my nose when it comes to that sort of thing." Brian took pride in hunting out food.

"I'll come with you." I stood up and looked at Paul, he had finished unpacking, so followed us as we tried to find the cookhouse. We had time to kill. Most of the ex-German barracks were arranged to a standard lay out, so we quickly homed in on the cookhouse and just caught the last few sausages and a cup of tea.

We were the last in to the classroom and had to stand at the back, still not knowing what our duties would be, what was our role. Surely it took years to train intelligence personnel, surely they had to be of the highest intelligence, code breakers, swots, doing the Times crossword over a cup of tea, the James Bond type, killing with one blow and disappearing in the night. What the hell could they want with us?

Captain Roberts came in; he looked like a desk clerk in a captain's uniform, nothing to distinguish him, no high forehead, no bulging muscles.

"Look men, we are very short on the ground." He looked around. There were about thirty of us, from all different units. "We have been short for years and now we're expected to put observations all over Northern Ireland. Your jobs will be to fill in on these observations, file reports and move around the city, eyes and ears." You could hear a collective sigh from the men sitting around.

"You will be doing static observations on the more mundane side of things." He went on. "Your training will start tomorrow. You need to able to observe and report, keep a close check on the mug shots and all the in coming intelligence." He then gave us some news which made every single one of us cheer.

"From to day, long hair and long sideburns, beards and anything else is in." Roberts smiled as a room full of squaddies cheered and whooped; he had to raise his voice to bring the room back to order.

"So we have a lot to do before we go. I want you all to look at the board over there." He pointed to the blackboard with lists of men's names pinned on it. "Find out who you're teamed up with; remember you train as a team, you work as a team."

There was a scraping of chairs as we all rose. I lit a cigarette and stood back, but most men pushed and shoved to find out who they would be working with. Eventually someone ripped his list off the board and started to shout names out.

24

I had gone into a little daydream remembering when I was younger, before we left Belfast. Would I meet my Gran, my Aunts and Uncles?

"Deery." I came to, to hear my name being called out.

"Deery." A small compact corporal with the uniform of the Royal Signals was calling.

"Here," I looked at him, "I'm Deery."

"I'm Corporal Kelly. There are five men out near the front door, one's fat and there's another one black, so you should find them." He then started to shout another name and forgot about me. I wandered out. The group was easy to identify and one of them was Brian. The coloured lad was about six foot four with an easy smile. I walked over and Brian was talking to the coloured boy.

"How the fuck are you going to fit in, in Ireland? I mean how many........." he looked for the right word and could not find it. "How many big black fuckers are there in Belfast?"

It was one of those moments when everyone wants to be swallowed up, or be somewhere else.

"Hi, I'm Billy Deery from 17th Engineers." I stuck my hand out. Brian was grateful for the diversion; the coloured lad took my hand.

"Smudge Smith transport Bielefeld." Brian, who was blushing because he had not introduced himself, just said, "Brian Fodden." Smudge just gave him a wink and this helped to take the awkwardness away. At that moment Kelly came out of the building with another man following behind.

He took charge. "Okay everyone in my section," he used his hands a lot; he pointed with both index fingers. "Make your way to room fourteen; it's on the second floor." The fingers were pointing towards the door we had just come out of, so we ambled back in and up the stairs. I continued to talk to Smudge.

"What do you drive?" I liked Smudge; he was self assured, he reeked of confidence and I wanted to be part of that.

"Oh, we have all sorts, mostly small stuff, but we got some big stuff as well, we got tank transporters an' all sorts, but my favourite is the Stalwart, I just love that ride."

We piled into room fourteen and found seats. Kelly had some notes.

"Settle down, we will be working together for the next five or six months and I want you to all stand up and tell us who you are, then I'll be telling you what's expected of you, I know this is all new and we don't have much time, so you start" he pointed at Smudge, Smudge stood up.

"I'm Gerry Smith but people call me Smudge, I've been in the Royal corps of transport for just over two years, and come from Dover, we're based in Bielefeld and I'm in the basket ball team." he sat down.

Kelly pointed at me.

I stood up "Billy Deery, Royal Engineers, bridging, building and blowing, mine warfare laying and breeching." I started to sit down and remembered "Oh and I'm in the regimental orienteering team" I hardly listened to the rest, but there was eight of us including Kelly of which two were full corporals.

"How many have driving licences?" We stuck our hands up, Kelly ticked off his list "And how many are radio trained?" We stuck our hands up again, more ticks "Good, and has anyone lived or has family in Northern Ireland?" I was the only one to hold my hand up, tick.

"Tomorrow morning were on the ranges, we get picked up at zero seven thirty outside the gym, full battle gear, piss pots and ground sheets the lot," he looked up "weapons will be issued at the ranges, and don't forget your mess tins and eating irons." He thought for a minute "I'm bunking down on the top floor of this building," he pointed to the ceiling, just in case we did not know where the top of the building was "room 211, and the other ranks bar is above the cookhouse." he gathered his thoughts again "so go and sort your kit out, and I'll see you all in the morning." There was a scraping of chairs and people started to talk excitedly.

"Deery." Kelly was talking to me, but my mind was on that camp bed "Deery." a bit louder.

"Yes corporal" I made my way over to him.

"What family do you have over there?" It took me by surprise, I had thought it was just one of those questions, but no, it was one of those questions.

"Well my Grandmother lives there, and maybe my Dad, but almost certainly a few of my aunties and uncles live there, I was born in Belfast." I let this sink in, he stroked his nose.

"You don't sound like you come from Belfast."

"That's because I was brought up in Liverpool." he pulled his nose again, I moved from one leg to another. At this point I thought I would give him a demonstration so I said "Come on Corporal Kelly, it's not the sort of thing you tell people." I had dropped into my home accent, I had not spoken in my home accent for years, I had in fact tried my hardest not to use it. I had adopted the local idiom as soon as I could possibly manage after moving to Liverpool.

"We moved to Liverpool when I was six or seven, my mother did a runner and that's where my accent comes from." all the time I'm speaking in my old accent.

He jotted some notes down.

"You do realise you could get an exemption from the tour?" he would dearly love an exemption, I had something he wanted. I pursed my lips. I think I was teasing him.

"But I want to go" what was the alternative, sitting back on rear party, hell on earth, an empty camp, a few losers left behind, no not for me, no I'm here for the ride, the sharp end, the deep end. I looked at him, almost insolently.

"Yes I want to go." I had gone back to my normal accent.

"Okay, I'll file this, go and sort yourself out" he nodded at the door, I was dismissed.

I made my way back to the gym, at one end of the gym someone had a portable tape player blasting Johnny Cash, Smudge and Brian had changed into civvies and was relaxing on their beds.

"You're a Paddy." Brian was laughing at his own joke "You should be in the Pioneers not the Engineers, but there's not much difference." he looked around for support.

"Hey don't turn your back to me when we're there." I had dropped into my Irish accent. I made a gun action with my hand pointed at Brian's head and blew imaginary smoke away. I started to get my things ready for the next day.

"Fancy a pint tonight?" I looked over to the other two.

Smudge was the first to answer "Yes suits me."

"Deery." There was someone was calling out my name, I looked around "Sapper Deery" I saw who was calling and stood up.

"Over here." I held my hand up and a young private from the intelligence Corp was approaching me.

"You're wanted by Captain Roberts now, follow me." I shrugged my shoulders at the other two.

"I'll see you soon." I followed the private.

"What do you think it is?" I tried to get an idea.

He took his time answering "not a fucking clue mate" we carried on over to the block.

"Just wait there." I seem to be waiting outside offices quite a lot lately, he disappeared into the office and came out quite quickly and walked off.

"Thanks mate" I put in as much sarcasm as I could as he walked away.

The door opened and Roberts head popped out.

"Come in Deery." I followed "Sit down." Well I'm not in the shit, you don't sit down when the shit's flying.

"Are you a Catholic?" That took me by surprise.

"No, well yes, but..." the army never pushed religion so I could not see where he was going and I was starting to sweat.

He tried another tack "Do you have family in Ireland?" that was better, now I felt I knew where he was coming from.

"Yes Sir, my Gran still lives there, and I lived there until I was seven, and I also have other people there like my Aunt." I was trying to please him, but he did not show any emotion.

"So why is your accent Scouse?" he corrected himself "From Merseyside?"

"Well we did a flit to Liverpool, just me and my mother," I started to relax "and I had to fit in so just started to talk like them, Sir." the wheels were turning in his head, he was trying to evaluate me.

"One last question, is there anyone in Belfast who knows you're in the army? Think very carefully" I sat there for over a minute, I knew the answer but my mind had started to think of the pint tonight, and I also thought it gave the question gravity.

"No Sir." I also thought that if this did not swing my way I could just remember someone who knew me.

"Look we need eyes and ears in the community, and we have to find people who can live and work on the streets," he's watching my reaction, "we need people on the streets, we need people who can fit in. I'll admit that most personnel who come from Ireland just don't want to get mixed up in this, to close to home I'm afraid." He sat back and let this lot sink in, there was a long pause. I'm a bit shocked, it's one thing to ride around in a team, but to pose as a local and rub shoulders with known IRA and UVF activist this was a different world. He could see the cogs turning.

"Of course you would be promoted to corporal."

"Do you mean full corporal?"

"Yes, and you will be trained, and your cover will be water tight."

I do want promotion, but I'm still not sure, now I was really sweating.

"Deery, this is a big step, but you will have twenty four hour back up, and if you feel compromised at any time we will pull you out." I was getting scared again, my mind was racing.

"What job have you got lined up?" I want to know more.

"I need someone on the buses, there is a good cross section, Catholics and Protestants a mix from both sides, but the O'Neil family work from that depot, and we want to keep an eye on them." He's watching me again, but giving me time to let all the information sink in, he knows that if I go away and think about it I will reject it, stripes or no stripes.

"We need to push on." He knows I'm under the cosh, but I'm stalling.

"How long is it for?" I wanted the stripes.

"No longer than the full tour," he was reeling me in like a trout. "after that, just back to normal duties, with two stripes."

It sounded easy, in a childish way I had always wanted to shout "Hold tight please and ring the bell twice." and run up and down asking for fares.

"Just go to work, keep you eyes peeled, and report back."
He was pulling me in further. "Do you want in?"

"Yes Sir."

Chapter 4. 14 March 1972.   32

The next morning everyone was ready for the ranges. I did not think they had plans for me, so I just got ready with them and lined up to get on the transport. The rain was coming in sideways with a cutting wind. We piled into the back of the lorry, the tailgate was up.

"Is Deery on that wagon?" I heard Captain Roberts ask.

The corporal on the tailgate looked around.

"Is Deery on here?"

I stood up.

"Could you send him into my office please." Roberts disappeared and I jumped down and followed.

"Come straight in Deery." Roberts was sitting at his desk which was covered in documents.

"You're booked on a military flight out of Gutersloh to Blighty, at fourteen hundred. You will be met by Sergeant Mackie. It's his job to make sure you are informed and ready for the task you have been given."

I sat there taking this in. "Then when you're ready, you'll be shipped off to Ulster. Do you have any questions?"

"No Sir." I had not had time to think of any.

"Right, you need to be at the guard room with all your baggage at eleven forty five. I have arranged for transport to pick you up. It's just over one and a half hours to the airport." He stood up and did something I was not expecting. He leaned over the table and shook my hand.

"Well done Corporal Deery, I'll see you in Belfast."

I left the offices and made my way back to the gym, it was still only just before eight. I felt scruffy, I had not had a shave, but orders were orders. I needed to make myself look like a civilian as soon as possible. Most of my kit was still packed, so I was ready to go after fifteen minutes. I got hold of a trolley and loaded my suitcase and kit bag and in the driving rain made my way over to the guard room.

"We're not the left luggage department." The duty MP greeted me. They were trained in being unhelpful; it must have taken years to reach this standard. I went to pick up my baggage.

"Put it over there." He pointed to the corner and I stacked the bag in the corner and opened the suitcase. I took out my cheque book from the left hand side. Once out of the Guard House, I left the barracks and made my way to the bank. Our wages had been paid into German banks for over a year by then.

"Gut morning." The cashier could speak English, which was good for me.

"How much is in this account please?" I handed over my cheque book and asked for forty Deutsche marks and forty English pounds. She left the desk and returned quickly with the money.

"Could I see your ID card please?" I handed over my card, she filled out the cheque and I signed it.

I made my way back to camp and to the NAFFI canteen. After a few cups of coffee and having read Readers Digest from cover to cover, it was time to go. The driver had not done the run to Gutersloh so I read the route card out to him but we made it in time. He dumped me at the main entrance. It was a long low building with not many people around. I made my way over to the desk and handed my ID card to a bored corporal from the Military Police. He looked at his list of names.

"Are you carrying any fire arms? You'll get checked at the other end."

"No."

"Do you have more than your allowance for cigarettes or spirits?"

"No," Shit, I had forgotten to get cigarettes. "Can I get any cigarettes here?"

"Normally you can, but today the duty free is closed, no civvy flights today." He pointed over to the far end of the hall, "Go and sit near the door, they'll call you."

I started to pick up my bag, but the MP called me back. "I can let you have them." He nodded in the direction of his desk, there was a full sleeve of Embassy. At ten marks it was above the shop price, but I had been caught short.

I paid for the cigarettes and went and sat down. Military flights are supremely unsophisticated. With ten minutes, to go an R.A.F. sergeant, with a clipboard under his arm, came through the glass doors which lead onto the tarmac.

"Two o'clock flight to Brize Norton," he announced. "Load your bags onto the trolleys just out here." He pointed towards two hand pull trolleys out side the door. There were only seven passengers and only one of them was wearing uniform - me.

I loaded my case and kit bag onto the first trolley and helped others load up and then the R.A.F. Sergeant and I pulled it to the back of Hercules, which had the tail gate down. The passengers walked up the ramp and found seats, while we loaded the cases onto the back of the plane. There were also about twenty five bags of mail, which although not heavy, still left me sweating by the time we had them loaded and strapped down.

A seat would be a loose description of what we were offered to sit on. They were just canvas strips, strung between two supports which could be pulled down like a cinema seat.

The flight was hell. We had to keep our seat-belts on for the whole journey; because we did not fly as high as commercial flights, we hit every bit of turbulence. The toilet was what could only be called a hole in the side of the plane.

I was glad to be back on terra-firma when we landed. We had to carry our own bags to the buildings. I was glad of this; it saved me doing all the donkey work. The mail was taken off by Royal Ordinance who then delivered the mail to the Post Office. I was not impressed by the airfield but we did not have far to walk to the two storey building. I was at the back of the queue. I lifted my bags onto the long bench and lit a cigarette while I waited for a customs man to get to me.

"Do you have any firearms, ammunition or ordinance?" I could tell he was bored; I was cold.

"No, Sir." I was not quite sure what to call him.

"Do you have more than two hundred cigarettes, one bottle of spirits or more than two bottles of wine?"

"No Sir."

"Open the case please." He ruffled around and I could feel myself blushing when he found my dirty socks.

"ID card please" He didn't look in the kitbag; I was through. It was always great to be back in England, everyone speaking English, you knowing the customs, you can read signs and understand the money without having to think twice and the air seems different, better.

"Corporal Deery?" I looked around to see the man who had spoken. He was short, stocky, with a face which could have been carved out of an old oak tree. He was dressed in the old battle dress style still in use at training Regiments, no rank, no regimental insignia. I had been told I was being met by a sergeant.

"Yes I'm Deery." I still had not got used to my new status of corporal.

"I'm Sergeant Gerry Mackie, everyone calls me Mack." He stuck his hand out; he had very strong hands. He did not grip me hard but I could feel the power. He picked up my kitbag and started to walk out.

"So do I call you Mack?" I followed him like a child.

He turned round and put the bag down.

"From now on you only talk to me with your hometown accent and yes 'Mack' will do fine, but you may be calling me worse things before long." We set off again to his car.

"We will be bunking at Chepstow. I'll be in charge of your training and preparation." We hit the motorway. "We have a lot to do and only ten days to do it in." I sat back and wondered what I had got myself into but comforted myself with the thought of my get-out clause.

As we went over a massive suspension bridge, he pointed down to what looked like an island just off the river bank. Even though we were on the other side of the bridge to the island and there was some mist I could see it was quite isolated.

"That's where we will be staying." We pulled off the motorway and made our way through Chepstow and back around to the camp. He carried my kitbag so easily, it looked empty and he swaggered ahead of me, into a two storey building. Inside was a doorman reading a book.

"Give me the key for room seventeen, George." The doorman handed over a key, "This is Corporal Deery," he gestured towards me, "ten days." The doorman nodded. I said hello as I passed him.

It was a shock to both of us, as the back of Mack's hand hit my nose.

"Irish, Irish, Irish." I was stunned. Mack's face was hard up against mine. "You will not get a second chance where you're going." He strode off, I followed, I was furious.

It was a single ground floor room with a sink. The bed was already made up.

"There's a TV room at the end of the corridor, evening meal is from five, and breakfast starts at six thirty. I'll meet you at the main door at seven forty five tomorrow." Mack looked me in the face. "You must think, dream, and even fart in Irish from now on. Everyone you talk to, even yourself, do you get that?" I took a deep breath and nodded. "And wear civvies in the morning, jeans or something." He slammed the door on the way out. I sat on the bed and wondered whether I really wanted to be there and after two cigarettes I knew the answer, yes.

I unpacked a few things, putting on my jeans and best Ben Sherman shirt. I dug out my eating irons and my chipped tin mug, and then made my way down to the front door.

"Where is the cookhouse please?" George the doorman gave me instructions and handed me a plastic holder with a pin.

"Put your ID card in that and pin it to your chest." He came out of his cubby-hole and pinned it on for me. When I got back from tea, George had been replaced by another man. I introduced myself.

"Do you want a knock in the morning?" The man found his list and jotted down six thirty, room seventeen. He looked up and gave me a wink.

I watched TV in the lounge, my first introduction to Monty Python. Lights out was at ten, so strictly observed I had to clean my teeth in the dark.

There was a light tap on the door, I could hear steps going down the corridor, tap tap, tap tap. I got up. It wasn't always easy to get up in a strange room and there wasn't much room as my suitcase was open and my kit-bag leaning against the sink. It was frosty on the way to breakfast, but the food was good and warmed me through and they sold news papers from one of the tables. I read in Irish, as I did not want to be slapped again.

Mack turned up five minutes early and inspected my clothes. To be honest, because I wore uniform most of the time and there wasn't much room in army lockers. I was like most young soldiers, not very well endowed with civvies. You need a suit for church and a few pair of jeans and maybe two pairs of shoes, not much more and this was all I had.

"Go and bring all your kit to room four."   He pointed down the corridor to the left. I scurried off to collect my bags. Room four was a small classroom with a blackboard and six tables and chairs and a table in the corner with a brew kit. The milk was dried. I put my bags down and Mack opened up the army suitcase. He started to throw all the army belongings on one table and the civilian things on another.

"Is that all you have?" I tried to remember whether there was anything else in my kit bag, I could add to the civvies pile, but could only conjure up a pair of sandshoes.

"Yep." I blushed, not much to show.

"Okay, pack that crap away, you don't need that." He started to make an address label.   "What's your B.F.P.O. number?" I tied the label on.

Return to unit.
Cpl. W. Deery,
17 Sqd, R.E.
B.F.P.O. 36.

I was never to see those bags again. Mack made two cups of tea; we sat down facing each other.

"What colour tie is Tim wearing?" I was a bit puzzled,
"The doorman." I thought a bit,

"Blue." It was a guess.

"How many cooks were working in the canteen last night?"
I could now see where this was going, I did a replay.

"Seven." Mack did not make any facial movements, I
watched him carefully.

"What is the registration of my car?" I could not even
remember looking at it. I shook my head.

"What junction number did we come off the motorway at
yesterday evening?" I thought about it and realised I had not
been watching. I shook my head again.

Mack took a swig of tea, I lit a cigarette.

"You have a long way to go sonny." He finished his tea.
Mine was still too hot to drink.

"Come on." I jumped up and followed him, as we passed
the doorman I noticed he was not wearing a tie. We climbed into
Mack's Ford Anglia and made our way out of the camp. I was
trying to take in as much detail as possible. He might test me
again.

He drove to Cardiff. I was nearly passing out in the attempt
to take in so much detail. We wound through the city and parked
up in a back street not far from the centre. There was a shop
nearby selling second hand clothes, books and brick-a-brack.
Once inside, Mack rapidly went through the clothes racks and
piles of clothes on the bench, picking out anything that fitted me,
an old pair of boots, a brown corduroy jacket, frayed shirts, scarf,
pullovers, and an old tweed coat. Then he pulled an old suitcase
off the top shelf with rusty hinges. Down another isle he found
two towels, a couple of tea cups, shaving mirror, some knives and
spoons.

"Oh come on there are better suitcases than that," I argued.
He ignored me. The shop owner followed helping to carry some
of the stuff. When he had finished he turned to the lady.

"How much for that lot?" She nodded her head as she
pretended to added up, but I could see she was really working out
how much she could get off Mack.

"Thirty bob." She looked at Mack to see the reaction.

"It's for a school play. I'll give you seventeen shillings or I'm off." He turned away slightly.

"A quid and you're robbing me. The case is nine bob and those cups are collector's items." Mack got his wallet out.

"Give me a shilling change and you have a deal." We packed the clothes away, and she wrapped the cups in brown paper. We dumped the battered suitcase in the car went to a menswear shop. This time Mack bought me two shirts, a black tie, six pairs of socks, underpants and a pair of slacks. Two doors down, we bought black shoes. Mack carefully put away all the receipts. The whole thing took less than an hour.

"Cup of tea?" We walked into a café; the heat hit you, damp, steamy and too crowded with tables.

"Name all the items we bought in the second hand shop?" I listed them.

"What unusual thing did you notice about the woman?" Mack was testing again.

I pictured her in my head "Only one earring." I ventured.

"Go on."

"Gold teeth, rings on every finger, and odd Wellingtons." I had not consciously picked that up, but as I pictured her in my mind, I remembered.

"Yes," Mack smiled "Odd Wellingtons." We left the cafe and made our way back to the car and camp. On the journey Mack kept up the narrative.

"One of the reasons men don't look around at other men is because it's threatening. That's why women are better at identifying people they have just met, because they observe more thoroughly." We turned off the motorway.

"I need you to start looking, and at first it will seem strange, confrontational, but that's how you can scan large numbers of people and remember individuals. Don't stand in the middle. Stand on the sidelines."

The camp was an army apprentice college, so apart from the training staff, most of the occupants of the camp were boy soldiers. However, two buildings at the lower end of the barracks was exclusively Military Intelligence. We parked outside one of the buildings and went inside. Up the stairs, there was a corridor. At the end, we entered the last room on the left. Inside was a

40

counter keeping us out and them in. We stood for a while, I read the notices. Mack introduced me to the Private behind the counter.

"This is Corporal Deery, he's going to Northern Ireland as himself, and he needs all the documents."

Mack turned to me. "Do you drive?" I nodded and got my driving licence out. The Private behind the desk went to a drawer and took out a sheet of paper.

"So, driving licence, national insurance card, medical docs, and school certificates." He looked up, "bank account?" Mack nodded. He ticked.

"Come behind here." He lifted up the end of the counter and opened the door.

"Sit there." He pointed at a chair with a white screen behind, then went over to a cupboard and brought back a box of wigs. I was taken aback by this.

"Find one you like." He went over to talk to Mack while I self consciously tried on a few wigs.

"Just look to the left." He pointed just in case I did not know which way he meant.

I was hustled back out to the other side of the counter.

"They will be ready on Monday."

"Well, make sure they are, he goes on Friday." We left the office and went downstairs, into another office. This had four tables with women working at each of them.

"Jenny." He greeted one of the women. The woman beamed back.

"This is William Deery he will be going over to Northern Ireland." She started to make notes.

"He needs accommodation in East Belfast, in the Catholic area paid up until July."

"Bed and breakfast?"

"No self contained." She pulled a face and took a long hard look at me.

"When does he go?"

"Next Friday." She scowled. Turning round she looked at the calendar on the wall.

"That's going to be tough." She made notes.

"He also needs," Mack looked at her sympathetically. "a union card for the Transport Union, a doctor's and a CUI card."

"Is that all?" She was being sarcastic, but it took me a few seconds to catch on.

"I'll leave it with you." Mack bent down and gave her a peck on the cheek.

We left the office and made our way out.

"A lovely girl."

"Do I need those things?" My mind was on all the attention to detail, surely I was going as an observer? Surely I would just be in the background?

"Do you want to go without them?" Mack had stopped to ask the question.

The next few days were taken up with observation, history of Ireland, land marks and maps, IRA membership and weapon training. We covered all weapons, theirs and ours. I also went to lectures covering all the political parties, local laws including the yellow card. Mack did not sit in on these information gatherings, but he would be waiting for me when I came out and question me about the people in the classroom; he never gave me a moment's peace. Every time we came out of a building the questions would start, but by then, I had started to observe properly.

I was given the Sunday off. This gave me time to think. Did I have the nerve for this? I could just back out, but I would be letting everybody down, I would be letting myself down and what harm could come to me. I was just an observer, working on the buses, just keeping an eye out and reporting back.

Monday 20 March 1972.

On the Monday morning, Mack was waiting in class four, the kettle was boiling as I arrived. I looked at the folder on the table.

"Keep your hands off that." He stirred the tea and brought the cups over.

I supped my tea as he opened the folder.

"I want you to know this backwards by tomorrow; we'll go through it now."

He handed me a Northern Ireland driving licence, it had been well worn, dog eared. I opened it. The photograph showed me wearing a wig. One endorsement had been awarded, to make it more viable I suppose.

The next set of papers were my release papers from prison, Walton Prison, Liverpool. Four months for burglary.

"We have put this in so you can explain your short hair." He handed me my union card.

"You will notice it is dated from your eighteenth birthday and is stamped in both Merseyside and Castlederg." Mack gave me a hand typed booklet explaining all the details of the two depots I was supposed to have worked at, including a list of busmen's terminology and practise. Next was the CIU membership. I had never even been in a working man's club, but here was my membership.

"Your medical documents will be sent to Dr Thompson, the address is in here somewhere." He rummaged through the documents, till he found them. He put two pages stapled together on the desk. There were more details, my National Insurance number, bank account and school certificates. Someone had been working very hard.

Mack got up and put the kettle on again.

"I'll give you till lunch to read this lot and then I'm going to check you on everything." He poured my tea. I looked down at the documents, there was a lot there to read, never mind memorise.

"You don't need to remember numbers, just the bare bones, but you do need to know dates, the people and the place names, just as if you had been there." He looked at his watch. "Two hours."

He closed the door behind him as he left. I lit a cigarette and read and I read between the lines; where there were details missing, I made them up. I read during lunch, hunched over my paperwork like a child hiding his answers in an exam. I was beginning to look very un-military with my face not shaven and my hair just a bit too long for most Sergeant Majors' levels of acceptance. Two junior apprentices sat at my table, I carried on reading.

"Hey, are you a gardener?" I looked up from the documents. I was annoyed but also pleased, pleased that I was being mistaken for a civvy. I tapped the side of my nose. Before they could ask any more questions I packed up and left.

I was sitting in the classroom before Mack came back, the kettle went straight on and I lit a cigarette to help me concentrate.

"So how long have you been driving?" Mack knew every little detail of my new life.

"Oh I got my bike licence when I was sixteen, but did not pass my car test until last year." I had picked up on that one, he smiled.

"Did you know the cash clerk at Castlederg depot?"

"Of course, old Seamus the bastard booked me in every shift for eight weeks." He was pleased again. I had noticed and remembered that I had only been at Castlederg for just under two months. We carried on like this for the next thirty minutes. I was sweating but Mack was pleased.

"Good." He stood up. "I want you to concentrate on maps of Belfast and public buildings, things you should know and I'll see you in here tomorrow at eight fifteen, then we do mugshots." I carried on reading, just going over a few things which had been difficult to remember, Mack had nearly found me out.

The next few days were more of the same, but as the training continued, I was becoming this new person, myself, but in another guise. Myself, as if I had never been in the army.

Chapter 6. Thursday 23 March 1972.   46

We worked through the day, polishing up on all the details and after a gruelling final hour of close questioning, Mack stood up.

"Well, if you're not ready now, you never will be." I was feeling much better. I knew myself, I knew the town, and I knew the people. I just had to go and do it.

"Do you drink?" Mack was looking at me.

"Does the Pope pray?" I smiled at him; he was inviting me out for a drink.

"Right I'll pick you up at seven thirty outside, you don't fly until two o'clock tomorrow, so we don't have to leave here until eleven."

He rolled up on the dot of seven thirty and I jumped into his car. He had, until now, always been in his uniform with no insignia. This, in a way, made him look like a civilian in khaki, if it hadn't been for his manner.

"I want you to stay in character tonight."

"Sure, no bother." My accent came naturally now. In the early days, I had to think before I spoke but now it just seemed normal. He drove down into town and we parked up in a side street and went into the pub.

"What you having?" Mack leaned against the bar waving a five pound note. I had become fond of Mack over the weeks. I looked along the bar, I only drank German beer and then only the small frothy beers typically sold in the bars near camp.

"I'll have a Lager please.

The bar man came over to Mack. "A pint of best, and a pint of lager and two whisky chasers please." Mack paid for the drinks and we went and sat down at a small table in the corner. Mack was relaxed and chatty. He picked up the whisky and downed it in one, I followed his lead. We sat and chatted, he told me stories of Aden and Borneo. Before I had got half way down my pint he jumped up, draining his glass.

"Two more pints with chasers, please." They were put on the table. I finished my pint in a hurry.

"So what was your training like?" It was like tickling trout and Mack was winding me in. I told him about the fat controller, a little moustached man who had made our lives a misery by bouncing us round the square in double quick time.

Mack jumped up and got them in again; I tried to get them, but Mack tapped the side of his nose.

"They're paying - just enjoy yourself."

We downed the whiskies and supped the pints, each telling our stories, his far better than mine. I was falling behind on the drinking front, Mack taking out nearly half a pint every time he picked up his glass. I staggered to the toilets, tripping on the step up. I also banged my head on the low beam on the way back.

"Come on, sup up, I'll show you a nice pub." Mack stood up. I struggled to finish my pint.

"Good night." We were outside and walking up the street. I wondered if I should ask him if I could just drink halves, my head was starting to spin. We went into the next pub.

"Best, Lager and a couple of whiskies please." I went straight to the toilets, it was running through me now. When I came back Mack was sitting at a table. He carried on with the chat, I was in crisis, and I sat there smoking not really listening to Mack.

He handed me a pound note. "Go on get them in. I staggered across to the bar.

"A pint of Best and a whisky." The barmaid started to pour.

"Are you out with your dad?' She had the small glass up to the optic, but was turning to face me.

"Oh no he's not my father; we're in the army together." I didn't notice. I was just doing my best to stand up straight. Suddenly Mack was standing behind me. I had not noticed, I was past noticing anything. Mack got a hold of my collar and dragged me onto the street. I was confused, I was up against the wall and I was getting wet. It was raining hard.

"What do you think would happen to you if you'd talked like that in a pub over there?" I was still none the wiser.

"What?" Mack's face was up close.

His were hands at my throat, tight around my neck.

"I don't know what you mean." I'd had done something, but couldn't work out what.

"You dropped the accent." He stood looking into my face, rain pouring down. People were passing us as they went into the pub, in a hurry to get inside.

We stood there while it sank in, both of us face to face. In my mind, I replayed what had been said. Slowly my body relaxed, as I realised what had happened.

"I'm sorry." His hands slowly released my neck, we both became aware of how wet we were. Mack pulled up his collar on his corduroy jacket.

"Come on I'll take you home." We made our way back to his car and he drove me back to camp in silence.

The whole point of the night had been made and no amount of lectures and warnings would sink in like tonight. I had to watch my tongue when I was drunk. He dropped me off outside my quarters.

"Be packed and ready to go at ten and just go through your things again and make sure there are no items to do with the army in your luggage." He drove away. I went to my room and slept badly.

The next morning I packed my things into my beat up suitcase, carefully checking each item. I found Mack in classroom four, he had two cups of tea on the desk and he was reading the newspaper. He folded the paper and placed it on the table.

He pushed his thick hair back. "I don't want you to worry, you've had to learn a lot in a short space of time, but I want you never to let your guard down." He sipped his tea. "You will have good back up, they'll have safety procedures in place and if you get into trouble, get out fast, get to the nearest police station, get in a taxi or jump in the nearest army vehicle." He slugged his tea.

We sat in silence for a while, smoke drifting up from my cigarette. Mack finished his tea.

"I don't want you to drink while you're there." He looked at me, I nodded.

"If you do get drinking and you will, because that's the way they are. I want you to spill it, pour it into the glass of someone who won't notice - or just swap the glass if you need to... do you understand?" I nodded.

There was a silence while we both went through things in our head. Eventually Mack took a piece of paper out of his pocket.

"You'll be met by Simon Adder, he'll show you the ropes. It's his job to watch over you." He went into his briefcase and brought out a receipt book.

"Sign here." He produced twenty pounds in Irish notes. "Your rent is paid and the gas and electricity are both registered in your name." It made me worried when I saw how much detail had gone into this operation, but like Mack had asked, did I want to go without it. But just how much would I be scrutinised over there?

We sat and went through some last details, about being transferred from Castlederg bus depot to the Short Strand depot, because the depot was fully staffed and had not taken anyone new for over a year so a new face would turn heads.

I sat and re-read the reports and details as we drove to the airport, more to take my mind off where I was going, but also to check I had got this absolutely massive amount of information into my head. All too quickly we were at RAF Brize Norton. We parked up and went into the main building, soldiers in battle dress with weapons, were sitting all over the place, doing what soldiers the world over are good at, passing time.

I had been growing my hair and sideboards since that first day and with my clothes and battered suitcase looked for all the world like a civvy, I could feel many suspicious eyes on me. They had been trained to watch out for my kind. I, on the other hand, felt like shouting, "Hey, I'm on your side." This was a feeling I would have many times over the coming months. I followed Mack through the hall. Eventually we found a Flight Sergeant who was expecting me.

"Ah, Mr W. Deery for the Belfast flight, you're on the two o'clock." He looked at his watch. "Well we're busy today; we have five flights to Belfast, so keep your eyes open."

Then he looked at Mack. "I'll keep him right." He walked away. I lit a cigarette, I was nervous and Mack could see it. He walked up to the canteen and got two teas.

"You'll be fine, just remember your field craft, don't talk about yourself and watch everyone."

Mack looked at his watch, he had things to do. He stuck his hand out which took me by surprise. I still had a cigarette in my hand, so I dropped it. His hand was strong and dry, my hand was damp but he held it while we said goodbye. Then he turned on his heels and walked off. I went over to the canteen and bought a newspaper, the woman inspected the Irish pound note very closely.

This flight was much worse. The only seat available to me since I was last to get on, was in between two very large squaddies who obviously did not like the look of the filthy civvy with the Irish accent. We landed at RAF Aldergrove, each man carrying his own luggage to the waiting customs men. I only had three packets of duty-free and had no weapon, but he still searched me thoroughly.

I walked through the long hut to the exit, feeling a bit lost. It was raining hard as I stood at the entrance trying to keep out of the way of the soldiers who were loading up into three tonners.

I saw Simon as soon as he came into the car park. He was as I imagined he would be. Tall, an athletic public school type, he zipped through the parked lorries and pulled up at the front door, no thought of taking one of the parking bays.

"Are you Deery?" I had picked up my case and was already walking to the back of his car; he opened the boot to allow me to place my case inside. He looked me up and down. "Do you want a wig?" My hair had grown some but still had that look, quite out of fashion. We jumped in the car and belatedly Simon stuck his hand out.

"Sorry, I'm Lt. Simon Adder, but you must call me Simon, it's my job to make sure you have all the things you need."

He pulled away and headed for Holywood Barracks. As we drove he talked.

"It's chaos at the moment, I've only been here three weeks and my job is to control four men in the field." He turned to have a quick glance at me. "We don't really have enough men out there." He pulled onto the dual carriage way and quickly gained a lot of speed.

"You will be staying at the camp for the first few days. There are a few last minute things and I want to take you around as much as possible, show you the sights and I do want you to think about wearing a wig."

He had another quick glance to see how this was going. "You can take it off after a few weeks."

We had not been driving long, when we pulled into the entrance to the barracks. Simon showed his ID card and we were let through. He pulled up at one of the blocks and we unloaded my case. I followed him into the building.

"This is your room." He opened the door. There were four beds, one of which had no blankets.

"I'll get that sorted for you, but I want you to come with me for now and I'll show you the Ops room and bring you up to date."

We closed the door and I followed him.

"That building over there is the cookhouse." We walked over to a two storey building covered in aerial masts. We went straight up the stairs, and into a large office.

On the walls were maps of Belfast with such detail that they showed even the shape of the back yards and individual lamp posts. There were a mixture of officers and other ranks either listening or talking to radios. I recognised Captain Roberts; he was on the phone and had not seen me. I carried on looking at the information boards. It was all stuff I had seen before but with a bit more detail, some of the mug shots had red pen through them with the word DEAD.

"How are you doing Deery?" Captain Roberts had noticed me.

"Fine Sir." I tried to smile, but he saw through that.

"You will be a bit nervous." He pointed to a seat next to him. I sat down.

"Yes just a bit."

"Remember, you're only doing observation, most of the time you will just be another conductor on the buses." Captain Roberts's phone rang. Simon gave me a cup of tea while I waited.

"As I was saying," he went straight back in where he'd left off, "It's low key, just keep an eye out and report in every night."

He fished around on his desk and found what he was looking for and re-read the information.

"I see they have placed you directly opposite the police station." He read some more. "You have an interview on Monday at the bus depot."

He put the piece of paper down. "Well I suppose Simon wants to show you quite a few things, so I'll let you get on." I was dismissed as he picked up the phone.

Simon beckoned me over to the other side of the room. He leaned against the bench.

"Let's get your temporary ID card sorted and your bedding and then we'll go for a ride, just to get the feel of the town."

As we walked to the Quartermaster's store, Simon told me about a shooting the night before.

Once the bedding had been sorted out, we picked up a temporary ID card for me. It had no photograph on it, so had to be used in conjunction with my driving licence. For the next four hours we drove around Belfast, which was surprisingly small. He showed me all the buildings I would be expected to know. We drove past where I would be living. I took heart from the fact that it was directly opposite a police station, which had three major lookout posts. That night I sat and read the latest reports, dossiers on IRA units and where all the army units had made camp. There was even a Squadron of Sappers in the bus depot I would be working at.

Chapter 7. Saturday 25 March 1972. 54

That morning Simon found me in the canteen eating a full army breakfast.

"Good morning." He sat down, he only had a cup of tea "I'll get you settled in at number 37 today."

"I think I need to go to Castlederg bus depot, I just feel someone may ask me about my last depot." I looked at Simon for agreement.

"Yes, busmen will be interested where you have come from." I carried on eating, pleased with myself.

"I think you should go and see some of your relations." Simon let this sink in. "They give you credence." I chewed my toast.

The thought of my Grandmother's house, with that smell of poverty, that smell of lentils and those worn out carpets. I knew he was right, so I nodded.

The rest of the day was spent travelling. Castlederg was small, but even so had a bus depot. We had a pint in one of the pubs, my first chance to talk to a local. Then we made our way to Derry for a quick spin round the town. I was reading the maps which had areas coloured to represent the various religions in the area.. Protestant, Catholic and mixed. Then we went back down the A6, back to Belfast.

We went into No. 37 Mount Pottinger Road, which had its front door on Madrid Street for some strange reason, but it was above the Post Office on Mount Pottinger Road, so that was the address. Directly opposite was the Police Station. At each end there were massive steel clad Sangers and you could just make one out on the roof. My flat was clean to a point and it had all the things I would need. I was glad to see a TV in the corner. I put the kettle on and realised that I had not done any shopping for myself.

"Why not go down and introduce yourself to the landlord, he owns the shop downstairs." Simon went into his pocket.

"No, I have money."

The doorbell made a loud pinging noise as I entered. It was the old fashioned type of shop where you asked for everything you wanted, whilst you stood on the other side of the counter. It had a small area glassed off, the Post Office, A large closed sign hung there.

"Hi, I'm moving in upstairs." He was a big Asian man and I got a shock when he opened his mouth, his accent was as thick as mine.

"Sure, no problem." He smiled at me. "It's been empty since February since some Pikey did a runner. I had to decorate from top to bottom."

I ordered all the things I needed and paid him with the money Mack had made me sign for.

I went upstairs with my little load of shopping. I realised that this was my first home, just for me.

"Do I need to keep receipts?" I looked at Simon as I passed into the kitchenette, he did not answer straight away, so I told him about the money Mack had given me.

"I'm not sure." We didn't mention it again.

He showed me a hidden phone in the bedroom; he peeled back the carpet and lifted two newly sawn floorboards and there was the phone. There was no dial for ringing numbers just a single button. He pressed it and was answered straight away.

"I'm just testing this line." Simon told the listener. I could hear the other person.

"Clear as a bell Sir." Having made contact and ensuring it was fully functional, he replaced the boards and carpet.

I carried on looking round the flat. The bathroom was small and the toilet was down some steep wooden stairs, but at least it was an inside toilet, so many of them were out in the cold back yards in Belfast.

That night I stayed in Holywood Barracks. On the Sunday, we started late. We walked around Belfast and had Sunday lunch in the Europa Hotel, Simon paid. Then we went down my memory lane visiting places which I only vaguely remembered.

Outside my old house, we were gathering too much attention, so we made a quick exit. My school, it looked so small now, had a burnt out car outside, half on the pavement.

The corner shop, which in my childhood was an Aladdin's cave, was just a dirty old shop, the outer windows boarded up with signs pasted on saying "Open for business."

"Do you want to see your Grandmother?" I shook my head. I was not quite ready for that. We made our way back to camp.

Simon had other people to look after, so when I'd collected my suitcase from the barracks, he drove me back to No. 37. We parked the car out of sight and quickly entered the flat.

Simon sat for a while and we went over last minute things.

"Where are you going to hide the mugshot book?" We looked around the flat and eventually decided on the cupboard which housed the gas meter. If anybody searched the house very thoroughly, I was in trouble anyway. Eventually Simon left, saying he would talk to me in the morning on the landline. I just sat there with the gas fire hissing and gathered my thoughts. I had never spent the night on my own, even when my mother knew she was going on a bender, she would farm my out to Mrs. Oxon, three doors down. I checked to see if the television was working. It was a small portable with twist tuning, but all three channels were clear and crisp. I finished my coffee and started to unpack, then watched the television for the rest of the night. Every time there was a noise outside, I jumped up to look out of the window, but otherwise I felt settled. Before I went to bed I practiced getting to the phone quickly. I did not sleep well and woke early. The question of the wig was beginning to worry me.

Monday 27th March 1972.

The Army had moved into the bus depot quite early on in the Troubles and the gate was manned by a couple of soldiers. I showed them my letter inviting me to an interview. They patted me down. I walked round the main building. There were busmen and soldiers all over the depot and one of them showed me to a rickety old stairwell leading to the top floor.

I introduced myself to a female clerk and she gave me a form to fill in while I waited. In the office there four women pushing pieces of paper around, waybills, time-sheets and engineer reports.

Eventually Mr. Jackson the depot superintendent came out of his office and invited me in. He asked all the questions we had anticipated, and I had my answers ready. He knew he had to give me the job, but he wanted to find out as much as possible about me.

"Well I can only offer you three day's training." He peered over his glasses to see my reaction.

"Oh that will be plenty. I've been doing the same job at Castlederg." I was feeling positive.

"And how is Billy O'Brian?" He asked the question I had been dreading. I sat there racking my brain to remember O'Brian.

"Oh he's always on about retirement, but I'm sure he'll be taken out of there in a box." I could feel the sweat running down my back. Jackson just laughed.

"Right then, you start on Wednesday." He jumped up to open the door. "Doris, fix Mr. Deery up with a temporary bus pass, he starts Wednesday, transferred from Castlederg Depot." He shook my hand and closed the door.

The office staff looked me up and down. They had not started anyone for over a year, jobs were hard to come by. They were curious.

Doris did all the paper work, temporary employee's bus pass, public service badge, uniform chit, pay records, and timetables. I was feeling relieved as she gave me instructions as to what to expect.

She sent me off to the clothing store. I was issued with two pairs of trousers, two shirts, one dust jacket, one tie, an overcoat and a hat which I didn't have to wear. I went round to the cashing-in office. Men were clocking on and off as the shifts were changing, so the cash clerk was not too happy about issuing me with a locker and a ticket machine, but eventually this was done. Like any other work place where men know each other well, the banter went on.

"Hey Billy." One of the conductors, who was cashing in at the end of his shift, shouted across the office, "You know that clippie from the Newtownards depot?"

"Aye the one that shaves twice a day." Billy knew exactly which woman he was talking about.

"Aye, well she's left her husband and run off with a barmaid from The Kings Arms."

"The dirty fucking cow." The two men carried on their comments with other men, making occasional remarks about the woman. I noticed one of my target men come in. I had only seen photographs of him, but there was no mistaking him, Tommy O'Neil had just walked in. He was the union convener for the depot, but most of all he was the commander of 'C' coy. IRA East Belfast. I could feel the power and hatred, and so did the men in the office. You always knew when you were in the presence of a sociopath. Everybody continued to cash up or clock on; nobody made eye contact with O'Neil. I busied myself with my ticket machine but I was keeping an eye on him, without staring. The man walked over to the cash clerk, suddenly the whole atmosphere changed.

"Clock me off Sam." O'Neil handed his money over.

The cash clerk deferred. He counted the money quickly. This gave me a chance to look carefully at O'Neil. So this was the man who ordered killings, bombings and still had over forty men under his command. The exact strength of the IRA was always hard to judge, active, passive, people who just made the numbers up. There was a huge sense of relief when O'Neil walked out of the office. I was excited, I had made a direct hit and I had not even started the job. I wanted to get back and report, but I knew that if I did that, I would be stuck in the flat until the next day, so I walked over the Albert Bridge and into town. I spent the next few hours riding around on the buses. I needed to learn the bus routes and know the layout of the city as well as possible.

It was a great idea. On the buses you can keep an eye out for everyone without raising any suspicion, observe, watch and gather nice low level intelligence to report back. I was feeling much better. The day had gone right to plan.

I got home late in the afternoon and started to get the flat clean, this was my army training kicking in. Simon came bang on time, but I still jumped a mile when the doorbell rang.

"How did it go?" Simon was smiling.

"You are not going to believe this." I could not wait to tell him my news. "I saw Tommy O'Neil. He came in the office while I was there." I wanted Simon to congratulate me, but he remained calm. He was pleased, pleased that I was enthusiastic, pleased that I had been listening and pleased that I had some sort of early success already.

"When do you start the job?" Simon was watching me, assessing me.

"Wednesday, very early, but I've already been out on the buses to have a look around with my free bus pass." I showed him my uniform, PSV badge, pass. I was like a child showing someone his Christmas presents.

"We may as well go back to the barracks." I packed my washing gear and some clean clothes in the brown paper bag from my shopping trip down stairs and we switched off the fire and left.

Wednesday 29th March 1972.

I got back to No. 37 at eleven thirty on Tuesday night. I had to be up early, so went straight to bed. I didn't really sleep well.

I arrived at the depot at five thirty in the morning, wearing my smart new uniform. It was drizzling. What was strange was the number of vigilantes still on the streets, watching everything and the army watching them. There were men on doorsteps, standing on corners, hands in pockets, scrutinizing everything that moved. The busmen were largely ignored, as they made their way into the depot.

Buses were moving onto the streets going to their various routes to start the day.

I clocked on, Denis, the duty clerk, handed me the running board, my timetable for the day. "You've been placed with George Megahey, I'll let you know when he comes in."

I made myself busy checking my ticket machine and filling out my waybill, but all the time quietly looking around. George arrived with four minutes to spare before we were due on the road.

"Hello Denis, clock me on."

Denis pointed to me and told George that he had got a trainee. His smiled. "I like it, I like it, some other bugger can run up and down the stairs." He came over to me and shook my hand. He was about mid fifties, greying hair, short, with nicotine stains on his right hand, but there was a relaxed air about him.

"I've been transferred from Castlederg." I said as an opening line, but he was more interested in how little he had to show me.

"So you've been on the buses before?" He checked my paper work over and pointed out that I had left off the duty number. We strolled over to the garage and found the driver, Danny Orr, doing his early morning checks.

"Hey Danny, I've got a trainee." George was beaming.

Danny shook my hand and jumped into the cab and the next thing, we were out of the depot and making our way over the Albert Bridge, passing the markets and down to the bus station.

The rest of the day flew by. I was being shown fare stages, routes and given all manner of information to do with the job. It's an interesting life, busily moving people from one place to another and there's a feeling of achievement at the end of the shift.

"Are you coming for a pint?" George asked me while we were cashing in. It was only one thirty and I was never a big drinker, I just couldn't handle the stuff. But would I just go home and stay there till my next shift I asked myself, or should I start to integrate with my work mates? I found myself agreeing.

The shifts were changing, men were clocking on and off, the cash office was bubbling. I noticed that one of my key target men, a young Catholic called Johnny O'Neil the son of Tommy O'Neil was clocking on. I logged it into my memory, ready for the night's report.

I drank shandy much to the derision of George and Danny, who after years of practise, could drink for all Ireland.

"Hell, he's a Prod, I'm a Catholic, but we don't let things like that get in the way." Danny was filling me in. "We've known each other for years, but I don't need to know where he prays." He lifted his beer and took a long draught. "But there are plenty around here who do."

Last orders were called at three; George and Danny got in another couple of pints and sank them fast. Even though I had only been drinking shandy, I went home with my head spinning.

They wandered off in the opposite direction to me. I just wanted to go home to sleep.

Simon was in the flat when I got to No. 37 and while I was having a coffee, I gave him all my information gathered that day.

"Johnny O'Neil came in to clock on, God he's an evil looking bastard." Simon already knew this.

He had the local mugshot book. "Look through this lot." We went though them but I had not seen anybody else out of the book, but it helped to refresh my memory.

The next morning I got to the depot thirty minutes early. This gave me time to stand around and watch the crew members as they clocked on. As usual, George and Danny bowled in with just minutes on the clock to get on the road. George checked my paperwork, off we went. As it happens, we had a long tea break, this was quite common. Good rest periods were allocated on most duties, thanks to the Union rules. The canteen was at the back of the depot; it was higher than the rest of the building to save ground floor space. I had to buy the teas. It was a rule that the conductor would always pay for the tea. Generally that was because he was the one who could make a few bob, by short changing or not giving a ticket out for a short journey, whilst the driver kept a watchful eye out for inspectors. At this point I had no idea how to fiddle, but they assumed I did.

George and Danny started a card school. I was sitting watching them and looking around at the canteen, which was a scruffy place. There was a lot of litter on the floor and the table was wiped with what looked like a floor cloth; everything had a fine layer of grease. The pool table caught my eye, I loved pool. I spent all my leisure time, back in Germany playing and I took the game very seriously.

There were two men playing; they did not have a clue. I chalked my name on the board, so I would play the winner. Eventually game ended and I went to set up the balls. We had just introduced ourselves, when Johnny O'Neil came in. I did not turn to look at him as he swaggered over to the counter. The local pool rules were spelled out to me. The game started. Now I'm the sort of player who wants to win, big style. I want to crush my opponent, which was not hard in this case. Throughout the game, Johnny was watching me. First I beat the winner, and then eight balled the next man. It was a nice table, it ran smooth and the balls were accurate, the cues were kept in good order. I was enjoying myself. All the time, Johnny's eyes were on me as I demolished the two no-hopers.

"I'll give you a game, these fucking wankers couldn't hit a cows arse with a banjo." Johnny was putting his name down on the board. I wondered how close Intelligence wanted me to get. I was smiling inside, but I didn't show it.

He was good, but erratic, which was how I liked it. I was making out that it was beginner's luck, just having a good day. It helped to wind him up.

"You're a lucky bastard, so you are." I put on my soft face, as Johnny put in another tanner, even though it was not his turn, nobody complained. I won again, he was getting angry and I was really enjoying the situation. We had four games and he won the last one. He played well and had started to give me some respect.

"Come on young'un." George was letting me know it was time to get back to work.

"Go on fuck off, now I've started to win." Johnny wanted more but I had to go. What a good story to tell Simon. The rest of the shift flew past.

When I got back to No. 37, I pulled up the boards and lifted the phone out and pressed the button.

'It's Deery here.' I did not recognize the voice that answered.

"I'll put you through to Captain Ellis." There was a moment, then a click.

"Captain Ellis." I recognized the plummy vowels of Ellis.

"Sir it's Deery, I'm just using my phone for the first time," I explained.

"Oh well Lt. Adder's not here at the moment, do you have anything to report." I went on to tell him about the pool games with Johnny O'Neil and that everything else was going fine.

"Well done Deery, I'll fill Simon in when he gets back."

"OK sir." I hung up and replaced the boards.

In the office, Ellis made a note in the large log, in his meticulous handwriting.

Wednesday 26 April 1972. Deery has made a good start, contact with John O'Neil C Coy E. Belfast, settled in well. Very promising.

We had a setback, Edwards has been sacked from Garson's Bakery, and so he will be posted to Londonderry where we believe we can get him a job with the council. We have some influence in that area.

McDonnell has settled in well at the Coach House in Strabane, and has volunteered for extra shifts at weekends, but maybe having a fling with one of the barmaids (one to keep an eye on).

BBC News, 31st April 1972

..A British soldier died this morning, after being shot in the Donegal Road area of Belfast four days ago...

The three days of training were over on Friday and George and Danny took me for a pint.

"I see you've been put with old Jerry Mason, well he won't throw you around." They both laugh. George continued, "He's never been out of third gear for five years." We drank the afternoon away.

Saturday 1st April 1972.

The next morning it was cold and raining but I had gone in early to make sure I had all the fare stages and other things in my head. I wanted to be ready for my first day with no guidance. I was reading the notice board, when I felt a little poke in the back.

"You'll not be so lucky next time." I turned round to find Johnny O'Neil scowling at me. It was still bothering him. He had not been turned over for a long time on the pool table.

"What time's your relief?" He was trying to see which duty I was on. I looked at the running board.

"We are off from ten thirty till eleven forty seven." I replied. Johnny smiled.

"Well, I'll be ready for you. I'm the spare conductor today and will be warming up all morning." He had a strange smile, the type you are instinctively wary of when you're a child. This is not supposed to happen. I'm supposed to just watch from the sidelines.

Denis the cash clerk was calling me over.

"Jerry this is the new boy, he's been transferred from Castlederg." Jerry looked round and took me in with one glance.

"Just keep the kids quiet on the school runs and get the teas in on relief and you'll do for me." He walked out into the yard to find his bus.

They were right, Jerry never went over twenty five miles an hour, not that it made much difference to me. We did a workman's special to Harland & Wolf, got a cup of tea at the canteen at Johnson's metal works, and then a scholars' run. The little bastards knew I didn't have much of a clue, but I didn't care, I knew I was not going to make a career out of this.

We were back at the depot at ten thirty, and Johnny O'Neil was sitting with his dad. I was not sure I want to be this close to these two evil men, but I smiled as I saw them.

"Two teas and a sausage sarnie please." The lady served me quickly but I was not in a hurry to sit down; I wanted time to think. I sat with Jerry.

"Hey." Johnny was waving me over. I didn't want to be that close but the pressure was on. I took my sandwich and tea and sat with them.

"So you've come from Castlederg?" I nodded at Tommy O'Neil. "Well, I'll have to send off for your union records. Do you still pay your dues at that branch?" I nearly choked on my sausage; my mouth went dry. At no point had anyone thought of my union records. The buses was a closed shop, you had to be a member of the union to be on the buses. Tommy was looking right into my soul, I lifted my tea to my mouth, just to give myself a few seconds to think.

"Yes, fully paid up member." I smiled, but my hands were shaking so I hid them under the table.

"I'll bring in my card tomorrow." What else could I say? He gave me a form to fill in while Johnny was setting up the balls on the pool table. I was glad that I to get away from Tommy. We started playing pool, Johnny was not giving anything away, so the game was slow and tactical. I ground out three wins. All the time Johnny was getting upset.

"You are the luckiest bugger alive." He was not used to losing but my mind was on the union records. I needed to get a message to Simon quickly.

"No more for me." I put the cue away. Johnny was furious. He wanted to win, to prove that nobody could make a fool out of him. I wanted to get to the phone under the floorboards.

"No that's enough for me." I smiled and made my way to the door. Johnny came running after me and caught up with me at the top of the stairs.

"What are you doing tonight?" He had his hands on my shoulder. I slowly removed his hands.

"Not a lot really, why?"

"We can go to the club. It's a better table there, come on, it's Saturday night." I was a bit shocked, but I didn't have an excuse so I agreed.

"I'll knock for you at seven." I was off, I had fourteen minutes to get to the phone, tell Simon and get back to the depot. I ran all the way and stumbled up the stairs of No.37 and into the bedroom. The phone was again answered quickly.

"Get me Simon." It seemed like ages before he answered, but probably only took a matter of seconds.

"Ellis here." I started to babble. "Sir, they are going to get my union records from Castlederg." He was silent for a few seconds, "Hmm…." Then there was silence. Every second seemed a minute. "Sir I've only got minutes to get back to the depot, I must go now." I slammed the phone down, put the boards back and ran like the wind. Jerry was standing at the depot gates, but I got there on time.

We got re-routed due to a suspect bomb, but time flew for me.

As soon as I got back to No 37, I was up the stairs and on the phone. Simon answered as soon as I asked for him.

"Yes, we forgot about the union records." He said calmly. "The union convener at Castlederg is ex-army protestant. He assures us that you will have two months records of full union dues, when the request comes through and we will get the union card to you by tonight." I was feeling much better, but just how many other things had we forgotten to cover?

There were still a few hours till seven, so I got some kip.

Johnny knocked very loudly on the door. I heard it clearly but I was ready for him.

We walked to the club, not the quickest way, Johnny didn't want to go though Protestant streets. Along the way, the vigilantes were out early that night, and most of them acknowledged Johnny.

The club was already quite full when we arrived and there were men playing pool. We took a seat and waited our turn. I studied everyone but not openly staring, just using the technique that Mack had taught me. How had I got myself into this position. I was supposed to be lying low and there I found myself in the lion's den, surrounded by all sorts of God knows who. I didn't know whether I'd done well or I'd stepped over the mark. Would they pull me out or what? I knew I was out of my depth, but didn't know whether I should just keep mouth shut and carry on.

Johnny went on to the pool table first. It gave me time to look around the club. I started making mental notes. I had already seen two familiar faces, who were on the wanted list and two from the report list.

The winner stays on the table, so Johnny had to win so that we could play. Johnny lost and I could see his pride was hurt. I had watched the other man play, so I identified his weakness whilst he did not know my game.

"Robert, he's a lucky bugger and he'll clear up if you give him a chance." Johnny filled the other guy in. I was thinking it might be a good time to lose; maybe he'd lose interest in me, if I played a duffer's game, but the fighting spirit got inside me as soon as we started to play. We shook hands at the end of the game and as the night wore, on people lost interest in the pool table. There was bingo and a singer came on at nine, rebel songs were going down the best, she knew her audience. But Johnny and I played on. When he won, you could see the jubilation in his face but I didn't let that happen too often. I knew he held me in high esteem, for no other reason than I could beat him at pool. He didn't even know me. At the end of the night, I deliberately missed the black. I did this because I knew him to be a sociopath and I had to walk home with him. It worked, he was happy and on the way started to sing. We were stopped by an army patrol and pushed against the wall. I gave them a bit of mouth. "Fuck off sunshine." The squaddie made me lean over even further. He knew this would start to hurt pretty quickly but we were kept waiting whilst our names and addresses were checked out. Mine took forever, because I'd not been there long.

"Spell that again." The radio operator had mispronounced my name. "Delta, Echo, Echo, Romeo, Yankee." My arms were killing me, so I tried to stand up a bit more upright.

"Don't fucking move son." The soldier holding me had a baton pushed into my back and they were very edgy, but this did not help my arms, which were starting to give way. I moved again, this time the soldier brought me down with a head lock, my face caught the ground and I started to struggle. I was wondering how it had come to this, but my mouth said "You son of a whore, fuck off to where you came from."

This was a bad mistake. A Land Rover was called up and I was whisked off to Mount Pottinger Police Station. I didn't know what had happened to Johnny. They let me go at four in the morning; the 'reasonable force' showing as blue marks all over my back and legs. I got straight on the phone, blood still on my lips.

"Get me Simon Adder."

"Hello?" The sound of Simon's voice calmed me down, he said he would be there soon and he was. I suddenly realised that this is what it was going to be like.

"I've been lifted by the army." I still felt sorry for myself. "I have to be at work in two hours." Simon listened, while I moaned on, "I'm black and blue." But then I remembered the four sightings and told him about them. Simon took the details down and before I fell asleep, he gave me my union card.

"I'll catch an hour's sleep and phone you after my shift tomorrow." I looked at the alarm clock. "No, later today."

Chapter 8.   69

I was not due to clock on until five past six, so I did get some sleep, but in the morning light the bruises on my back and legs were spectacular and I limped to work. The day passed over with no real happenings, but I did hand in my union card to Tommy O'Neil. At the end of my shift, I made my way to No. 37. I took some aspirins, which I bought from the shop downstairs, and sat looking at the Police Station over the road. I realised I was looking on them as the enemy, looking out of their Sangers, dominating the scene. It was a strange feeling. Then I went straight to bed, planning to sort out the reports later.

I was woken by banging on the front door. I rushed to pull on my pants and then walked down the stairs.

"Who's that?" I had a frog in my throat.

"It's me." Johnny was talking in one of those loud whispers. Johnny had come to find out what had happened, and he was very impressed with the bruises. All I could think of was Simon suddenly phoning or worse, appearing.

I put the kettle on as I told Johnny what had happened.

"Four in the morning and will you look at that." I was showing him my legs. The bruising look good enough to get a load of sympathy, but Johnny was not the sympathetic type. He did, though, like other people to hate the army as much as he did.

"Well, we'll get them one of these days." Johnny made a pistol with his finger and pointed it at me and fired. There was a quiet knock on the door; I leapt out of the chair and sprinted down the stairs. I did not ask who it was, but just opened the door. Simon tried to walk in, but I put my hand forcibly against his chest as he walked up the steps. At first he was surprised.

"No, they don't live here anymore." Simon nodded and walked away. I had said this more for the benefit of the person who upstairs than for Simon and closed the door noisily. I ran up the stairs and straight into the kitchenette and finished off the tea.

"Do you want a biscuit?"

"Yes."

"How many sugars do you take?"

"Two."

"Who was that?"

"It was just someone asking for the people who used to live here." I desperately wanted to change the subject.

"What happened to you last night?" Not that I gave a toss, but I managed to feign interest in how the night had ended for Johnny, after I was shuffled away.

"They'd had their fun, so I was soon on my way." He took a drink of tea and looked at me, "I went straight home and told my dad."

"You still live with your parents?" I forgot, not everyone has to get out as soon as they can walk.

Looking hurt, Johnny replied, very defensively, "Of course I do."

I wanted to get rid of Johnny.

"Do you want to go out tonight?" Johnny asked.

I was knackered and bruised and I wanted to get to the barracks, not just make a phone call report.

"No way, I'm black and blue. Do you want to beat a man who's wounded and anyway I'm on an early start tomorrow."

Johnny finished his tea and left with my promise that I would give him a chance for revenge soon.

I was on the phone before Johnny had got to the end of the street.

"Tell Simon I'm coming in." That's all I said, when my call was eventually answered.

I got the number eighty six bus to Holywood. I did not use my staff pass and the bus conductor did not know me, but I still got off two stops after the barracks, preferring to walk back, rather than get off nearer to the barracks. I had no ID so had to wait at the guardhouse until Simon came to identify me.

As we walked back to the offices I gave him all the details as to what had occurred. Simon was just listening and calculating the effect of these changes of events.

Captain Ellis, joined us in Room seven.

"So you've bonded with a known IRA sympathizer and you have not even been in position for a week!" He looked pleased. I had mixed feelings.

70

"Obviously we don't want you to rush things." Ellis could afford to be relaxed he didn't have to be out there. "But to be close to some one the likes of O'Neil, it's a big plus."

He looked from Simon to me. Simon was trying to look encouraging.

"It could take years to get to this position again, you've done really well lad." But they could see it was lying heavily on me.

"I do my best." I smiled weakly and was given no further instructions, other than to keep doing what I was doing.

I made my way to the canteen. I thought I might as well get a proper meal while I was there. The cook sergeant wanted to know who I was; my hair was getting long as were my side boards. I explained I was MI and it would be foolish to carry an identity card.

I walked back up a few stops to get the bus home and was in bed by nine thirty.

Wednesday 19th April 1972 BBC News.

A British soldier was shot today in the Lower Falls area of Belfast, while on foot patrol, his next of kin has been informed...

In the OP's room at Holywood barracks, the radio operator turned round and announced "One shot Willy has done it again." All the men in the office knew it meant another mother would be getting a visit from the Army.

I had done a week of early and a week of late shifts and was well into my second week of early shifts. Life was settling down and a pattern was evolving. Johnny and I played pool every Wednesday and Saturday night, plus we got a few games at work when our paths crossed, which was quite often, because we were on the same shift. One of the really good things which I had not even considered. I received two wage packets. I was allowed to keep my bus wage and the army paid my wages into the bank in Germany and they paid my rent. I felt rich. Simon said "Well you need money to live, don't you?" I didn't think he knew how much I could have earned, with a little bit of overtime, so I kept schtum.

It was amazing how much I saw on the buses. I kept writing the reports and spotting things which army patrols never saw. Both Protestants and Catholics kept a close eye on the army – when they were planning anything. The problem was how slowly my information got to those who need to know, but it was better than nothing.

We were diverted regularly on the bus route because of a suspect bomb here, a demo there, sometimes even gun fights occurred. A lot of this was not even newsworthy.

Jerry the driver just plodded on, nothing fazed him. He had been a merchant sailor in the war and lost a lot of friends one way or another, so this little tiff didn't worry him. Most of his stories started "I remember the time" and he was a great raconteur, remembering dates, names and places in great detail. I asked him once, when we were standing at the terminus waiting for the return journey, whether he ever expected to die whilst he was in fighting.

"Oh yes, every time we left port, I used to write my last letter to my mother. She couldn't face opening them until I was back, I never understood that." He looked into the distance, miles away, remembering the distant conflict.

On Saturday, when Johnny knocked, I was wearing a new shirt and feeling very flash.

"Electric blue, you look like a Belisha beacon."

Johnny was not impressed with my new shirt. I'd also bought myself a two piece pool cue and carrying case, which I hoped would improve my pool.

"Just wait until this little beauty starts to talk." I was winding Johnny up, he was inspecting the cue while we walked to the club and as he was putting it back in the case, a foot patrol soldier came around the corner. We carried on walking, but the section leader decided that we perhaps might be carrying some sort of weapon. I could see it coming and they may have checked us out even if we hadn't had the cue box with us, but that just tipped the balance. Why they had to lean us against the wall and kick our feet around I don't know, but with the best will in the world it got us going.

"You just leave my bollocks alone you puff." Johnny was getting indignant at the process and I couldn't blame him, I felt my own temper rising.

"Have you no home to go to?" Johnny kept up the pressure, I did not want another beating, answered their questions.

Eventually, we were allowed to go on our way. Johnny was furious. "Well that makes my mind up." I looked at Johnny quizzically. He said, "I'm going to join my dad's unit."

"What do you mean?" We were getting close to the club and as we entered he said slowly, "I'm going to join the IRA." I nearly said, that I thought he was already a member, but managed to hold that in.

Sitting at the bottom of the club house, we watched the other pool players as we waited our turn.

"My dad has always expected me to take more of an active part, but until now I never felt the need." This information went directly against all the intelligence reports I had studied.

"I go on the demos and to the funerals, but not any real action, but now...," he tapered off, a grim look on his face.

I played badly all night. The new cue was not doing anything for my game. There was a subdued atmosphere to the night.

The next day, news got to the O'Neil's that Paddy McVeigh, a family friend, had been shot by an under cover British Intelligence Agent, from a passing car, in the Andersonstown part of Belfast. Johnny was away from work for six days, to mourn the death of his friend.

I went into Holywood for a night of R&R on the Wednesday night. Fat Brian and Smudge were on their night off and the film Soldier Blue was showing in the canteen. We had more than two cans that night. I slept in my bunk, which had not been re-allocated.

I read the reports before I went back to No. 37. A soldier, who had been shot by a sniper two days before, was in intensive care. There were some of my reports on the list, which made me feel proud.

Johnny came back on the Friday, you could see some change in him and he was full of hate, so a bit scary. We just saw each other briefly, whilst passing in the yard, and arranged to meet up on the Saturday night.

That Saturday, I had only just finished reporting and put the phone away, when Johnny knocked.

"Fancy a night in town?" He was imploring me to go into Belfast for a pub crawl.

"No problem mate." I put on the electric blue shirt and polished my shoes, while Johnny watched the TV, then we walked through the back streets to Albert Bridge.

He was back to normal and we were chatting away about how many girls we had been with, both exaggerating about our exploits, as we got to the first bar.

I'm not a big drinker, so I had to make sure that I didn't drink too much. Bar after bar we visited and even though ever time Johnny turned his back, or went to the toilet, I poured some of my drink into his or any other glass near to me, I could feel I was slowly getting drunk. I suggested we have half pints at each bar, but Johnny ridiculed me.

"Are you a queer?" I was shamed into drinking more than I could take. My guard was going down. We fell all over the road on the way back, Johnny picked me up.

"I'm going on training exercise next week." I tried to comprehend this piece of information.

"Where to?" My head was spinning but I knew that I had to listen.

"Three days, out in the sticks." Johnny was holding me steady and watching my response. I needed to look dumb; it was easy because of the beer.

"My dad has arranged for weapon training and I want you to come." I could not believe what was happening. I let myself fall to the floor, to give me time to think.

"Come on, you hate the bastards as much as me." Had I been acting that well?

"I'm just a bus conductor." I wailed.

"We have to make a stand." He was really putting the pressure on. "They need us." I was sobering up very fast here. "I can't be taking time off work. I've only just started." My mind was racing, what would Simon advise me to do?

"You get three days off next week I've already had a look at your duties." He was serious. The adrenaline was kicking in and at that moment I knew that the army would like to have me there.

"OK, but don't expect me to be any good."

He hugged me. Here was I, having just agreed to join the IRA, standing on the streets of Belfast, being hugged by a man who, for all the world, wants me to shoot and maim my own side. You could not make this up.

I didn't report in that night, it would not have been worth it, I would have been incoherent.

The next morning with my tongue rasping on the top of my mouth, I spoke into the phone. "Get me Simon." Simon was there.

"I've just joined the IRA." There was a long silence and after a while I explained how the night had gone and why I had agreed to the offer.

"You need to come in. I'll have things ready when you get here."

"I start work at two thirty," I reminded him. "I have other things to do, besides running up to Holywood every five minutes."

"I know, but we still need a full report on this." I looked at my watch. I supposed it could be done.

"I'll be on the ten thirty bus." I could get my breakfast in camp.

"No we'll pick you up in twenty minutes. Be at the junction of Mount Pottinger and Madrid Street." There was a new firmness in his voice, which told me how important this was.

Brian was detailed to pick me up and was a bit frosty with me. He didn't like having to taxi me around and I did not want to be explaining things to him, so there was an atmosphere in the car.

"Oh, it's just a general reporting session," I lied. Well could I really say that I was about to go on an IRA training course?

"They seemed a bit anxious, that's all." I shrugged my shoulders and changed the subject.

"How are things going with you?"

"Every minute feels like an hour." He was not having a good time.

I told him that the buses were a lot more interesting than I expected. We arrived at the camp and went straight in, no messing this time. Brian dropped me at the door.

"See you later." I tried to be friendly, but I felt he saw through me.

Bloody hell, they had brought in every Tom, Dick and Harry to listen to my report. We were in the room at the end of the corridor, which was a bit larger. There were seven of them, one was a half Colonel. There was an air of excitement. I still had a hangover and still wasn't sure I had done the right thing.

Ellis asked the questions, everybody else just listened. I was sweating.

"Do you think it was the beer talking?"

"No Sir, he'd looked at my duties, so it was premeditated."

"You know things are going very fast here, but you have to go with the flow." I nodded. I was ambitious and wanted to do my best, but also knew that it would be very dangerous to continue. Everybody in the room knew that.

At this point, the colonel opened his mouth.

"We feel because of the responsibility you are taking on, that you should be rewarded, so as of today you are now Corporal." Not very long ago, I was a Sapper, now I had suddenly become a Corporal, I was receiving two wages and my head was spinning.

After every one had gone, Ellis and a tough looking man in civvies, who had not said a word during the meeting, stayed behind. He introduced himself as Captain Lunn of the SAS and actually shook my hand. His hand shake was firm and my hand was wet through with sweat, but he did not appear to notice.

"We need to go though certain things. You need to make it look like you are unfamiliar with weapons and we need to know where the training takes place." I nodded my head and listened as closely as I could. Out in the corridor, the Colonel was giving instructions.

"Put Mr Adder on this one full time, I don't want him distracted by anything else."

"Yes Sir."

"And get the techs to bug Deery's flat, we need to know what's going on in there, without his having to report it."

"Yes Sir." The wheels started to turn.

Back in the big room, Lunn gave me pointers, which were obvious, but it helped focus my mind. I was offered coffee, to help me concentrate. The mugshot book was out and Lunn pointed to his main targets. At last they were finished with me.

"Do you want a bed?"

"No sir, I wouldn't mind grabbing a meal, and then I'll get back to my flat."

It had been a long day. I could feel my batteries running low.

"Ok, go to the mess, get a bite to eat and we'll organise a lift." Ellis was patting me on the back, as I made my way to the door.

"Well done, Deery," Lunn said. I felt very proud at that moment.

I wandered out to the mess and felt the cold of the night. A heavy dew had fallen and there were no clouds to keep the temperature up.

Ellis sipped his coffee as he filled out his report, which then was sent directly to The Secretary of State for Northern Ireland.

Outside the vigilantes stood on doorsteps, men moved weapons and bombs from one safe house to another, doors were kicked in and heavy boots stamped up stairs. It was just one more night in the province.

Brian came to my table with a large cup of tea and the morning paper and sat down.

"A couple of our lads were in a gun fight last night."

"Do I know them?" I was happy to talk about anything except what was happening to me.

"Yes, do you know that fat bastard from Two Troop, Johnston?" I nodded.

"Well it was his section, they were on patrol and all hell broke loose down on McAuley Street, someone had a rifle and a few hand guns, shooting from an old warehouse." He started to chuckle. "They ran out of ammo, didn't hit a thing."

He finished off his tea and we made our way to his car. He drove me back to my place, dropping me off in a back lane.

"Be careful," he said as he drove off. I went to my cold bed.

Chapter 9. Friday 28th April 1972.   80

My shift on the buses went over that night without much to tell, but I was sure Jerry's driving was getting slower, or was I just getting impatient. When I got home to No. 37, something was different. I sat and looked about the room. I could not put my finger on it, was that glass there before? Was the door just like that? Was there a smell? I decided I should start to take precautions. There were two ways into the flat and I needed know if anyone came in while I was out. I put a tin can behind the back door. If this moved, I would know that someone had been in.

I was on a late shift that night and as I went through the gates into the yard, I bumped into Tommy O'Neil.

"Here's your union card." He handed over the card and looking at me closely. "There's a funeral for one of our boys on Monday, I'd like you to be there." I was taken aback, but managed to say, "I'll be there, is Johnny going?"

"Yes he can pick you up at ten thirty."

On the Monday morning Johnny was at the door bang on time, and we walked to the stop where the forty one bus would take us up Falls Road to Milltown cemetery.

As we went along, he told me of the training which was to take place that weekend. He knew that it was my long weekend, so I would not need to take time off work.

We arrived at the cemetery and walked past the Police Station, which was heavily fortified with barbed wire and sand bags. You could clearly see RUC and army officers photographing everyone one who entered.

In the cemetery, a big crowd had gathered and we fell in with them. The cortège meandered down the path, the family at the front weeping quietly as we all gathered around the grave. We were at the back. A tricolour had been placed over the coffin and as the body was lowered into the grave, I saw six men with black balaclavas and green army styled jackets, line up next to the grave. Suddenly they pulled out pistols and with one of them shouting out the time, fired six shots into the air. Immediately the RUC tried to move in, grey Land Rovers rolling down the path, to where we were milling around. The gunmen ran down in the opposite direction and climbed quickly over the fence. Meanwhile the men in the crowd blocked the road and were banging on the windows of the vehicles, generally making things difficult for the RUC. Tempers were rising and some of the men started throwing stones and branches which were lying under the trees. The RUC started to pull back and then the army came down another path with riot shields and batons. As the RUC retreated, we got braver, pushing hard. It ended up as a stand off, with the RUC and the army outside the gates and us just on the inside. Photographers had been running around most of the time, largely ignored by the crowd, but snapping away. We didn't know whether they were press, army or IRA sympathizers and I didn't care. I was close to Johnny all the time. If anyone had asked who I was, I knew he would vouch for me. There was great excitement amongst the men, we stood around and going over the whole event. Everybody wanted to get to the pub for the wake, so the first of the brave souls left and we saw them being allowed to leave, without any retribution from the RUC. We followed them out and down the Falls Road to the pub.

"Did you see them run?" Johnny was full of himself. We arrived at the pub, which was full to the brim with people ordering drinks and recalling their part in the day's action.

"What you drinking?" Tommy O'Neil was getting the order in. I was trying to remember as many faces as possible without looking too obvious.

A man, who Johnny referred to as Joe, was telling his tale. "Then did you see me hit that bastard with that rock." He was beaming and excited. We listened to him telling the story, exaggerating the victory over the RUC and army.

The pub was now full and suddenly a big cheer went up. I could not see at first, but six men were pushing through towards the bar. They were the six men who had fired the salute at the graveside. They were being patted on the back, drinks were set on the bar, the noise and excitement increased, songs were being sung, stories of the deceased were being told and people got drunk. I was watching, listening and making mental notes. I also had a shift on the buses that night.

Tuesday 2nd May 1972.

The next morning Johnny knocked on the door while I was reporting to Simon on the land line. I had to quickly put the carpet down and hide the phone, to get to the door.

"Have you seen this?" He was holding out a copy of Belfast Today. He pushed past me and went up the stairs. I followed.

The headline read, "Mob protects gun men" and there on the front page was a picture of Johnny and me, he was throwing something and I had a snarl on my face. I didn't remember snarling. The photographers had been from the press. Johnny was delighted, I was wondering what Simon and Ellis will think of this.

In an office back at barracks the radio operator listened and made notes. The wire had been installed. That was the someone who had been in the flat.

"Look at your face, you look as though you're going to bite them." Johnny was pointing at the picture of me.

"Aye, but you'll get lifted for that photo, not me." I quipped.

Johnny sat and read parts of the report, reading out loud bits that vaguely had anything to do with us.

"It says 'the crowd at this point turned ugly.' They are talking about you." He was like a child with a new toy. I put the kettle on and made two cups of tea, he shouted through to the kitchen.

"Hey, it says the wake went on until the early hours, you're not joking, I never got home until three in the morning." He tossed the paper down and leaned back.

"Come on, let's go for a game of pool." I was on the middle shift, so I had a few hours spare.

"I'll only thrash you." I was trying to wind him up.

"Fuck you, I'll play you for a pint and I'll be pissed in an hour." He stood up.

82

"You always did get pissed easily." Its part of the game, make it important to the other player, so he tries too hard. I picked up the cue case and put my coat on. There was a fine drizzle as we walked to the club.

While we were in the club, Johnny told me that we would be getting picked up on the Friday at six thirty, for training.

At Holywood barracks, in the large training room, Major Ellis was talking to all ranks. There were detailed maps on the wall behind him.

"As you know, sadly, we lost another man to One Shot Willy and we have to make finding this man, a top priority. It could be there's more than one man, but it's doubtful that they have more than one with these skills." He glanced down at his notes.

"He's currently taking out a man every ten days, with a single shot to the head. His average distance from target is two hundred and seventy five yards." He looked up.

"This is very high calibre shooting, even with a specialist rifle and taking all things into account, this man is a top notch marksman." There was a murmur from the men assembled, Ellis went on.

"We don't have much, but I will tell you this, we think that he's been brought in from abroad, probably East Germany or Poland and he works for money. Of course we have to keep an open mind and it may turn out that they just have more than one operator and they may be local." Ellis stopped to think for a moment.

"We do have our ears to the ground and all intelligence on this subject is being collated by Captain Lunn Special Forces." He pointed over to Lunn. "If you have any information, no matter how tenuous, you think may be linked to this problem, you must pass it through his department." He turned the page on his notes.

"Now I want to cover the riot involving the Para's on Crumlin Road. I want to say that they acted well within the rules of the yellow card...." He went on to other business.

Monday, 29th May 1972.

The rest of the week passed by, my driver, Jerry was off ill and I was given a young driver called Kerry Howell. We left late and arrived early on every trip, he was throwing the bus around but he made up for that with his wit.

"I like my girls to have a pulse and still be warm." He was girl mad. Often he would slow the bus down and open his window to wolf whistle, even when we had a bus inspector on board.

"Hey love, fancy a good time?" I started to blush, but this easy going attitude with girls, was part of his life.

On my last shift, before we went to the training with Johnny and the IRA, Kerry and I were on the number twenty four route, which went from Dunmurry to the city. We were waiting at the terminus for the return journey. Two of the loveliest young girls got on the bus. Kerry had seen them and had come from the cab and to sit in the back with me. He was chatting away.

"Where are you two lovelies going then, on the town?' They were enjoying the attention.

"None of your business." The older one replied, but she still kept eye contact with Kerry, obviously wanting the conversation to carry on. Kerry was not put out of his stride one bit.

"Well I'm off tomorrow, if you would like a good time?" He gave an easy smile, not taking his eyes off the girl. She was about seventeen, purple mini skirt and her coat was even shorter.

"Do you think we go out with any old man who asks?" She was smiling; her friend and I were just watching this go on.

"Well do you want a drink then?" Kerry kept going; the girl looked at her friend, who took a sly glance over to me. I had got what I thought was my best face on.

"Well you'll not get me drunk." She was defiant and started to lay down conditions. Kerry knew he'd scored.

"Would I do that?" Kerry looked more roguish when he was trying to look innocent, but everyone understood, that he would try and she probably would get drunk. He now wanted to draw me and the other girl in. I at this moment, remembered I had a date with the IRA.

"I'm sorry I can't come." I didn't want to look like a party pooper, so added that I was going home to my mother's for a long weekend.

"Sure your mum will let you out for once." Kerry felt as thought he was loosing it.

"Sorry, she lives in Liverpool, I'm getting the ferry across and won't be back until Monday." What could I say, if looks could have killed, I would have been dead meat.

Kerry tried to salvage something. "Me and you could go out?" He looked at the first girl.

"What me? Go out with the likes of you, I've got a reputation to keep." At this moment an old man got on the bus and looked at his watch.

"I thought I'd missed it," he said.

"God look at the time." Kerry jumped up and left saying, "We'll meet you at O'Donnell's at eight on Wednesday."

The journey back into town must have broken a speed record. Even though we picked up a passenger at almost every stop, I never really had time to speak to the girls again, but the young one smiled every time I passed. Later Kerry quizzed me about the trip back.

"Did they talk to you?"

"No, I was busy."

"So they did not say they would not be there?"

"No." I was getting impatient with him.

"Where did they get off?"

"Bedford Street and they walked towards City Hall."

At the end of the shift I went to No. 37 and reported to Simon on the phone.

"Will you be monitoring me?" I wanted to know whether I would be followed.

"No I'm afraid you will be on your own, you'll have to be very careful. If you want to get out of this at any point, get yourself to a phone and we'll pull you." Simon knew this was a golden opportunity, but that it was me taking the risks.

"Report in as soon as you get back and don't take any risks." This was stating the obvious.

I slept quite well considering and the next morning I just hung around the house, trying to relax.

Friday 2nd June 1972. BBC News

Another British soldier was shot today by a sniper in the Ballymurphy area of Belfast, whilst on foot patrol… …

Friday 2nd June 1972.

"Have you got a sleeping bag?" Johnny enquired as he came through the door.

"No, what do you think I am, a Boy Scout?"

"You'll have to take a few blankets rolled up then." He went past me into the bed room and stripped off the only bedding I had and made a neat roll, tying them with a belt. He looked down at the two pillows on the floor, where I had been resting my head while reporting to Simon.

"Have you been sleeping on the floor?" I blushed.

"No I was going to wash the sheets before we go." I picked the pillows up and placed them on the bed, I was not a good liar.

"You also need some warm clothes." Johnny was sitting on the bed and I was thinking that I didn't like him being too close to the phone and I wanted him out of the bedroom.

"Hey you're like my mother, get the fuck out and make a cup of tea." I pointed towards the kitchen. He went though and put the kettle on.

I filled my duffle bag with some clean socks and a warm pullover, collected a few things from the bathroom and I was ready.

Johnny looked at his watch. "We've got twenty minutes".

I told Johnny about the two girls and at the mention of Kerry's name, I could see he did not get on with him.

"Kerry's a lad, so he is." But he didn't mean that, he meant he was a fucking proddy bastard, who got all the girls. I made a mental note not to mention Kerry again.

It was raining as we went to the pick up point. I was feeling self conscious about my blanket roll, I felt like some carpet bagger.

86

We were picked up by two men in a Ford Capri; we threw our stuff in the boot and were on our way.

The driver was about thirty years old, but the man who sat next to him was much younger, barely eighteen. Johnny ran the conversation, "Hiya, this is Billy Deery." He pointed at me; I leant across and shook their hands

"What's your name?" Johnny was looking at the young man.

"Rory." He did not give us his last name.

Johnny knew the driver. "So Hugh, how are things?"

"Not so bad, Johnny boy and yourself?" We were heading out of town, and the windscreen wiper on the passenger side was all but useless. As we left Belfast, I started to consider my position; it could have turned into a full blown panic attack. Were these men were my execution squad? Imagine if they had known all along who I was? Were they going to take me to some dark corner of Ireland and leave me dead?

The radio was on, I remained silent. I was watching where we were going for one, and two I was starting to think too much. After an hour and a half I sat up.

"Hugh, can we stop for a piss?" I was not sure I wanted to go to the toilet, but I sure needed some fresh air, he went on for a further five minutes then pulled in.

It was not a lay-by but there was cover. We got out of the car stretching our legs and lighting up cigarettes, I walked into the trees. Now there were all sorts of things running through my head and one was Simon saying not to take any risks. I felt as though something was wrong, I didn't have any evidence, just a gut feeling I was going to end up in a ditch.

My experience so far was telling me that if I ran and they found me, that's where I'd be. If I stayed the course and they were who they said they were, then I would gain some very valuable intelligence.

"Hey Billy, what the fuck are you doing?" I was brought back to the present by Johnny.

"Move yourself, you're not on your father's yacht now." He had a lovely way of saying things. I trudged back to the car, not having the nerve to make a run for it. Needless to say they gave a little cheer as we crossed the border. We arrived at our destination about fifteen minutes later, driving along a very tight lane and going over a hill to a farm.

I was surprised at how many people there were at the training camp. We were met by an old man, who checked us off his list.

"Just park over there." He pointed to where four other cars were parked. We picked up our bags and things and followed him to a barn. By now it was completely dark, there were no lights at all, and only the old man had a torch. Inside there was a single bulb lighting the whole barn. About a dozen men had already taken the best sleeping places. Half the barn was stacked with bails of hay; the other half had old tractors and bits of very old farm machinery lying around.

"When you've got yourselves sorted, there's a meeting at eight in here." He disappeared into the dark.

Rory was still outside trying to wipe cow shit off his boots.

I went and got a bail of hay, dragging it over to where I planned to sleep. I cut the rope and spread the hay level, then getting my blankets out, made my bed for the weekend.

"You've done this before." Johnny was watching and copying me.

"Aye a regular Boy Scout that's me." I really should not have looked so useful, but the army training kept kicking in.

"There's a pub not far from here, after the meeting I'm off for a pint." Johnny smiled at the thought of it.

I knew what sleeping rough was like and a few pints inside always helped. "Count me in. Does it have a pool table?"

"No, but the music's good and the landlord does not have a watch."

One more car arrived after us, but there was only the driver inside. He came in and without saying anything, he set out his camp bed. He had a gas light and some home comforts, a folding chair and the biggest chunky sleeping bag I've ever seen.

Not long after some men came into the barn. One young man called us all together.

"Get yourselves over here." We all gathered at the other end and they did a roll call, very military.

"Right you're here for basic training, reveille is six thirty, you can get washed in the farm and breakfast is in two stages."

At this point he read out the names of those in the first and those in the second shift for breakfast. Johnny was on the first and I was on the second. I was not displeased about this, I would have more opportunity to look around and make mental notes, remember names and faces.

The young man continued and told us that we would be covering basic discipline, small arms, organising riots and how to deal with the forces.

He then introduced us to the other men who would be training us that weekend.

As soon as the talk was over, Johnny said, "Come on, off to the pub." We made sure everything was packed away.

There was not much light and Johnny tripped on our way to the local. We arrived at the village, it was not really a village, no more than a few houses but they had a pub. We stumbled in and were hit by the warmth and light. You have to give it to the Irish; they are well blessed with homely welcoming ale-houses

There were quite a lot of people inside, dogs lying in the middle of the floor, a heavy pall of smoke hung around and on one of the tables, a fiddle and a few penny whistles. Some of the men from the farm had already beaten us down there. We got our pints and joined them.

"We're from Derry, Bogside." The oldest man said by way of an introduction. He was in his late twenties, with long dank hair and that pinched mouth look that only poverty can bring.

"I'm Johnny and that's Billy.' Johnny introduced both of us.

"John, Pat and I'm Seamus." He pointed out the other two and they nodded.

Hugh and Rory came into the bar and ordered pints, and we made room for them.

"You two must have sprinted down here," Hugh observed looking at Johnny and me.

"Hey, we're not wasting drinking time." Johnny opened a pack of cards, "Anyone in for Crash?" He started to shuffle the cards. Soon the musicians started playing over in the far corner. A guitarist and a small harp player came in later during the evening. We all rolled back to the farm late, stumbling and laughing, and fell into our beds. I slept well.

Saturday 3rd June 1972.

The next morning I could hear the rain falling, I did not want to get out of bed. The lone man who was dressed like a hunter was up and dressed. All of his things had been packed away.

A voice in the gloom said, "Come on get yourselves up." I struggled out of bed and walked across the yard. In the bathroom, there was only one cold water sink and the door was missing. I waited my turn, decided against shaving, just rinsed my face and had a quick brush of the teeth and I was out. While Johnny was at breakfast, I had a chance to study the last man to arrive. He'd bedded down on the other side of the barn. To my knowledge, he had not spoken to anyone. He was sitting on his camp bed reading a paper backed book. He wore black boots, which tied a long way up the leg, a camouflage jacket with a hood and dark trousers. His watch was one of those big heavy duty things which could probably go down to a hundred yards under water and tell you the time in every country of the world. He was not very tall, but had an air of strength, confidence and looked very sure footed. I was trying to work out why this man would be on basic training, when Johnny came back from breakfast.

"Fucking lovely," he was smiling, "as much as you can eat, eggs, bacon, sausage and every damn thing you could want, go on get yourself in." Johnny jumped back onto his bed. I went off, but I noticed that the quiet man, the Hunter, did not come in.

It was like the monkeys' tea party, people grabbing tea and toast and generally making pigs of themselves.

"Yes I'll have another slice of toast if you don't mind," announced one of the men who had eaten the most. I was glad to get out of there, but not until I had taken a very good look at every face at the table. I still had a job to do.

The rain was easing off as we paraded, although 'parade' would be too strong a word. We stood in two lines with three men out in the front. The Hunter stood off to the left, smoking a cigarette, his hood up, he was becoming interesting.

"OK, we are going to break you up into three groups of six and in that way, you'll circulate from one area to another over here in the big barn. We'll be doing tactics. Out here, we'll be marching and practising parade stuff." He pointed to the yard.

Parade stuff? I nearly burst out laughing.

"Over that hill to the left, about half a mile, we'll be using the guns and things." Johnny and I were put in the barn for the first part of our training and the young man, who had done most of the organizing, led us there.

"Hi, I'm Noel Dougal; I'm the adjutant of 'D' company. I want to take you through the tactics of resistance. We have to be organized, we have to be disciplined and above all we have to be smarter than the Loyalists and the army."

Dougal delivered a great two hour lecture. He was young, but he was passionate, intelligent and dedicated and he definitely motivated the men in our group.

"Remember, be smart - use the situation to your advantage and don't take stupid risks." He looked at us and stood up. "Has anybody got any questions?"

I wanted a cup of tea and didn't want a long question and answer session to make it hard going. The rest must have felt that way too, because when one daft sod asked, "Do we get identity cards?" Johnny gave him a swift clatter on the back of the head.

We all strolled out of the barn and as we rounded the end, the other group was standing to attention. The rain was that type of drizzle that soaks you through before you realize. We went straight into the kitchen, there was a bit of a fight to be first to the tea urn, so that we could get a good seat next to the stove. I was at the front and sat next to the window, just the right distance from the fire, and lit a cigarette.

"So if you've got your ID and the army pull you over, do you just show him your pass and go on your way?" Johnny was taking the piss out of the daft lad, who blushed.

The lad tried to defend his stupid remark. "I meant so that we could prove to other members that we were on the same side."

"For fuck sake," Johnny kept up the attack, "just turn out your pockets son, next thing you know you'll be in The Maidstone eating gruel." Johnny took a long drag on his cigarette, he was feeling pleased with himself. At this moment the men who had been doing foot drill poured through the door, there was a mad rush for the teas and as they sat down and made themselves comfortable, Johnny started to recount the story of the ID card to them. To our surprise, the young lad jumped up and gave Johnny a punch to the face. For a moment I thought Johnny was just going to take it, but in an instant, Johnny was up and at him. Most people in the kitchen didn't know what was going on. As they both fell to ground, Johnny was on top and the other men were trying to pull them apart. Eventually, and not before Johnny had given the lad a head butt, they managed to separate them. In this incident, Johnny showed his killer instinct. He had had that look a man gets, when no matter how large or small the insult, something snaps.

I always do the same thing when men fight around me, hold my pint or tea out of the way and wait to see who's going to win, this was no exception. It could have been interesting, a big strong lad against this wiry little psychopath! But the fight was stopped. I took Johnny outside, with him declaring that he would have killed the bastard. I knew he would have.

"Come on, save it for the army, we don't want to be fighting amongst ourselves." He was still flushed from the fight and had a trace of blood in the corner of his mouth, from the first blow.

"I hope he doesn't stand in front of me, when !'ve got a gun." I remembered that we would be having the experience of small arms later.

"Calm down, he's just a boy."

"Well the fucker started it and I'll finish it." That threatening look came over Johnny's face again.

At this point, the men who had been over the hill, doing small arms, came into the yard carrying an assortment of weapons. One of them held a Tommy gun, which must have been forty years old. They were smiling and joking.

The Hunter was at the back carrying a rifle and a green case, he looked just the part. The men stacked the guns on a ground sheet, just inside the first room and piled in to get their tea.

I went back in with them. The lad was nursing himself in the corner.

At the end of the break, Noel Dougal asked us to line up in two ranks.

"I'm sorry, but some of us have to go, there's trouble at Derry and we have to be there, the prods are marching." Dougal added, "If anybody wants to come with us, they'd be welcome."

Dougal turned and made his way into the farm house.

Johnny turned to Hugh and Rory, who were in the same transport as us. "Well do you fancy it?"

Hugh, the driver said, "I'm going." The excitement was tangible. Men were hurrying back to the barn. We went in and packed our things. I noticed the Hunter sitting on his bed, carefully cleaning his rifle, a Lee Enfield with telescopic sights. It didn't look as though he was going anywhere.

Within a few minutes we were packed and making our way to the car. Noel Dougal came across to talk to us.

"You'll have to come into the city from the north, the army have road blocks all over the place." Hugh got out an old map and they poured over it while we sat in the car. It had started to rain and the inside of it had one of those wet dog smells. With the directions sorted, Hugh tried to start the car, but there was just a clicking sound when he turned the key.

"Fuck, come on, get out and push." We leapt out and started to push the car back across the farm yard, a few more men came across to help. It started on the second bump, we were on our way.

We travelled north, with the radio on. Reception was a bit poor in that area, so it took a while to find anything out, but what we did hear sounded like big news. The main story was that a land mine had killed two soldiers in an attack at Rosslea. We all gave a cheer. I found it hard, but nobody seemed to notice.

Rory was map reading and Johnny and I were in the back, chain smoking.

We entered the city and almost immediately came to a road block. I just knew we would get pulled over. Well what could you expect; we were four men of the right age group. The soldier pointed to a side alley, which we pulled into. Several soldiers immediately started to look under the car with mirrors. Hugh wound down the window and a young soldier leaned in.

"Where are you going?" Hugh handed over his license.

"We're off for Saturday lunch with my sister." This went right over the top of the soldier's head.

"Can we see in the boot?" The traffic was starting to build up and the soldier was in a hurry. Hugh jumped out and opened the boot. The soldier had a quick glance, pushing a few of the bags around.

"OK sir." We were on our way.

"We need to get parked up soon. We can walk from here."

Hugh seemed to know his way around. I had only been to Derry once with Simon. We pulled off the main road, parked up and started to walk towards the city centre. As we walked along we talked excitedly about the events which were about to unfold.

"We can kick fuck out of them prods." Rory was expressing what the others were thinking.

"Come on down this road." Hugh lead the way, we walked through blocks of flats, through the maze of alleyways, eventually arriving at a street of small terrace houses. He knocked gently on the door, eventually it opened slowly.

"Hugh Dolan, what are you doing here?" The man who opened the door came into the street and started to shake Hugh's hand. He had a big smile on his face.

He nodded in our direction. "Who's this lot?"

"We're here to see the prods off, they're marching sometime today. That's Billy, Johnny and Rory. Rory's dad is Jacky Docherty. Remember he worked at the factory on Antrim Road in the early sixty's. The man looked at Rory. "Oh yes I remember him, always singing at the top of his voice." Rory smiled, recognizing the description of his father.

"Boys, this is Seamus." Seamus smiled.

"Come in, come in." We were waved through the door into the smallest front room I had ever seen, somehow they had managed to fit two large sofas and a small table into the room. The place had a damp smell and had obviously not been decorated for decades.

"Mary, put the kettle on." Seamus called to his wife in the kitchen. He was about fifty and had dirty, grey hair. There was no collar on his shirt and his braces had lost most of the elasticity and had been adjusted to take this into account. We squeezed into the seats and made ourselves as comfortable as we could.

"Are you working now?" Rory enquired.

"Hell no, there's no jobs here for the likes of us." He looked to us for sympathy and we nodded knowingly. "But the Prods walk into a job anytime they want."

At this moment Mary came in, carrying a pot of tea and a plate with biscuits, she returned quickly with the cups and milk and sugar.

"Could you put the three o'clock news on the radio?" Rory asked. I noticed then that they had no television. In fact there was precious little, except the sofas, in the room. The radio was switched on as Mary poured the tea and we helped ourselves to sugar and milk.

On the hour, the bleeps told us it was time for the news.

"Shush, Shush, listen." We all stopped talking.

"The marchers will be leaving the Irish street area of Derry at about three o'clock. They are protesting about the No-go areas in the Bogside and Creggan. William Craig has spoken these words "We are no longer protesting, we are demanding action.""

We started to talk over the broadcast on the radio.

"Well that'll get the bastard re-elected." Seamus's face had a look of disgust, we all had sympathised with him.

Rory jumped up. "Come on, let's get at them." I bolted my tea down and grabbed a handful of biscuits and before I knew it, we were making our way round the city walls.

As we got closer to the bridge, we saw the army were all over the place, every street corner had men with full riot gear and weapons at the ready. There were armoured vehicles with men on high alert, sitting inside. We came down Aberckon Road and could see that they had fenced off the bridge at both ends with barbed wire and a six foot fence. Nobody was going over that bridge today. I was relieved, Johnny was disappointed.

"Let the fuckers come." Johnny was joining in with the rest of the crowd.

The army had put a roadblock of barbed wire and fencing at the junction of Harding Street and Aberckon Road but we all pushed as close as we could. Soldiers were facing us and we cursed and goaded them. The press were taking photographs of everything that happened.

Suddenly a bottle was thrown by someone at the back of the crowd towards the army. At first it looked as though they wouldn't respond, but they were waiting until two Land Rovers with half a squad of men were in place behind us. They marched up towards us, close to the temporary fence. We were spitting and bad mouthing them. Then they pulled the barricade to one side and charged and at the same time a snatch squad jumped out of the Land Rovers and was baton charging from the back.

It had the right effect; we were running everywhere to get away from the soldiers, who were using their batons indiscriminately. I stumbled on the corner of the pavement and went down like a ton of bricks, catching my right eyebrow on the ground. My biggest fear was to be trampled under foot, while I was down, still dazed from the knock on my head. The soldiers passed me by, but as people fled, the soldiers re-grouped and came my way again. I stood up and blood was pouring down my face, two squaddies lifted me up, pulled my arms around my back and marched me off through the barrier. I was aware that some of the protestors were trying to stop them from arresting me, but the soldiers closed ranks and I was quickly through the barrier, but not before the press had taken some fairly good pictures of me covered in blood being choked by an arm around my neck.

There was a big temptation to shout "I'm on your side." Then I was in the back of a Pig with two squaddies sitting on top of me and another holding a loaded gun to my head. The Pig was hammering up the hill to God knows where. The driver knew, but I didn't. The Pig swung into a yard full of Army vehicles. I was dragged out and rushed into what turned out to be part of the library.

"What's your name boy?" I was being questioned by a corporal from the military police, at the end of an aisle in the library.

"William Deery."

"Address?"

"37 Mount Pottinger Street, Belfast."

"Date of birth?"

"11th December 1951."

"What are you doing here?"

"I was minding my own business, when you lot picked me up."

He leaned forward and snarled, "Shut the fuck up, we've got witnesses who say you were the fucker who was throwing bottles. I'm probably going to do you for grievous bodily harm." He stepped up close, but he didn't know that better people than him had breathed their bad breath over me and I had been threatened by better men than him.

"You were handed over to me covered in blood, no one will notice a bit more."

I didn't flinch. He stormed off.

"Keep an eye on that twat." I stood in the aisle, while he went off to check my details. I had a chance to check myself over. The blood had stopped running down my face, but I had a nasty cut above my right eye and this had a swollen and felt puffy to it. Someone had stood on my left leg while I was down and they were trying to escape from the soldiers in the initial charge. All in all, I felt rough.

I leaned against the wall at the end of the aisle, resting and thinking of the events of the last few days. I was exhausted. When the military policeman came back his attitude had completely changed, he was carrying a cup of tea and a chair.

"Sorry mate." He placed the seat down and handed the tea to me.

"They're sending someone to see you." I looked at him to see if he knew what was going on.

"Who's that?" I asked suspiciously, staying in character.

"Dunno mate, but the word has come down to look after you." He started to walk away.

"I'll get someone to clean you up, give me ten minutes." And with that he was gone.

The tea was hot and sweet and I sat there having a smoke and just resting, the toil of leading a double life had at last caught up with me. I reflected on what I had been first directive, just observe from the bus what was going on in the city. That was my only task. How things had changed.

After thirty minutes a medic set about washing and bandaging my head.

"How's that?" he enquired, standing back to survey his efforts. He had been very careful, only two butterfly stitches and some liniment on my leg.

"The bandage will need changing in two days, so go and see your doctor."

He thought I had a doctor, my documents were with the M.O. in Germany, I had better get that sorted, I thought.

After a while a Captain from the Fusiliers came down the aisle.

"They're sending someone from Belfast to see you, do you want a rest?" He didn't know what my status was but he knew I was important and people in high places wanted me to be kept safe.

"Yes please." I kept the accent going, but I was beginning to relax.

"Could I have something to eat?"

After steak and kidney pudding, chips and several cups of tea, I was taken through the library and up the stairs into an office, where there was a lone camp bed for me.

"Get some rest." The officer disappeared and in the warmth and safety of that office, I soon dropped off.

Chapter 10. The same day. 100

"Billy…. Billy." I was being shaken gently and wakened by Simon Adder. I sat up and stretched.

"Whoa that's a nasty bump." Simon sat back on a chair, while I gathered my thoughts.

"I fell over while we were on the barricades in Aberckon Road, it was chaos and I was trampled under foot. I thought I was a goner."

I liked to exaggerate and I wanted to make sure he realised how hard it was out there.

"Can you remember where the training camp was?" Simon needed to catch up, he needed information.

"Of course I can." I became indignant.

"We need to get you back to Holywood and debrief you."

"Hey, hey, I need an alibi if you're going to make me disappear for a while. These people are not stupid." If I'd got to go back and face these people, I wanted a good cover story.

"We have a choice here, we could release you and you could make your own way back, or we can cover your back by putting someone in Crumlin Road for seven days with the story that you attacked a screw." He was testing my feelings on the subject. But he needed to know my decision. "It's your call. What do you want to do?" I took my time weighing things up.

"I need to make my own way back. It sounds tempting to have seven days out of it, but I need to get back out there before I lose my nerve."

There was silence while we both pondered as to what to do. I wondered if Johnny and the car would still be around. Would it be safe for me to walk through Derry on my own? If we put someone in Crumlin Road, as me, would we be able to keep my identity a secret?

"You know, I was only put on the buses as an observer." I looked at Simon. He thought for a while, choosing his words carefully, he knew I needed some encouragement.

"I know, but because of the situation here, we don't have many people on the ground. We have the R.U.C., but everyone knows them and their judgment is clouded by past prejudices. We have informers, but who can trust them?" Simon lit a cigarette and leaned back. "And we have plants like you and by chance you have dug the deepest in the quickest time, we could not have planned that." He looked at me, right into my soul and I knew I had to go on.

"I feel as though I'm going too fast, that I'm out of my depth." I dropped my head, I felt weak.

"Go for the jail option then. We can get a cover body in jail for you and you could be back in Holywood in two hours." He could see the strain on my face.

"No, it's too risky. If word gets out that it's not me, bang." I made a pistol out of my hands. "I'll push on." I stood up and put my jacket on. "If my ride has gone, I may need a lift to where I can get a bus back to Belfast."

We left the office and walked down to the main door. It was drizzling as I walked down the road, trying to get my bearings. As it happened, I was very close to the home of Seamus. The streets were still full of people. There were army vehicles patrolling but not many other cars on the streets. I was not absolutely sure which door we had gone into, I just had to guess. The man who answered pointed to the next house along, when I asked if Seamus was in.

"Fuck me, it's the hero." Seamus bellowed into the house, when he saw me at the door. Johnny was the first to look over Seamus's shoulder.

"Get the lad into the house."

Hugh patted me on the back as we got off the street and into the house, everyone asking what had happened.

"They had me standing against the wall for hours." I was making it up on the spot.

I mimicked the interrogator. "What you doing here? How did you get here? The whole fucking lot, I told them I came on the bus for a day trip." Everyone in the room was looking at me, as though I was some sort of hero.

"Come on, let's go to the pub." Johnny wanted a drink after the day's events, everybody agreed and we poured out of the small terrace house and walked round the corner and into a bar.

"Here's the boy who kicked fuck out of the army." Hugh was holding up my arm, I wanted to just keep a low profile. Not much chance of that though, the beers just kept coming. We carried on re-writing history all night, by the end of which, we had ripped down the barricades and seen off the army, the prods, everyone.

We left the city by roads going north, which meant a long detour through Strabbane. We managed to get petrol once over the bridge, just scraping the money together for a few gallons.

"Fucking seven and six a gallon, the robbing bastards." Johnny always worked out how many pints he could buy for the same money. I fell asleep in the back. Hugh woke me outside my front door, it was still raining, and I let myself in. The seal on my door had been broken. I went gingerly up the stairs, all my senses wide awake, but nobody was there. I went into the bedroom and looked under the floorboards as quickly as possible.

Sunday 6th June 1972.

"I'm back." Simon was on the other end of the phone. I told him how we got back and how I had been greeted as a hero.

"When are you due back on the buses?" I thought hard.

"Tomorrow, middle shift, eleven thirty I think."

"Well we need you in here as soon as possible for a report, it may take some time." Simon pushed.

"Well I'm knackered; I need a kip before work. I can't see where I can fit it in for days."

"No, we need you in now." Simon was positive about this, but my batteries were running low.

"You'll have to cover my shift tomorrow and give me a cover story." I always had to look after my cover story.

"Oh that'll be easy, just get to bed and I'll get that sorted."

I put the phone down, had a bath and then open a packet of soup. There was no bread, but I did have some crackers which had gone a bit soft, but I was famished. Even though the bed was cold, I soon warmed up.

Monday 5th June 1972

I was fast asleep when the front door was smashed in and big boots stamped up the stairs. When you think you're going to die, the rush of adrenaline makes your mouth go dry, you have the strength of five men and everything appears to happen in slow motion. My blankets were ripped off, showing the world that I slept in my vest and underpants and I was still wearing yesterday's socks. My clothes were thrown at me, as they shouted and bawled at me to move myself. I was pushed down the stairs with shirt still unbuttoned. The vigilantes were out quickly, there were three Land Rovers with soldiers deployed in the street on the corners and in a defensive position, the vigilantes were shouting and banging dustbin lids, people were pouring out of their houses.

I was unceremoniously thrown into the back of one of the Land Rovers and driven off. I still did not understand what was going on, but when we arrived in Holywood barracks, Simon was there to meet me.

"Sorry mate," he said, as he helped me out of the back of the vehicle. We went up to his office, then up to the main op's room. I looked at the clock on the wall; it was five thirty in the morning. Captain Lunn from the SAS was there.

"Hello Deery."

"Hello Sir." He flicked the switch on the kettle and sat down on one of the chairs. Simon followed me into the office and patted me on the back. "Well done, but we have to get things recorded before you forget. We'll start with the mug shots."

Over the next five hours Simon, Lunn and I went over the events of the weekend, careful notes were taken, mug shots were scrutinized and maps were studied. There was constant stream of coffee being supplied by one of the office crew.

I told them of the strange Hunter figure, who never spoke. I recounted all the practices in training and described all the men I had worked with there. They were very interested in Noel Dougal.

Then we went over the events in Derry, addresses and characters. By eleven, my concentration was flagging.

Lunn looked at his watch. "Well, that's enough for now, Simon can you find a bed for Deery, I don't want him with the lads."

Simon said he would find a spare bed in the mess and as we got up to leave Lunn said, "Well done Deery."

"Thank you Sir." I could feel myself blushing, he shook my hand. "Go and get some sleep and be back here at four, that gives you five hours." Simon led the way.

We went down to the cookhouse, which was always busy, men coming in from patrol, men getting ready to go out on patrol. There was a continuous flow of troops being fed. I had forgotten that I now looked like a tramp, my hair long, I hadn't had a proper shave, sideburns down past the bottom of my ears and my clothes could have done with a good boil wash. There was also the matter of the dirty bandage on my head, covering the two stitches on my eye brow.

Simon walked in and loaded up his plate, I followed a short way behind, feeling a bit self conscious. Men were looking at me, some of them seemed to half recognise my face.

"We don't serve civvies in here mate." One of the cooks, was in one of those moods.

Simon lent over the counter, "Shut up and serve and don't ask questions." The cook put a fried egg on my plate. "Can I have two?" I held my plate out whilst I loaded up with beans and a couple of sausages. We sat down at a table in a corner.

"So who do you think the Hunter is then?" Simon opened up the conversation.

"I don't know, but he was not the normal run of thugs. I never spoke to him, he always kept himself to himself and he didn't come with us to Derry." I loaded my mouth again.

Simon was looking into the distance, thinking. "It's a pity that the Derry thing came up, you may have found out more had you stayed longer at the farm."

There was more silence as we ate and drank our tea.

"What will happen to the info I've given?" Simon thought for a while.

"We'll pick them up one at a time and they will be interned."

I thought about this for a while. "I hope it can't be traced back to me? If you pick up everybody I come into contact, with it won't take them long to figure me out." I was starting to get nervous and looked at Simon for reassurance.

"We're not that stupid and anyway it takes months to find out their movements, so they can be lifted." He wiped the last bit of sauce off his plate with a piece of bread and popped it in his mouth. "Most of them will just go on the watch list."

We walked back to the quarters and Simon let me have his bed, throwing a sleeping bag at me.

"I'll come and get you at three thirty." I went to sleep thinking about everybody I had just fingered, and how deep into all, this I was getting.

Inside Lunn's office, he and Captain Ellis were pouring over the weekend's work. They were both coming to the same conclusion, which was that I had got myself into a position that could have taken years to achieve.

"We must look after this boy." Ellis nodded, Lunn went on, "I want an around the clock watch on his house, with a rapid response team ready to go in at the first sign of trouble." Ellis looked at the notes.

"I see we have a telephone landline directly to our office and two microphones in the flat and the Police Station is directly opposite."

Lunn thought for a minute. "How do you think Simon Adders is handling the situation?" Ellis pushed his glasses to the top of his nose, to give himself time to consider the question.

"Simon has a good relationship with Deery and seems to bring the best out of him, but he does have four other operators to run, but his others haven't made any breakthroughs like Deery."

Lunn made some notes. "Well ask Simon to concentrate on Deery, even if it means he has to lose sight of the others somewhat."

In Lunn's report, which would eventually end up on William Whitelaw's desk, the good work being achieved was mentioned, even they were coming from a long way back. There was a long passage about Agent alpha7, my code name.

I was awake when Simon came in shortly after three thirty.

"God you need a bath, mate, it stinks in here. I'll get you a towel and soap."

My personal hygiene had slipped quite a bit over the last few days. I chose to have a bath because of the bandage on my head, but oh it was nice to lie there in a bath nearly full to the top. Not for long though, I had to get a move on. I only had five minutes to get to Lunn's office. I arrived there still damp.

We went over the mug shots again. They definitely wanted a picture of the Hunter, he was the unknown person and part of the story, but either he had no driving license, or he was not from Ulster. All driving licenses in Northern Ireland had a photograph, with a copy on file, which was a great source of intelligence, but try as I might I could not find a photo of him.

"We want you to go in the slow lane for while." Lunn knew things had been moving too fast, I knew what he meant. "Obviously take your chances while they're there but just keep your head down a bit." It was good advice and I wanted to slow things down myself. I determined to be as invisible as possible, and just watch was happening, but I didn't write the script. I had been in the press twice recently. I had been the only person to be arrested in Derry on the day and I didn't want to be on the fast track. But the script was being changed all the time.

"How are you getting back?" Simon thought he was being helpful.

"How would anybody lifted by the army get back?" I looked him in the eye. "Well I suppose they would make their own way back." He answered.

"Well there you go then." I was slipping back into my other persona.

It was nine eleven and there was a bus in sixteen minutes back to Belfast, so I had a smoke as I walked to the bus stop, it was drizzling but somehow it helped to clear my head. I didn't know the driver, which spared me the obligation of standing at the front of the bus explaining what had been going on.

Tuesday 6th June 1972.

Stepping off the bus, about 150 yards away from my flat, the drizzle had turned to rain, it was just getting dark and I wished I had taken Simon's offer of a lift home. I had a sense of foreboding as I approached the corner and saw my front door was ajar. I didn't know what to expect. It wasn't wide open, but as I got nearer I could see the lock was broken. I remembered the army had smashed their way in to lift me. God that seemed days ago that had happened. I stood at the bottom of the stairs and listened, no sound, no light. Slowly and with my heart in my mouth, I went up the stairs. Bravery is doing what you don't want to do and I did not want to go up those stairs. I switched on the light in the living room. The place was a mess and the television was gone. I listened, all was quiet. I switched on the light in the kitchen, the toaster was gone. The bedroom was a mess but at least the carpet was still in place. I lifted it and the floor boards. The phone was still there, good.

"I'm just checking my phone is still working." The duty clerk had answered very quickly. "Is Simon there?"

"No."

"Well can you tell him that I have been burgled and I'm still checking out what's gone." The clerk sounded as if he didn't give a flying f. about me and my problems.

"Will do."

I checked the flat over, someone had gone through there quickly. It was not too bad, socks and underwear on the floor. I couldn't remember how tidy the flat had been but was sure I hadn't left them lying around. And then, how much had the army done. I had the feeling that the T.V. and toaster were enough for the people who had entered and then a quick exit. Not much use calling the police, but I could feel my anger rising. I went down and had a look at the lock on the door. Why did I think the army would have made good, after they had kicked my door in, most of them would not have known who I was, so why should they? I went back up stairs to the phone.

"Can I have Simon now" There was a brief pause while the duty clerk passed the phone over to Simon.

"Yes." Simon sounded unconcerned.

"I want my front door repairing, now." There was a pause, I sensed that he would be looking at his watch and thinking things through.

"Someone has been through the flat and my TV's gone. To the best of my knowledge, I don't think they found my phone."

"Can you wedge the door for tonight?" I could feel my blood pressure rising. I felt at that moment, that it was just me putting in all the effort.

"No, get some handy man from the camp down here, some engineer, anybody who knows how to fix a door with a new lock." Now that's not the way to talk to an officer, but needs must. I wanted that door fixed before I went to bed. I had plans for the evening.

"I'll see what I can do." I had to bite my tongue.

"No Simon! I want this fixed to night, I'll be out for an hour." I slammed the phone down.

It was still drizzling as I walked around to Johnny's house. As I was knocking on the door, I looked up the street; vigilantes were standing on door steps and I knew I was being watched. The door was opened by Tommy O'Neil; he was a thick set man, who always wore a tie, but never looked smart, but again, never untidy.

"Come in boy." He had a newspaper in his hand. He was not the type to relax too often, keeping up with the news, was the nearest he would get to relaxing.

"Johnny, your mate's here." O'Neil shouted up the stairs.
"Who?"

"The Deery boy." I could hear Johnny getting dressed.

"Sit down." O'Neil pointed to a chair on the other side of the table to him. This was a big test for me, I was sitting on the other side of the table of the most powerful man in East Belfast, commander of 'C' Coy and union rep for the bus depot, obviously a man who takes the rights of the workers seriously. It would be hard to pull the wool over his eyes. I needed to be on my guard.

"What's happening?" It was a simple question, but it opened up a can of worms for me.

"Well, I was lifted by the Army, they must have been informed by people in Derry and while I was answering questions

108

in Holywood, some twat has emptied my flat." I looked at him
to see how this had gone down. He pulled on his pipe and thought
for a while.

"Did they take much?" I thought he would have started his
questions with the knock to my head, or what had the Army
wanted with me, or how did the training go, but no, he started
with the only thing he didn't know about.

"Well the only things that seem to have gone are the TV
and the toaster, but they're not mine, they belong to the
landlord." At this moment Johnny came downstairs.

"What's up?" Johnny opened a bottle of beer and sat
down at the table.

"The bastards have robbed me, my TV's gone and they've
been through my house and the army lifted me for over a day,
questions, questions, questions." There was a silence.

"Johnny, go and find Spencer, see if he's seen anything." I
was way down the pecking order from Tommy O'Neil, but he
obviously he felt he had to help this new young lad. Johnny was
not in the mood to go round the streets at this time of the night.

"Get to fuck, I'm away to my bed." At this point
Tommy's voice took on a menacing tone, Spencer was a local
fence, selling a bit of this and a bit of that, and he always knew
what was going on in the area.

"Oh shit, it's pissing down." Johnny clearly didn't fancy
running around at that time of night. He took another pull on his
beer and slammed the door on his way out. He had been away for
no more than three minutes when he returned with a name.

"Danny Steele." Johnny looked at his father, O'Neil
sucked on his pipe.

"Well I might have guessed, right up his street this one."
Tommy turned to me.

"Do you want me to have a word?" He didn't know what
was running through my head. He didn't know that I was going
to make my mark that night or die. I had a plan.

"Where does he live?"

"He's a tricky feller; he has a lot of family near by. It's best
I sort this one out for you." O'Neil sucked his pipe some more. I
turned to Johnny.

"Where does he live?"

"I'll come with you. I've had a few run-ins with this twat."
Johnny pulled on his coat and we left the house, but he first
picked up a heavy stick from behind the door.

We didn't have to go far, just round into Moira Street,
which was close to the bus depot.

We didn't knock on the door. The lock didn't give much
resistance, one kick and the door flew open. We walked into the
house, down a small corridor and into the back room. These
were very small houses, two up and two down. Danny Steele was
well named, the house was stacked with stolen items.

It was a shambles. There rolls of lead rolled clearly off a
roof, old bikes, even the engine of a motor bike in the corner.
Steele had a knife in his hand and his back to the kitchen door.
We hadn't left him enough time to run into the kitchen. My TV
was on the floor and the toaster on the table. It only took me
moments to spot them.

"What the fuck do you think you're up to, you cunt?" It
was Johnny's way of letting him know we weren't happy with
him.

Danny had the look of a cornered rat, he was terrified,
which made him dangerous. A red mist came down over me and
I'm not too sure what happened next, but according to Johnny, I
pulled the stick out of Johnny's hand and flew across the room
past him and smashed Danny's hand, which was holding the
knife. He went down and all in one movement, I had my knee in
his Adam's apple. Two swift punches to the face finished off
Steele. Seconds later, a woman came running in the room,
yelling at the top of her voice. She went for Johnny, but he had
no compunction, he just backhanded the woman to the ground. I
turned back to Steele, who was still on the floor.

"If I see you in my street again, you'll be fucked, do you
understand?"

This was a power struggle. I wanted an answer from him
and I wanted submission; it was important that he knew his
position in this matter. Steele nodded. He knew he couldn't keep
out of my street, but he sure would keep out of my way for the
time being, until the tables were turned and he had more fire
power than me. I picked up the TV and told Johnny to get the
toaster. We laughed and laughed all the way back to my flat but

110

as we approached, we could see an army Land Rover outside my house, with squaddies posted all over the road. We both suddenly went quiet.

"What's happening there?" I got the question in first. I knew that the army were fixing my door, but I didn't want Johnny to find out how much pull I had with the army.

"Put the toaster on top of the TV and get yourself away. I'll see you later." Johnny patted me on the back and turned for home. I managed to call out my thanks to him just before he got round the corner. He gave me a wave and went on his way.

I pushed past the man repairing the door. The TV was starting to get heavy and I struggled up the last few stairs. I was really feeling the strain of the last four days and just sat on the sofa with my eyes shut, till the engineer came up to join me.

"That's the best I can do." He passed me three shiny new keys on a ring. I went down with him to have a quick look at the job. It was better than the original; the door appeared to close better than it had originally.

Before I went to bed, I lifted the carpet and picked up the phone.

Simon had been waiting for a call. He wanted to know what had been happening. I told him the story and Simon sighed.

"What's that for?" I said, I could feel his displeasure.

"Well, don't you think you should be keeping your head down a bit. You've only been out there for a few weeks and you've been in the papers twice, arrested in front of hundreds, hob-nobbed with IRA leaders, and been on training courses. Don't you think that beating up the local hard man, may be just pushing too far."

I was silent for a while. I felt as though I had done something wrong.

"I had to take my chances." I said defensively.

"You're right, and no one has done better, but try to slow down a bit. I worry about you out there.

I still felt a bit down, as I put the phone back under the floorboards and replaced the carpet.

But I set my alarm clock and was soon asleep.

When I awoke I felt a lot better. I had a shower and a shave and took the bandage off, carefully cleaning round the wound. It didn't look too bad and I thought the fresh air would help it heal more quickly. I nipped down to the Post Office below for fresh milk, cornflakes and a small jar of coffee.

Sid, the only Asian man with an Ulster accent, who was also my landlord, had a ready smile.

"How are you and how's the door?" He had heard of the damage done when it was kicked in by the army.

"Oh the army had the wrong man, they were looking for someone else, and so they repaired the door." I tried to play last night down.

"And how is the new job going on the buses." I didn't know whether he was just being nice, or trying to find out if I could pay the rent, but he said it with a smile.

"Great, I love it." I paid, then left Sid to serve his next customer and got back upstairs.

When I arrived at work, Kerry was in the office; he was the spare driver, so was just hanging around until needed.

"Wow, what's happened to your head?" I could see the clerk, waiting to clock me on.

"Just wait a mo." I went over to the duty clerk.

"Clock me on for one hundred and four duty." The clerk gave me my running board for the day and I got my ticket machine out of the locker. I went back to Kerry.

"I hit my head on a curb stone." I didn't want to go into it too deeply.

"Were you pissed?"

"Oh yes." When you're lying, keep it simple. That's my motto.

I wanted to change the subject, so asked him if he'd seen the girls again.

"Oh yes." A big smile came across his face. "I've got a date with the pretty one."

"They were both pretty, are you blind?" I wanted a piece of the action, "When's your date?"

Kerry gave a dirty little smile. "This Friday." He leant back against the bench.

I had to go. "Look I'll try and catch you later. Let's make it a foursome."

He winked at me.

I saw a few of the faces of people who were wanted, later that day and I filed the normal report. A pattern of their movements was emerging.

There was a knock at my door about that evening. I knew it would be Johnny picking me up for a game of pool. We'd been playing most Wednesday nights, as well as at work. I threw on my jacket, as I went down the stairs.

"I fancy a night at Jenson's."   Johnny looked at me to see how this had gone down. I was not sure I liked it at all.

Jenson's was the meeting place of the IRA's local leaders, the atmosphere was deadly. I didn't know if I was ready for it, but I knew I could just keep my head down and play. It would be a good place do some observing.

"Yes fine."   I tried to put on a smile, but my heart sank at the thought of the night ahead. It was warm as we strolled along. The vigilantes were out sitting on their doorsteps and we nodded to a few of them. Our reputation was growing.

From the outside of Jenson's it looked derelict; all the windows were boarded up and painted brown and the door had galvanized steel screwed onto it. Nobody was going to break that door down easily.

We entered, to find it was full. Johnny's dad was in his usual seat over in the far corner; a heavy pall of smoke hung in the air.

"I'll have a Murphy's."   According to Johnny, I was buying the first round. As I waited to get served, I looked in the mirror behind the bar, to see if I could recognize anybody from the mug shots.   But this was not the time to start eyeing everyone up; they were watching me.

I nudged Johnny and told him to put his name up for a game. He went and put a penny on the pool table, and then went back and put another penny down for me.

I had already picked out two known IRA men from the mug shots. It made me wonder how they moved around so easily without being picked up by the army, but because everyone left their doors open, they could duck into any house on the street and be out of the back door, before the soldiers got anywhere near them. As well, all the street lights had been vandalised long ago.

"Hi Da." Johnny acknowledged his father. Tommy gave a nod, but clearly, had other things on his mind. I, on the other hand, was looking around in amazement; it was wall to wall with all the people you would not like to meet on a dark night, even if there had been no Troubles. But in these times, they were the people who were doing the business, the people who craved for and could indulge in violence.

We stood at the bar drinking slowly, and I started to settle down.

Johnny was on the table first; he got into a long drawn out tactical battle on the pool table.

I got the pints in and stood watching from the end of the bar. I was at this time, trying not to make eye contact with anybody. Tommy O'Neil waved me over to his table. I picked up my pint and ambled across.

"How are you?" I said as I sat down.

"Fine and you?" he replied.

"Oh my head's getting better." Tommy pointed to the man on his right and introduced him.

"This is John." I looked towards him; I knew who he was, John Anderson bomb maker and bank robber, he provided funds for the IRA. He could have been anybody's uncle or brother, the man who does the plastering or roof repairs, but he was not. He was one of the most ruthless men operating in East Belfast. He had big strong hands, broad forehead and had not shaved for a few days. I shook his hand and told him my name; my hands were damp and weak and I was breaking out in a cold sweat.

"So your mother lives in Liverpool?" He was digging into my past.

"Yes, we did a runner from Belfast when I was about seven, but I never settled over there, so after I got out of prison, I came back here." Keep it simple, broad strokes, I thought to myself.

"What school did you go to? I've got a sister who's a teacher up there." John was digging deeper.

"Holy Child in South Green." John nodded his head, he knew the school. Johnny came up to the table and gave me a nudge.

"You're on." He handed me his cue. He had been beaten and I was on the table. I was so relieved to get out of the line of questioning, but because my mind was not on the game and my hands were shaking, I was soon beaten and on my way back to the table. I sat down with Johnny at his father's table.

"Did you put your name down again?" I nodded.

"It's your round." I nodded towards the bar. Johnny went over to the bar. John Anderson had been biding his time to tell me the news.

"We've a special job for you and Johnny." I felt pleased that he was satisfied enough with my cover, to give the job to us.

"Don't forget me and Johnny haven't finished our training." I was trying to make excuses, but he cut me short.

"Look you'll be able to do the job, but you won't have enough time to do the buses as well." Anderson looked round at Tommy and then round the pub, to see if anyone was taking any interest in our table, but they were all getting on with enjoying themselves. He went into his pocket and pulled out a big roll of five pound notes. Without counting them, he peeled off about a third and whilst putting the rest back in his pocket, he gave me the money. I was so surprised; he'd only just met me. But I wasn't sure about giving up the buses.

"I can't take that." I hid my hands so I couldn't take the money. I looked at Tommy, hoping for some sort of help.

But he urged me to take it. Tommy was in with this plan, he knew what was coming, he must have also known what sort of job Johnny and I were going to be asked to do. How much did Johnny know? At that moment he came back from the bar. The pints spilt a bit, as he sat down. He must have expected that I was fully informed, by the time he got back.

"Are you in?" Johnny had known all along. He hadn't come here by chance.

"I don't know what the job is yet." The money was pushed into my hand; it was almost an acceptance of the job, but what job?

I took a long slug of my pint, looking into the eyes of Anderson. In another time and another place this man would not be doing these things, but you don't get choices sometimes.

Johnny jumped in. "We have to look after ourselves and fight for a united Ireland, Catholics have been held down too long." Johnny meant this but he was also a loose cannon. He was really just looking for adventure in a drab cold world.

I was cornered, but also I had to think of what Simon would want me to do. He wanted people on the inside. I felt he would be shouting for me to accept this, but it was way past what I was expecting to do.

I put the money in my inside pocket without counting it, I smiled as though I was happy, and shook the hand of all the men at the table. I was dancing with the devil.

Johnny sat quietly at the table, as Anderson explained what was expected of me.

"So, you'll look after the gun, make sure that all the exits are clear, and carry the gun to and from the site. You'll help to pick the best sites and don't forget that for every hit there is a bonus." Anderson carried on with his instructions, but my mind had gone numb. In that pub, round that table, with everyone else enjoying themselves, I was being give instructions, on how I was going to help a sniper to kill my own comrades.

"You knew this was coming, didn't you?" I challenged Johnny.

"Oh yes, it's the best opportunity we'll ever get." He was defiant.

"I don't see this as a job opportunity. I don't see this as a career move. I see this as getting way out of our depth." Johnny had a wild look in his eye.

"We have to strike back at the people who attack us, we have to look after our own and if that means the others, get hurt so be it. If you don't want to get involved, then you're not the person I thought you were." He went back to the pool table.

It gave me a little time to think. I would never get another chance, to get this far into the IRA and I'd be able to bring valuable information back; it was just a question of my morals. Could I really go on active service for the IRA? Could I help to hunt down one my own kind? I reasoned that if I didn't do it, someone else would and then again, it might lead to my gathering much more intelligence, so it might lead to a quicker defeat of the IRA, an end to hostilities. My speculations were brought to a halt by Johnny.

"You're on." He stuffed a cue in my hand and started to set the balls, he had won his last game.

"You're not chickening out are you?" He said it with such fire, such menace, I was reminded what a wildcat he was.

"No," I said, "but you have to admit it's not every day you get asked to pack your job in and run guns." He roared with laughter and hit the pool ball right off the table. Another rebel song came on the jukebox and the beer started to kick in. As I looked around the pub, I couldn't believe that I had come so far, in such a short time.

We carried on drinking and playing pool, until last orders, and then we staggered off home, back to our damp little homes.

As soon as I got in, I went straight up the stairs, into my bedroom and onto the phone. It was answered immediately.

"Get me Simon." There was a short wait.

"Hello?" Simon must have been quite close.

"I've got a lot to tell you, do you want to do it on the phone, or shall I come in?" He was impatient to find out what had been going on.

"Just give me a brief outline on the phone. I'll make a decision after that." I told him the gist of what had happened. He asked questions just to confirm certain points.

"So are you sure it was Anderson?"

"Yes, I recognized him straight away."

"And how much money did he give you?" I still hadn't looked, so pulled the money from my pocket. I put the phone down, while I counted the notes. "Twenty three five pound notes." I told Simon, leaving him to work out how much that was.

"A hundred and fifteen pounds." Simon mused, "A month's wage."

"I think you should come in. I want you to look at mug shots and identify all the people in the bar tonight."

"How shall I get in?"

"We'll pick you up at the corner of Madrid Street and Tower Street in twenty minutes." I looked at my watch.

"Don't leave me waiting too long, the vigilantes are always watching." It was going to be a long night. I slipped out quietly, crossed the road and passed Mount Pottinger Police Station.

You would think there wouldn't be much out there at that time of night, but you would be wrong. Men were standing on their doorsteps, even though it was cooler by then; they were fully alert, waiting and watching, all sorts of skulduggery was going on. People were ready to go on to the streets, at a moment's notice.

I came out of the shadows and had walked through the back lanes for the last few hundred yards. The car was stationary, with its engine slowly ticking over. I jumped in the back door and rolled down onto the floor. The car pulled away and I lay there while the car left the city and took the road to Holywood.

"It's okay, now you can get up." With relief, I recognised the voice.

I sat up in the back seat, glad to get out from all the fish and chip wrappers and empty cans of pop, I'd been rolling in on the floor.

"How's it going, hippy." Brian was driving but he also had Kelly in the passenger's seat. He was happy not to be sitting in some hide, doing something more exiting to help to pass the time.

"Oh, I'm surviving but only just." I didn't want to tell them too much, but I couldn't think of any reason to hold things back.

"Are you still on the buses?" Of course, they wanted to know how I was getting on. They were probably jealous. Even so, I didn't think they would want to do the job, if they knew what was really going on.

"Yes, fares please ting ting." I wanted to create the impression that things were just ticking over and I was going in for a normal debrief.

"You get to meet some very nice girls on the job." I was trying to keep it all very superficial.

"Oh you lucky fucker." Kelly's imagination went overboard. "You've got your own pad too, your own spider's web." Kelly looked over the seat at me and grinned.

I thought that if I asked them about their jobs, they'd leave off any more questions about mine. "How's it going on your jobs?" There was silence, as they both thought about it. Brian was first to answer.

"Well if you like sitting in a car, with everyone around knowing just who you are, its fine." Kelly was nodding his head in agreement.

"But we've had our moments." Brian tried to make it sound exciting.

"Yes, the time we walked in on a hold up at a Post Office on Castlereagh Road and the two stupid arses who were doing the job, only had pick axe handles. We were there with our Browning. We'd only gone in for a stamp. We managed to pocket fifty quid each, in reward." They both burst out laughing.

We arrived at the camp in Holywood and as we pulled in through the gates, the guard gave me a long hard look. I didn't carry any army ID, but was given the nod.

Simon was in the main office, as I walked in.

"Get the kettle on." He was smiling, he offered me his cigarettes and I took one and he lit it. He was in a very good mood. I looked round, it was busy. I could hear radio operators giving instructions to units on the ground. There had been some small arms fire heard in the Divis Flats area, patrols were checking people out on the streets, reports of a shooting in the Markets area, and a Land rover had broken down along the Falls Road. There were also reports coming in from static observation posts.

"So you've been into the lions den, you're trusted then?" I looked around the crowded operation room. With me living in this cagey double sided world, I found it hard to open up and tell the story. Simon picked up on this and took me down the corridor to find an empty room. I was carrying my steaming cup of tea and a cigarette was hanging out of my mouth. I was still feeling the effects of the Murphy's. Ellis's room was not being used and we settled down to talk about the new developments, Simon made notes whilst I looked through the mug shots.

"I saw him a few days ago in Moira Street." I pointed to a photograph of Billy Toolan, Simon leaned over and made a note on his pad that Toolan used the bus at about eight in the morning to go into town. He would be picked up at a later date and probably slammed into Long Kesh.

"Do you know what you'll be doing in this active unit?" Simon wanted to get information on the job I had been given.

"All they said was that we will be carrying a rifle for a gun man and we had to make sure all the exits were clear. We will be picking the sites, or at least helping to pick the sites." I apologised to Simon that I couldn't be more specific. At that moment the door opened and Ellis came in.

"Don't stand." It had never occurred to me to stand, so it's a good job he had given us leave to stay seated. He sat down beside Simon, who gave him a quick update.

"You'll have to run with this. It means, you know, that from now on, you have the responsibility of being our deepest penetration in East Belfast. Tomorrow, hand your notice in at the bus station."

I sat forward, "But Sir…." He was ready for this.

"No buts. I want you on hand there at all times," he had already thought I would complain and was ready "I want you to hang around in all the bars and clubs, rub shoulders with as many as you can. Get your face known, use all the contacts you have, make as many friends as you can."

He gave me a sympathetic look. It doesn't happen too often in the army.

"The Police Station over the road from you, has special orders to watch your flat. If you ever feel the need to pull out, you can be over the road in a flash and that will be the end of things."

What could I say? To pull back from this position, would be a missed opportunity. I could see that. But why couldn't it be someone else.

Ellis jumped up and shook my hand. It helped to let me know, that they realized how dangerous it was and it helped me to go that one step further. After Ellis had disappeared, Simon said "Come on, are you hungry?" We went down to the OP's room.

"Make sure the transport is back here in fifteen minutes." Simon gave the order to a radio operator, pointing at his watch. We strolled down to the cookhouse, and after an early breakfast or a late supper I jumped into the back of Brian's car.

"Home James." I was feeling in a better mood, but still apprehensive.

We chit chatted on the way back to Belfast and it was nice to see them but it did not take long to get back from Holywood so I was being dropped in a back lane not far from Mount Pottinger in no time. The house was a bit cold but it did not take long to get to sleep.

I went to the bus depot on the Short Strand the next morning, and went straight up the stairs to the main office.

"You want to hand your notice in?" The girl could not believe what I had just said. She looked round at the other office workers.

"Mr. Deery wants to hand his notice in." The girl was going to make a fuss. She had turned round so her voice reached the whole office.

"You've not been here very long. You'll still have to work your notice. It's company rules." She was not going to make this easy for me.

"How much time for holidays do I have left?" I stared hard at her; it was now becoming a battle of wills.

"Just stay there." She went off to check my records.

"Jesus, where do you think I'm going?" I said sarcastically.

She walked off to the filing cabinets at the other end of the large office. I saw her talking with one of the more senior women and after a few minutes, she returned with a pencil and pad.

"You have seventeen days holiday." She looked puzzled because she knew I had not been at the depot that long.

"I had some holidays from my last depot. They came with me, when I transferred," I explained. I was thankful someone had done their job properly. I'd never even been to the other depot.

"Well you could use the holidays for your notice, but that doesn't give us much time to replace you." She knew she had lost this one. But as a parting shot she added, "The work can go to someone who's grateful."

"Fine, when do you want me to come in for my pay?" I was leaning against the counter and getting cocky, when the door to Jackson's office opened. I stood up quickly.

"Hello Deery." Jackson never missed a thing.

"Oh, hello Sir." I just wanted to get out of the place, with the least amount of fuss. I really didn't want to have to start explaining what was going on.

"How's the job going?" He was just keeping his finger on the pulse, passing the time.

"I have to leave sir, my mother's not well and I'm going to Liverpool to help her out." I hadn't thought of a good reason, I was hoping to just get in and out again.

"Oh, I am sorry, is she very bad?" He looked concerned. Now I was really on the back foot.

"She's never really been all that well since she lost my small brother." Another unnecessary lie, I usually tried to keep it simple.

"How sad," Jackson had a look of great sympathy, "if you do come back, come and see me." He shook my hand and patted me on the back. I was touched. He walked off as the girl came back. She had a form for me.

"Could you fill this in, and I'll see when your money will be ready." She went off to consult with the senior woman again. As I completed the leaving form, she came back.

"We can pay you this afternoon, if you want to come back later." Her tone had changed. She had overheard the conversation between me and Jackson.

"Yes, I could get back and it would be helpful to wrap things up quickly." I was feeling a bit better this had started to go to plan.

"Don't forget to bring in your uniform, badge and bus pass. Go down stairs and hand in your ticket machine and get the clerk to sign here." She pointed to the form.

As I went down the stairs into the daylight, It came to me, that I had been in the pay of the British Army, the IRA and the bus company all at the same time. At the bottom of the stairs I bumped into Tommy O'Neil. He'd seen me go up and had been waiting.

"Did you hand your notice in?" He was puffing on his pipe.

"Yes, and I'm getting seventeen day's holiday pay." He looked around to see if anyone was within earshot, and took the pipe out of his mouth.

"We want to keep you away from normal operations, do you understand?" He had an intense look on his face. "You have to stay out of trouble, keep yourself well away from the normal day to day harassment of the army, this job is special." He looked around again, "that's why you have been chosen."

I had to keep a smile off my face, he didn't know anything about me, where had all this trust come from? Looking back now, he probably didn't have many people he could trust, and I had shown as much get- up and go as anybody.

"I'll do my best." As I looked at him, I realized he wasn't doing this for profit or selfish reasons, he was doing this because he thought it was right. He was doing these things because he wanted to improve the lot of the people he lived with. It was why he was a union leader, why he struggled with paperwork long into the night.

"I want you and Johnny to look after one another." He was standing close to me now. "People are dying, people are getting hurt, and I don't want you two running unnecessary risks." It's strange that a man, who can order shootings, beatings and all manner of punishment for the smallest indiscretions, could be so protective of people close to him. The bottom line was he wanted me to look after his son.

I gave him a friendly punch on his shoulder, "Oh we'll be okay." At that moment the heavens opened.

"Go and see Johnny." He held his newspaper above his head.

I started to make my way to the main gate, and waved as I ran off, glad to get away. By the time I had got to Johnny's, I was wet through.

"I've been to hand my notice in," I said, as I went though the door. Johnny was in his underpants and had just got out of bed.

"Shit, you're in a rush. I'll do that when I'm ready." He wandered into the kitchen and put the kettle on the stove, I followed him in.

"So what happens now?" I felt Johnny must have all the plans.

"I don't know at yet, but we'll be told soon enough. Do you fancy a game of pool?" He was smiling at the thought of no work.

"Get your kecks on, I'm going to thrash you." Johnny smacked me on the side of the head, as he went past.

"I want three sugars and no milk." He skipped off up the stairs, and I could hear him getting dressed. The kitchen was a simple affair, Belfast sink with a network of cracks in it and a wooden draining board, a kitchen table with two chairs and a stool. The cooker was out of the ark, but it was spotlessly clean. I couldn't find the milk, but three sugars made it drinkable. Johnny came running down the stairs, and then we sat and drank the tea.

"It's going to be great, not having to get up in the morning. I hate those early shifts." Johnny was putting on his socks, his feet were filthy, but the house had no bathroom, only the sink in the kitchen. The tin bath hung in the backyard on a six inch nail. Johnny's feet showed that he didn't get the bath down very often. I was glad to get out of the house and onto the road.

"I bet you don't even win one game, I'm on form at the moment." Johnny was eager to start the game. We crossed over Mount Pottinger Road and headed for the club, which I expected would be full of men, who had no job. The only place to get out of the way of the wife or the mother was the club. We went down Madrid Street, across the road. I saw the army patrol, so did Johnny, but we had nothing to worry about, we were clean. Even if we got pulled over, a quick check on the radio and we'd be gone.

"Excuse me sir." There was heavy sarcasm in the soldier's voice. Johnny had been slightly in the lead, so he was the focus of the soldier's attention. He put Johnny against the wall; I decided to carry on walking. The next soldier along the road had moved up close by now; he pulled me over. It was Barry Thompson.

"Get your hands on that wall." We recognised each other straight away, but I could see there was confusion on his face. He had no idea what I was doing walking along the streets of Belfast, with my hair long and unkempt and unshaven. He spun me round.

"Billy, it's me, Barry." I looked over at Johnny, who had his own problems. He'd been spread eagled against the wall. The soldier was kicking his legs wider and wider, making life uncomfortable for him.

The army were not going to tell everyone who was on undercover work. It was a fluke, that I had been stopped by one of my own Regiment. I had to think fast.

Barry didn't know what danger he was putting me in. He was about to blow the whole operation. I turned my back on Barry and put my hands on the wall, I just needed a few seconds to think.

"My names William Deery." I wanted Barry to pick up quickly.

"What the fuck are you on about?" Barry spun me round again, I spat in his face. Barry's temper was legendary; he reacted just as I'd hoped. He brought his rifle down across my face, I went down. Another soldier from the squad had come across the road to help out.

"Hello, Charlie One to Alpha One, over." The radio operator had an edge in his voice that made Alpha One answer quickly.

"Alpha One, over." It was the plummy voice of an officer.

"We need a mobile at the junction of Madrid and Edgar Street, over." There was a long pause.

"Alpha One to Charlie One, Roger." The voice replied. "The wagon's on its way." I was still lying on the floor, I wanted to stay down. Barry lent down and whispered into my ear.

"What's going on?" I could see that Johnny had his own problems and was not listening to us.

"Barry what ever happens do not lift the other guy." Barry looked over to where Johnny was being frisked, and at that moment a couple of Land Rovers came up the street. They screeched to a halt and six more bodies poured onto the streets, taking up defensive positions. I was thrown into the first one and a couple of soldiers got on the back standing plate. As we pulled off, I could see Johnny being pushed away, they had released him.

The Land Rover raced through the streets, throwing everyone around, but it didn't take long till we were pulling into the back yard of Mount Pottinger Police Station. They left me in the back of the Rover for a few minutes, but eventually I was pulled out and taken in through the back door, down a corridor and thrown into a cell. The door was slammed shut. After half an hour, the door was opened and a Sergeant came in, he had a pad in his hand and took out a pencil.

"Give me your details, son." He licked the end of his pencil and sat waiting for the information.

"Get me Lt. Simon Adder; he's in Intelligence at Holywood Barracks." He wrote this down "If you can't get in touch with him, speak to Major Ellis." He started off, obediently, "Oh and bring me a cup of tea, two sugars."

I lit a cigarette while he was away. It was half an hour before another soldier brought the tea in.

"Can you come through?" There was a markedly different attitude. He didn't know who or what I was, but the atmosphere had changed.

The phone was lying on the desk, and the sergeant pointed to it. I lifted the phone and said, "Hello?" Simon was on the other end.

Simon said, "In the shit again?" I smiled.

"Yes, I was stopped by an old friend and he nearly gave it away, but I don't think Johnny picked up on it." Simon thought for a while. "Are you sure?"

"Well you never know, but he had his hands full at the time, having his balls felt."

"Have you had any more instructions?" Simon was keen to find out more.

"No, we were just off to the club for a game of pool. Johnny's expecting things to start to happen soon." There was a pause, while Simon got an instruction from some one else, who must have been listening.

"Go to the club, tell O'Neil that you were mistaken for Seamus Deery from Anderson Town, he may know him. Can you put on the duty Sergeant."

I offered him the phone, and sat down. The Sergeant stood there nodding his head while listening and after a few minutes, put the phone down. He went over to his log and jotted down the time and a few more details and then looked over to me.

"Which door do you want to leave by?"

I was soon at the club it was smoky, warm and full of men who have nothing better to do. I walked over to Johnny, two pints in my hand. He was leaning over the table taking aim. I waited for him to take his shot; he missed, and came over to me.

"You know how to upset the bastards, don't you?" He lifted his pint, he was relaxed, no sign of distrust.

"The daft twats thought I was John Deery from Anderson Town, and that cunt that lifted me, he's given me trouble before." I watched how this went down. Johnny just turned to the other men.

"Hey they thought he was Deery from the other side of the water." Everyone started to laugh.

We played pool all afternoon, slowly getting drunk. Johnny would get angry, if he was beaten, but most of the time he was happy, he was playing well. I was listening in to as many conversations as possible, and generally picking up snippets hear and there, logging faces, evaluating. We were both happy.

At about half past five, Tommy O'Neil came in. I had my back to the wall, on the far side from the door and was playing cards with two older men. I clocked him straight away. He bought himself a half of beer, and leaning against the bar, looked around, nodding at people who greeted him. After a while he managed to make eye contact with Johnny. He made a nod to a quiet corner and Johnny nodded back.

It was the only time I have ever seen Johnny set someone up, for an easy finish. He shook hands with the winner and strolled over to where his father was sitting, reading some notes. I watched as they put their heads together. Johnny was being give instructions. From the movement of his hands, Tommy was obviously giving directions to somewhere on the other side of town. Then he looked at his watch, put his documents away in his well-worn briefcase, finished the last mouthful of beer and left.

Johnny looked around to see where I was. I was still playing cards, with my head down.

"Hey Doc Holliday, come on, we have to leave." I looked up, as surprised as I could manage.

132

"Give me a mo, I've still got this." I pointed at my pint.

"No leave it; you'll have plenty of time for that later." I jumped up, without even finishing the hand of cards.

It was early evening as we left the club and there was a light drizzle, as we walked over the Albert Bridge with hands in our pockets. We kept off the main drag where we could. This was in a period of frequent drive-by shootings. They happened for no other reason than someone thought the victim was 'one of them'.

We weaved through the streets, until suddenly we were at the foot of Divis Flats. It was a monstrous mass of concrete and glass, already showing early signs of wear and tear. Johnny looked at the signs, 106 to 142, with an arrow down that way, 143 to 162 this way, and led the way. Eventually, he knocked on a door. We were about five floors up, the windows that faced the corridor had newspapers stuck on the inside, not very house proud then.

"Who's there?" The occupant was being careful.

"It's Johnny, I've been sent by Anderson." Johnny was looking up and down the landing. The door opened, inside there were no carpets, but the man who answered the door, I recognized straight away. It was The Hunter from the training camp. He shut the door and bolted top and bottom. I passed the small kitchen as we went through, just a bottle of beer standing on the work top and a few dirty cups in the sink. In the living room, cheap curtains hung on string, held up by three nails. There was a bed in the corner, no other furniture, just a radio on the floor and two more empty bottles of beer, next to the radio.

"I'm Johnny, this is Billy." He held out his hand. The little man took Johnny's hand and shook it.

"Jonas." He shook my hand. "Please, sit." He pointed to the bed, unmade of course. We sat down, it felt damp, the sheets and blankets were old and not very clean.

He came back from the kitchen with three bottles of beer, pulled out a bottle opener and gave us one each. He sat on the floor on the opposite side of the room, leaning against the wall.

"My team have been arrested. Do you have police records?"

We both thought for a while, trying to figure out how much to tell him.

"You must be truthful." He could see we were undecided.

"Well, I've been lifted a few times," Johnny came in first, "but I've never been in court." Johnny looked at me; I was busy trying to separate my two roles.

I had been given a caution by the police, but that was in Liverpool, and I am not that same person today, but it still took me a few seconds to think about this. I shook my head. "No, I'm clean as a whistle." I put the bottle to my mouth. It's a good way of giving yourself a few more seconds to think, when you're lying.

"It's very important that you don't get involved with other things." He was looking intensely into our eyes, "We have to get on with our job, we have to go quietly about, and we have to be invisible." He was laying down the ground rules.

"We have to look very carefully. It's a big job, and if we are not careful," he drew his hand under his throat. We both lifted our beers and looked as solemn as possible.

Jonas carried on laying down the rules and we nodded to show we understood. After repeating the instructions a few times, he was happy and we left.

The door slammed behind us, we said nothing until we were out of earshot.

"Ve haft to be carefool." Johnny mimicked Jonas, they must have heard us laughing all over the flats.

On the way back, Johnny was ready for more beer, but I was running out of steam and I wanted to talk to Simon.

"I could meet you in a couple of hours?" He gave me a wink, "Okay, I'll see you." Johnny carried on to the club. I made my way back to No.37.

As soon as I got in, I put the kettle on, and then went into the bedroom to the phone.

"Get me Simon please." I could hear the sounds of a busy office.

Simon sounded as though he had just got up. I heard him ask for a coffee.

"What's happening?" Simon was starting to focus.

"I've met him." I was so excited, I forgot names.

"Who?" He was getting annoyed, and I didn't blame him, it was a shit way of getting your message across.

134

"Remember the Hunter. Well he's the sniper." I let this sink in.

Simon was really waking up now. "So do you think he could be One Shot Willy?"

"Yes I do." I was elated, but tried to hide it from my voice. We were both silent for a while, both enjoying the possible glory. This was like winning the pools, marrying Miss World and becoming Mr. Universe all in one go. We both came down to the ground at the same time.

"It will get dangerous," Simon said seriously.

"I know."

"Tell me every thing." Simon was settling in for a long chin wag.

"Well I think he's from some sort of Iron Curtain country, and he's only here for the money, and he's mad about security. The more I think about his accent, the more confused I get." Simon was listening, but I could tell he was also signalling for someone to listen in. I knew it, but it didn't bother me.

"Did he tell you his name?" Simon wanted to build a picture of him.

"Jonas, but he didn't tell me his surname." I gave a quick description of the man, and the address, where we had met him.

"What are your plans?" It was his way of letting me know I was in charge, to a certain point.

"Well, I'm going back to the club in about an hour, meeting up with Johnny and then I'll just go with the flow." I didn't ask for approval, but I wanted it.

"Yes, just see how things go." Simon was encouraging, "but at anytime you feel you need to pull out," a pause from him, "just say the word."

I was feeling a bit weary, I wanted to rest. From now on, I needed to be alert.

"We're meeting Jonas tomorrow at nine, he wants to train us in his ways."

"Ok, get a rest, then keep me informed. I want you to report in tonight."

After I'd hung up, Simon strode down the corridor and knocked on the door.

"Come." Simon opened the door and entered.

"Sir, I think you should know what's happening," Simon said to Major Ellis, who lent back in his chair and put his hands behind his head.

"Its Deery sir, he's been recruited into an active unit, but he thinks he's working with One Shot Willy." Simon waited while Ellis thought about this.

"How sure is he?" Ellis leaned forward.

"Well he's not sure at the moment, this only started today, but he does think the man is from Eastern Europe. They will be working as a three man squad. He's under orders not to get involved with any normal street activities, and he was ordered to finish his job on the buses. I sanctioned this." Simon waited for more questions.

"Well, we'll see what happens. Could you put it all in a written report and keep me informed." Ellis had work to do, so Simon left. He had things to do as well.

Ellis filled in his weekly report which would go directly to William Whitelaw's desk. It would inform him, that they had six men now directly in active cells for both sides, stretching from Londonderry in the north, to Newry in the south. As well, there were over fifty men in civilian locations, bringing in intelligence with no local RUC bias. He leaned back in his chair feeling pretty pleased with himself.

Meanwhile, Simon logged his report and put it in his out tray. He then ordered a vehicle to pick him up in thirty minutes outside the office.

"No, I don't want to go in an unmarked car, I would prefer a Pig if not, a Land Rover." Simon dashed off to get a shower. Twenty five minutes later, he was climbing into a Land Rover with two escorts on the back, riding shotgun.

"Take me to City Barracks." These buildings were on the opposite side of a main junction to Divis flats, and sounded a lot more impressive than they were. In reality they were no more than a disused yard, which had been commandeered early in the troubles. There was a tunnel entrance, a high wall of brick with a higher fence covered with hessian and corrugated iron. The latter, stopped the yard from being over looked by the nearby high flats. Even this was not very effective, and staying out of sight, was one of the preoccupations of everyone who walked across the yard. There was the normal line up of Pigs and Land Rovers parked in the yard. Most of the outbuildings were used as barracks, stores and cookhouses. The main offices were in effect the outer walls and had to have steel covers on the windows, as pot shots at the barracks, were a daily occurrence. They were an easy target, with a multitude of escape routes. People based here, were living on the edge. Simon, wearing his combat uniform instead of jeans and shirt, which had become his normal daywear, made his way to the OP's room.

"Good morning Sir." Simon saluted as he entered a small room, which was just a boarded off alcove, with a makeshift door. Every spare part of the wall was covered with maps, lists of units and call signs. Major Blyth greeted him. He was in the last years of his career, having worked his way through the ranks over a period of thirty years. He was well over pension age, but was building on it every year.

"Good morning, sit down." He pointed to a chair which had a jacket on the back and a pair of boots on its seat, Simon put the boots on the floor and settled in. "I've come to let you know what's happening over the road." Simon then informed Blyth about the sniper, and how I would probably be working from the area, and that I might need help at short notice. Blyth sat making notes and after Simon had finished, assured him that he would let the OP's room know.

The next morning Tommy O'Neil opened the door as soon as I knocked. "Hi ya." I walked past him and through to the kitchen. Johnny was leaning against the sink, eating his breakfast.

"Do you want a cup of tea?" The big old kettle was simmering on the stove.

"I'll make it; you eat your bacon butty." I poured myself a tea.

Tommy came into the kitchen, "Johnny, you need to hand your notice in today, I'm sick of them asking when you're coming in." He slammed the door on his way out. Johnny burst out laughing.

We made our way across the Albert Bridge and through town, Johnny leading me in such a way that we came in from the back of the Divis flats, he was being careful. We didn't even have to knock on the door. It opened just as we got there and Jonas closed it behind us.

"Did you check if you were being followed?" Jonas asked us, as we settled on the floor.

"Do you think we're stupid?" Johnny looked hurt.

"Well you can't be too sure." Jonas went through to the kitchen and put the kettle on, he came back with two cups of tea, with the tea bags still in them, we didn't complain.

"The way we work is this." Jonas glanced down at us, to see if we were listening. "We'll spend a lot of time finding a place to shoot from. We'll make a good escape run, it's best to go though houses, at least two streets, do you understand?" We both nodded. "I only have one shot, no more, and then we go." He made a hand movement showing it was a fast exit. "I always go the different way, and you two will go hide the gun, wash your hands very carefully, and leave, do you understand?" We both nodded again.

"We'll collect the gun later and then we get paid." Jonas sat back on the bed and shrugged as if to invite questions.

"How do we carry the gun around, we can hardly walk the streets toting a sniper's rifle?" Jonas sat up.

"We carry the gun in two parts, I carry the…." He had to think hard for the word. "..telescopic sights." He jumped up and started to put his coat on.

"Come, we will go to see the gun." We took another slug of tea, I was glad to leave most of mine, and made our way out. Jonas left three minutes later and met up with us at the top of the street. We then followed him, about thirty yards behind, as he made his way through the streets. He stopped every now and then and watched, sometimes stopping at a bus stop, sometimes just looking in shop windows, but all the time watching. He headed back over the Albert Bridge and turned left down the Short Strand, past the depot where Johnny and I had worked.

"Do you fancy a quick game of pool?" Johnny nudged me, as we passed the depot. Suddenly Jonas disappeared, he'd squeezed through a hole in a wooden fence, and we quickly followed. Behind was a big expanse of waste ground, with a brick building over near the river. This was some sort of warehouse, but had clearly not been used for sometime. We all climbed in through one of the smashed windows, Jonas stayed behind for about twenty minutes, looking out of the window. We sat on old boxes, waiting and had a cigarette.

"Better to check." Jonas was satisfied we hadn't been followed. I had no idea where the best place to hide a rifle was, but in a warehouse, in the middle of waste ground, didn't feel right. At the far end of the building, were some internal offices. The offices windows were all smashed, but a couple of old desks and a filing cabinet, had been left by the last occupants.

"Bring that up here." Jonas was pointing to an old wooden ladder with rungs missing. We obediently lifted them upright and Jonas climbed up and stepping carefully, disappeared over the office roof. He reappeared holding the rifle bag. We went into the office and watched Jonas unpack the rifle, from what appeared to be a home made rifle bag. He unrolled the carrier, to reveal a stripped down two piece weapon. The wooden stock had been removed and round the barrel was one layer of string, wrapped where your hand would hold the weapon. The butt was removable and snapped together with a male and female locking device. The butt had been hollowed out at some point in its life, making the weapon very light. Jonas quickly fitted the gun together, then opened the cleaning kit which had some pull through material. He expertly tore off a piece of four by two which he threaded this through the draw string and holding up the gun to the light and looking through every few pulls, checking for some piece of dirt or some sign of pitting on the inside of the barrel. When he was satisfied, he went back to the bag and out of one of the folds, brought the telescopic sights. "Good optic." He then started to show us the basics, like a training sergeant.

"You must be able to do everything in the dark. You have to be able to strip the gun down and put it back together with no light, it may cost you your life." Jonas began his lecture. "This gun has been modified to take NATO bullets, seven six two millimetre, easy to get hold of," he explained, "and they can penetrate any jacket, but I always go for the head." I gave a little shudder it brought it home to me what I was getting involved in.

"You have a go." Jonas handed the gun to Johnny, who held the gun to his shoulder and took aim at some point at the far end of the warehouse. He bent down and unlocked the butt from the rest of the weapon, placed the two parts together and in a jiffy the weapon was ready again. He handed it to me. I was surprised how light it was. The balance was not very good, but for a single shot attack, it was perfect.

"How do we get it around town?" It was the same question I was going to ask, but Johnny beat me to it.

"It is always difficult, but the last team used golf bags and tool bags, with other tools inside, or they just hid the thing, under their coats, but never the same method twice, even in taxis." Jonas couldn't tell us much more; the rest was up to us.

"The others were arrested, but not because they looked like they were carrying guns. You have to be careful not to raise anyone's suspicions." Jonas started to put the gun away, carefully packing every thing into its proper place and tying the two ends of the bag. Then climbed up onto the office roof and disappeared, as he hid the weapon at the back, out of sight.

"Come, we have a lot more work to do." We left the way we had come in, but before we went through the fence, he told us to follow him about fifty yards behind. We went through the fence, and back towards the city. All the time, he was checking to see if we were being followed. We walked through town, until Jonas found what he was looking for, he nodded towards us, and we caught him up. He had noticed a row of disused shops, the windows were smashed and the entire lower floor was boarded up, but it had a good field of fire; you could see all the way down the road, to the factories at the bottom. We went round the back of the buildings. There was a gate, with no lock and the bottom hinge had snapped, but the top hinge held it in place. Carefully, we looked around the back yard. The back door was unlocked and easily swung open to reveal what we wanted, stairs up to the floor above.

Jonas lead the way up the stairs, old bits of rubbish and bricks littered the way. On the first floor, off the small corridor, were four rooms and a bathroom. This had been trashed and pipe work taken. The toilet had been smashed, but the sink was still intact. The windows of the two front rooms were out, but most importantly, it had a very good view of the road, the junction to the main road being about one hundred and fifty yards away.

"This is good." Jonas liked what he saw and carefully removed a broken pane of glass from one window, which would be in his line of fire. Then he went into one of the other rooms, but didn't find what he wanted.

"Go and bring me a piece of wood, about twelve feet long, I want to put it across there. He pointed from the mantelpiece to the furthest window. "And you," he looked at me, "can clean the stairs, we need to be able to get out of here quickly, without tripping up."

Johnny and I set about our tasks.

"Make sure the yard is clear as well, for a quick exit."

Johnny left and I shifted an old bike frame and some broken bricks from the pathway between the gate and the door. Johnny came back with two lengths of wood, one was shorter and thicker the other was longer but flexible. Jonas set about fixing the long piece as he had planned, and used the shorter piece to support it. Soon he was happy. He kicked some rubbish to clear the place where he would be standing to take his shot. It was a small arc of fire that he was interested in, just at the end of the street, on the junction of the main road, just the sort of place the army would patrol regularly.

"Now we have to think of our retreat." We made our way downstairs and out of the yard and into the back lane of some terraced houses. These were small two up and two down dwellings. Some of them had numbers painted on their back walls. We walked down passing about five houses. We stopped at one, where Number forty three had been chalked on the wall. There were all sorts of bits of rubbish around in the alley. Johnny banged on the back door, no answer; he banged again, still no answer.

"I'll go round the front." We returned along the back lane and went round to the front door. Johnny again knocked on the door and after a short while, it opened a little. A man poked his head out.

"Hi Jacky," Johnny said as brightly as he could. When the man recognized Johnny, he opened the door all the way. He stood on the step and looked up and down the road, then he gave me and Jonas the once over.

"Hi Johnny, what's happening?" The man clearly knew this was not a social call.

"We need your doors open for two hours tomorrow, between four and six." It was half an order, half a request. The man now looked harder at me and Jonas.

"I don't want trouble for my mother." He had his hands dug into his pockets, his body language was saying "no."

"We'll just be passing through." Johnny insisted. "Jacky, we need this. See you tomorrow." Johnny turned on his heels and walked away, we followed.

Next, we went over the road and knocked on a blue door, it opened quickly and a fiery looking woman of about fifty, took one look at Johnny, glanced up and down the street and beckoned us inside. She disappeared into the house and we followed. From the front room, she led us down a passage to the kitchen. We all stood in the kitchen, the woman leaning on the sink, with her arms folded.

"What do you want?" She was looking at Johnny.

"We may need to come through here tomorrow, between four and six so both doors need to be open, and with nothing in the way." Johnny could see that was not a problem.

"Also," Johnny sucked on his teeth, "we need to leave a gun here for a day or so, do you have a hidey hole?"

"I've been a Republican all my life," she said as she lit the stove and placed a big kettle on the top. "My father and his father before him, were head to head with the Orange Men. I'll give you any help I can. Do you want a cup of tea?"

We needed friends like this; we all started to relax.

Johnny now remembered introductions. "That's Jonas and Billy. She looked at us both. "This is my aunty on my mother's side, Kathleen Kerry." Jonas and I nodded at her.

"Sit down the pair of you; you're cluttering the place up." We did what we were told, squeezing in at the small table. A loaf of bread stood on the chopping board with the cut end down; a bottle of brown sauce stood next to the salt and pepper. The table cloth was covered in breadcrumbs. As the kettle came to the boil, Kathleen set out four cups and went through the ritual of tea making, heating the brown teapot before putting three heaped spoons of tea into it. She filled it with the boiling water and left it to brew. We sat and watched in silence, enjoying the quiet scene.

"We hide things in here." She had opened a small cupboard in the kitchen, and pulled back some old tarpaulin beneath there were a couple of loose floorboards. She pulled them up and we peered in. You could smell the damp rising from the hole. It was big enough to hide the gun.

"That'll do fine," said Johnny and smiled. We sat down and finished our tea. Johnny and Kathleen talked of family matters; Jonas and I just listened.

"Well we need to get on." Johnny gave Kathleen a kiss as we left, we smiled and thanked her for the tea. Once back on the streets we walked to the main road.

"Meet me at two o'clock on the back stairs of the shop, have the gun in place before then. I'll bring the scope and the ammo."

Jonas walked off and as usual, kept checking that he was not being followed.

144

"Fancy a game?" Johnny was feeling pleased with himself, but I wanted to report in, before I forgot all the details.

"Come on," Johnny knocked my head, "let's go to O'Donnell's."

"Yes, but we haven't sorted out how we're going to get the gun through town?" I was getting jittery at the thought of going on tomorrow's operation.

"We'll get a taxi, you're paying." Johnny was walking at a brisk pace, obviously keen to get the first pint down his neck.

The bar was full for that time of the day. I start to take in all the faces, logging the ones I knew well, and then trying to pull the new ones off the mug shots. There was some very hairy company that day.

Johnny was chin wagging, as he waited for his turn on the pool table. I ordered the pints, and made sure I ordered a shandy for myself.

I used the mirror again, to hide the fact that I was studying faces in the crowd.

"We're on." A jab in the kidneys from Johnny, told me he'd got the table set up. It was a game of doubles; not an easy game to play, but we won easily. I played safe and Johnny cleaned up after they set him up.

"Fancy playing for pints?" Johnny was chalking his queue, as he asked the next couple up for a game. One of the men playing was on the files, I watched him carefully.

"Okay, but I'm drinking double gins." But Johnny has missed the signals.

"No bother." The winners break off, so Johnny gave them a good whack, the balls landed badly, wide open.

"Go on Ivan," someone called out. Oh shit, I had thought I knew his face, but now remembered his name, Ivan the Terrible. He was thought to have tortured many poor Orange Men, drive-by shooting was his specialty. Yes, the army would love to know where this man was. I could feel myself tense up; I wondered if I should throw the game? Then I decided, what the hell, I'll pay for the drinks. Ivan had an easy four balls but then the fifth was a hard shot and he missed.

It was my turn and none of my shots were easy, so I played safe, much to Johnny's disgust. Ivan's partner potted two balls from an impossible position, and we were staring defeat in the face.

We slowly but surely worked our way back into the game, Ivan getting more frustrated with every shot. I was tempted to play a loose ball, but something inside me wanted to win. Johnny punched home the last ball.

"Yes." He thrust his queue into the air, I smiled and shook Johnny's hand.

"Two pints of the finest, he's paying,"Johnny shouted with a nod towards Ivan, who had already sat down.

"Fuck off, we were playing pool not snooker," Ivan said, with a hardening look on his face. Johnny's quick temper immediately showed itself.

"Get the fucking beers in." Johnny was pointing to the bar. I looked around for any possible allies, but there was no one in the bar who fancied this one. Once again, Johnny could not control himself. He leaned over the table and slapped Ivan in the face. In a flash, chairs were being pushed back. Like a shot, the manager was around from the bar, but not before Ivan had head butted Johnny. I had done a half dropkick on Ivan from behind, not very successfully because he quickly turned round and gave me a one, then two to the face. I was on the floor holding my head. Johnny was being held down and about five men were holding Ivan back. We were on the street in no time.

"You're barred for a week." No manager wants to lose a paying customer for too long, but he had to show he was in charge, so we were out.

We re-played the action all the way back to Johnny's house, I claimed I'd done a full dropkick and that's how he caught me, but Johnny claimed he had given a full punch to Ivan's face; it was just a slap really.

Much later my face was still stinging, as I picked up the phone.

Simon answered and I gave him my report.

Chapter 15. Friday 16th June 1972. 148

I woke early, and staggered into the kitchen and filled the kettle. It was nice and sunny outside. As the kettle boiled, I caught sight of myself in the small mirror hanging on the window. I don't bruise easily, so to have a yellow patch on the cheek bone with a darker bit at the centre, I knew I had been hit hard.

I sat listening to the radio, drinking my tea. The announcer said that a body had been found on Shaw's Bridge. Then there was some news about the Olympic Games, which had just finished.

I continued to sit listening and trying to relax but it was difficult, I felt very nervous about going on my first active duty for the IRA.

In Holywood Barracks, Major Ellis was finishing a meeting. The room was full of operations officers from around the province. Sitting around the large table, each officer was reporting, giving details of their successes and their weaknesses.

"We have two in Strabane, one works in a bar on the main street, one in a bakery, but both of their tours of duty come to an end next month." The officer looked at Ellis.

"Yes, this does seem to be a problem, no sooner do we get someone in than their tour finishes, we need to look into this." Ellis picked up his papers and started to put them into his briefcase.

"Well gentlemen we'll meet next week, same time, thank you." There was a scraping of chairs, as everyone stood up.

"Oh Simon," Ellis was looking over the crowd, "my office in five." Simon nodded.

He went to the OP's room, just to check all was well, and at that moment, I picked up the phone.

"Simon please."

"You mean Lt Adder don't you?" But before I could say, "just get him", Simon had taken the phone.

"Simon, I don't want to do this." Simon looked at his watch, he knew it was a big ask, but he also knew I was in deeper than all but one other operator. My penetration into the interior was being hailed as a great success, but it relied on my being in this active IRA unit.

"We need you in this squad, if you weren't in there, someone else would be." Simon let this sink in, as he tried to think of more reasons why I shouldn't go.

"I'll have a squaddies blood on my hands." I was near to tears; Simon could tell and his mind was racing.

"We have lifted over fifteen dangerous men, who, had it not been for you, would still be on the streets. Just last night, we shifted two very evil men off the streets. There are people, who are now locked up in Maidstone, for a long time, because of your evidence."

I listened. I told myself he was right, but my hands were shaking.

"Okay." I took some deep breaths and slowly calmed myself down. I needed some sort of justification for what might happen.

"Okay, I'll be okay."

"Do you want to come in tonight?" Simon asked. I needed time to think about this.

"No, not tonight, I'll just carry on." I put the phone away. Simon walked into Room seven.

"I've just had Deery on the blower sir, he sounds a little shaky."

Ellis looked up. "What's the problem?"

"He's on his first mission today and he's feeling the pressure." Simon sat down. Ellis thought for a while.

"I think we'll bring in Lunn, he has a great deal of experience of this sort of motivational work." Ellis picked up the phone and dialled Lunn's number.

"Hello Gerry, it's Michael Ellis here, I'd like you to help Deery. He has a self doubt problem." Lunn listened and he remembered Deery well.

"How soon do you need me?" Lunn turned around and looked at the wall calendar, he had a full month of training ahead of him.

"Pretty soon, could you do a night call? He's got himself well placed and we need him to stay exactly where he is." Ellis waited for Lunn to consider.

"Could you bring him in on Sunday?" Ellis had his diary open, and decided that should be enough time.

"Yes that'll be fine, thanks Gerry." Ellis put the phone down.

"Come on, Simon, let's go and see Ivan and McDavid before someone kills them." They made their way to the prison cells.

By nine thirty, I couldn't stand waiting any longer. I grabbed my jacket, ran down the stairs, slamming the door behind me. I looked both ways along the street, no one was in sight, so quietly opened the door slightly and lodged a matchstick in the gap of the door. At Johnny's, his mother opened the door and we went through to the kitchen. Johnny was up and eating toast.

"Do ya want some?" He waved his toast at me, I felt too sick to eat at the flat, but the smell of his, now, made me change my mind. His mother was already cutting the bread.

"Yes please missus." The kettle went on and I soon had a brew in my hand and a big thick slice of toast with jam dripping off the side.

After we'd left Johnny's house, we didn't talk too much. He was carrying a duffle bag with a pair of squash racquets sticking out of the top. We made our way to the warehouse on the waste ground and squeezed through the fence. For now, we were only trespassing, but soon we'd be carrying a gun. I was sweating but took comfort from the fact, that if I got caught, it wouldn't mean years in jail. We climbed through the window and quickly recovered the gun, from its hiding place.

Johnny split the gun and handed me the barrel. On its own, it didn't look that much. I took my coat off and we taped the barrel to my back on the right side, winding the tape round my body a few times. I put my coat back on, and Johnny inspected me.

"You can't tell." Johnny then took an old pair of plimsolls out of the bag and tied them to the bottom of the strap of the duffle bag. Then he put the butt of the rifle into the bag. Some of it was still sticking out, but with an old tee shirt over the top and the two handles of the squash racquets sticking up even further, it would take a full search to find out what really was in the bag.

"Better than a violin case eh?" Johnny smiled. We were running early. We made our way out of the warehouse and straight across the road, to the bus stop. The conductor didn't take our fares; he knew our faces and was probably not aware that we had left the buses.

"Off for a game of squash?" The conductor came to talk to us, but we didn't want too many questions.

"Aye, we're just learning." Johnny replied hoping that would stop any follow on questions.

We sat on the bus until one stop further than we needed. It gave us a chance to survey the area as we walked back.

"Fancy a game of pool?" Johnny patted me on the back of the head, trying to make me loosen up. We entered the pub, Johnny ordered two pints and we went to sit down. At this point, I realised I had the barrel still strapped to my back. Johnny put his bag under the bench seat, out of sight and set the balls up on the pool table. I left my coat on even though the sun was streaming through the high windows. The time passed slowly, my play was severely hampered, but eventually the clock struggled round to half past one.

"Come on big boy." Johnny picked up his bag and we made our way out onto the street. The sun was high in the sky.

Before we entered the building, we checked the back door to Jacky's house was open.

Jonas came down the back lane, and quickly glanced behind him before stepped into the back yard.

"Did you have any difficulty?" he asked as he joined us.

"No, it went okay." I answered.

We all made our way up the stairs, Jonas cleaning up every small piece of rubble, as we went. Everything upstairs was as we left it, the baton across the room was still in place. Jonas quickly slotted the gun together and gave the gun a pull through. He fixed the telescopic sights to the gun, then took a round of ammo out of his pocket and carefully polished it, and making sure, as he put it in the breach, that his fingers didn't touch it. After he had rubbed down the gun to make sure his finger prints were cleaned off the weapon, he took a length of cord out of his pocket and strapped the gun to the baton, twice round the gun with a reef knot. The gun stayed suspended pointing up to the ceiling. Then he went into the bathroom; the sink had been smashed, but the tap still worked. Using a piece of soap out of his rucksack, he carefully scrubbed his hands, washing them three times. His last bit of preparation was to snap on a pair of yellow rubber gloves; he was ready. All this time, I was leaning on the back wall of the room, and Johnny was sitting on an old set of drawers, smoking a cigarette and looking out of the window.

The pattern for our working day was set. Jonas was ready, he stood there silent, like the hunter he was, focused, poised, and ready to pounce.

As time passed, I slowly calmed down. It was easier for Johnny. To him, our targets were the enemy, to me they were my comrades. Nothing was said, the air was thick with smoke, time passed slowly. At exactly six o'clock, Jonas snapped off the telescopic sights and put them in his pocket.

"Same time tomorrow, same place." He took his rubber gloves off, while Johnny started to strip down the gun, packing the butt into his duffle bag. At this point, Jonas pulled out a small wad of pound notes and gave both of us seven pounds. Johnny put his in his pocket and carried on packing up and strapping the barrel on to my back. By the time we had finished, Jonas had gone.

"He's not happy," I said as we went down the stairs.

"Well, he only gets paid when he does the job."

"Oh, that explains it," I replied. We left the building as we found it and went across to the back of Jacky's house, the door was open, so we walked in, closing the back gate.

"Hello, Jacky?" I closed the back door, but there was nobody in the house, so we just left the front door with the latch on and walked over to Kathleen's door, which was open.

"Fancy a cuppa?" The big kettle was already simmering.

"Does the Pope pray?" It was Johnny's stock answer for "yes". "We're back tomorrow, can we leave this here?"

"Of course, put it under the boards." She nodded in the direction of the cupboard. We unstrapped the barrel from my back, and then Johnny lifted the boards and placed both parts of the gun and the duffle bag with the squash racquets in the hole. He replaced the boards. By then the brew was ready.

"How did it go?" Kathleen asked.

"No one passed by, a total waste of time," Johnny said.

"Well are you going on the march next week?" Kathleen was trying to keep the conversation going.

"No. We've been told not to do anything, this is too important. We have to keep out of the limelight." She poured the teas out and we sat and enjoyed the quiet moment. Then as she helped herself to a biscuit, Kathleen casually asked me, "Where do you live Billy?"

"Oh, not far from Johnny." I realised this would not be enough, so after a slug on my tea, I told her, "37 Mount Pottinger, above the Post Office, opposite the Police Station." I let this sink in, hoping that would be the end of it.

"Don't you live with your parents?" I'm now mentally scanning my file, the sweat was running down my back.

"No, my mother lives in Liverpool. She works in a tyre factory, she's on good money, and my dad did a runner when I was three." She looked deep into my soul, but I held her gaze.

"What about your grand parents?" I so regretted not making the effort to see my Gran.

"I never knew my Grandad but my Gran is Ella Ward, she lives just off New Lodge Road." Kathleen's face lit up.

"I know her we used to go to bingo." This was getting out of hand, but luckily Johnny was getting bored with my family and suddenly jumped up.

"Come on, we've things to do." He gave Kathleen a hug, I drank the rest of my tea and gave her a peck on the cheek.

"See you tomorrow."

Next thing, we were out on the street, I was so relieved to be out of that grilling, Johnny didn't see it that way, and to him it had just been two people reminiscing.

I thought, I must get more information on my blood line, but Johnny wanted to get to the club, a game of pool on his mind.

We jumped onto the bus, straight upstairs and lit a fag.

I reminded him that we were still banned from O'Donnell's. Johnny jabbed me in the ribs, "I'll see my dad."

"What do you mean?"

"It's the best table in town, I want to play there tonight."
My eyebrows rose.

"I'm going in tonight." Johnny had that determined look on his face. I needed to talk to Simon.

"Look, I'll go home and get something to eat. I'll see you at the club for eight." Johnny looked at his watch and pulled a face, "Okay, but don't be late."

"Simon?"

"Yes."

"I need more info on my family." Simon wanted to know what had caused me a problem.

"Oh, the red haired lady, Kathleen Kelly, she knows Ella Ward, they went to bingo together."

"I'm onto it. What else happened today?" I quickly gave him all the details.

"I'll be around to see you in an hour." I looked at my watch.

"No time Sir, I'm supposed to be at the club by eight."

"OK, I'll be with you at seven tomorrow."

Johnny won at pool all night, my mind was on other things, and we staggered home at just gone eleven, having decided not to stay for the lock in.

17 June 1972 Saturday.

My front door slammed shut at ten to seven. I jumped out of bed and grabbed my piece of wood, but looking down the stairs I saw Simon picking up some mail, he had a couple of files in his hand.

"Put the kettle on." My heart was still thumping. I went into the kitchen, put the kettle on the stove, and rushed into the bedroom to get dressed. Simon was laying out the photos on the living room table.

"Yuk, I don't take sugar, do another one." I went and made another tea. I sat down and we went through the usual mug shot book.

"He was in the club last night." I pointed to a picture, "and he was in the botched bank raid at Newtownards."

"Was that the one where the bystander was shot in the leg?" Simon knew the job.

154

"Yes, and he was with him, bragging about some gun battle in the Lower Falls." I fingered another one.

Simon was taking notes.

"And he's in 2nd Battalion West Belfast." I pointed out some more.

"I'll get those sorted, now look at these." Simon opened up the other folder and showed me my family tree. Someone had done a lot of work.

We sat there, reading, studying for about two hours, pouring over driving licence photos, old newspaper cuttings, addresses and copies of birth certificates.

"Remember, these people have not seen you since you were very young, chances are they won't remember you." I sat back, I wasn't too sure. We had another cup of tea. Simon told me which people to keep a particular look out for and reminded me of the reasons why I should carry on with the sniper job. There was a knock on the door, we both jumped up and started to pack up the documents.

"Go and answer the door," Simon said. I went down the stairs and opened the door, Johnny was standing there.

"Bloody hell, you're early." I leaned out of the door and looked both ways up and down the street, trying to stall and give Simon more time to hide things.

"Come on, let me inside." Johnny tried to push past me.

"Slow down, what's the hurry?" I ambled up the stairs and was relieved to see Simon had cleared all the documents and hidden himself as well, I just hoped he had not hidden in the bathroom.

"The kettle's boiled, I'll get dressed." I disappeared into the bedroom. Simon was hiding as best he could, but anyway Johnny was not the type to go into someone's bedroom and if he did, it would be the last thing he would do. Johnny was replaceable, I was not, and his death would be just another tit for tat killing.

I threw my clothes on as quickly as possible and went into the living room, Johnny was busy making tea.

He told me he fancied having a look round town before we headed for the warehouse; that was why he had come early.

"We could do." I suddenly glimpsed someone's birth certificate peeping out from under his chair. Now I could explain most of the documents we had been looking at, but a birth certificate belonging to some one else, I didn't fancy that one.

I stood up and walked to the window, pulled back the curtains and looked out over the Police Station across the road.

"What the fuck is that?" Any port in a storm. A new type of army vehicle had just pulled up outside. Johnny came across to me, while he was looking; I went over to his chair, picked up the certificate and put it in my pocket.

"That's just a Sarrason they're replacing the old Pigs with those." I had what I wanted.

"Right, I'm going to have some toast, do you want some?" I went into the kitchen and put the grill on. I was in a hurry to get out now, but before I left, I went into the bedroom and threw the paper on the bed. Simon realised the significance of this and gave me a wink, he had a Browning pistol in his hand and I realised the significance of that.

We wolfed down the toast and left.

As we walked up the street, we passed Danny Steel, the man who had burgled my flat; I made a mental note to finger him at the next meeting with Simon.

BBC News....

*A man who suffered two gun shot wounds on Bloody
Sunday has died. His family claim that he died from the wounds
suffered on Bloody Sunday. The Prime minister, Mr Edward
Heath is expected.....*

We made our way over the Albert Bridge and into Belfast
City. After Johnny had done some petty pilfering from
Woolworth's, we ended up in a small cafe down a back street. It
was a lovely day.

"Two teas please."   Johnny was looking at the pens and
rubbers that he had stolen.
"What do you want those for, you can't even write?"   He
slapped the side of my head. I felt my blood rise, but managed to
take the blow without reprisal.
"Do you feel nervous, when you're going on a mission like
this?" I asked Johnny.
"Hell no," He was serious, he leaned forward over his tea.
"Look, they come here, and they wave their guns around, they
don't know the history of this place, they don't know who's
being held down, the B specials kicking shit out of the people
they don't like, jobs for the Prods and not for us. Well bring it on.
I'll do for them."   He leaned back, fire still in his eyes, a look
that reminded me what was really going on.
Exacerbated by school segregation, the ghettos where
people were almost a hundred percent separated by their religion.
It was an us and them situation. I must have shown it on my face,
because Johnny leaned across the table and grabbed my arm.
"Don't worry I'm going to look after you."   He meant it,
he had formed a bond with me, which I did not deserve, which I
did not want. I was confused, my loyalties were being pulled.

Just as this was running through my mind, the door opened and Kathleen Kelly walked in, she was with a man. She looked at us and didn't the least bit surprised to see us. They ordered coffees; the man seemed familiar. I immediately started going through the mugshots stored in my memory. He was skinny and had watery eyes, not quite sure footed. He wore a suit jacket, but his trousers didn't match; neither had been to the cleaners for many years. Kathleen paid for the coffees and they came over to our table. She led the way, he following, spilling some of his drink as he made his way through the tightly packed seats.

"Fancy meeting you two here." She sat down and we made room for the man. I tried to the photos I had been shown, I had seen that face recently.

"This is Alphonsus." Kathleen nodded to the man, I nearly did a summersault. Yes, I remembered. He was my uncle, his photo was amongst all those documents Simon had strewn over my coffee table. It was the name that did it.

"Are you my uncle?" I asked him.

He took a long hard look at me, "Why it's wee Billy, I haven't seen you for years." His eyes rolled upwards while he tried to remember, "It was your Aunty Jo's engagement."

She wasn't really my aunt, but she was always in our house, my mother's best friend, and yes I remembered too, that that was the last time I had seen him. He had been singing old songs in the corner with the older folk at the party.

At that moment Jerry Mason, my old bus driver came into the cafe. I jumped up and went over to him, while he ordered a tea.

"How's it going?" I smiled at him. It was really nice to see him, I was pleased to get my mind off other things.

"I finish the buses next week," he said, while stirring his tea, "but I'm not sure I want to, now it's time."

"Come on, you've waited all your life for this." I tried to encourage him. We sat down at a table near the window

He looked into my face, "Why are you hanging around with the likes of him?" He nodded over to Johnny, straight to the point was Jerry. "He's bad news that boy." I didn't have an answer.

"Aw, he's not that bad." But that was not going to change Jerry's mind. I now felt uncomfortable on more than one level, so I patted Jerry on the shoulder.

"Look, good luck, it was nice to see you." I stood up to go.

"Watch your back Billy, just watch your back." Jerry gave a little nod and I made my way back to Johnny's table. They had nearly finished their drinks.

"What's that old twat want?" Johnny had a nice turn of phrase.

"He's finishing the buses next week, he's been on the job since he was a young boy." I drank my tea.

Kathleen stood up. "Shall we go and see your Gran Billy?" I had been putting off going to my Gran, but now seemed as a good a time as any.

"Yes, good idea, but I have to out by one o'clock." I looked at Johnny but the look on his face, told me he was not up for it.

"I'll see you at Kathleen's at half one sharp." Johnny said as he stood up to leave us.

We left the cafe and I followed Kathleen to the bus stop. Alphonsus said his wife, Mary would be making his dinner and he didn't want to be late, so wouldn't come with us. I think Kathleen was happy for him to disappear, he wandered off. The bus came straight away and we jumped on. As we went past the street Alphonsus had turned down, I had a quick glance and saw him go into a pub on the left, he was going to drink his dinner.

At Gran's, she knocked on the door and it opened slowly. Gran hadn't changed much. Kathleen was standing in front of me, so it took her a while to notice me.

"Eeee, Eeee, will you just look at him." She stood and held both my hands, "God he looks just like his father, will you look at him so tall." She gave me a hug.

Her house had not changed either, still the worn out carpets, the smell of barley, cats running all over the place and the effigies of Christ over the mantelpiece.

"Do you want a cup of tea?" She disappeared into the kitchen.

Kathleen was beaming "Are you glad you came? She's delighted to see you."

"Of course." What else could I say?

She came back in with a tea pot on a tray, and put them on the table, then came over to give me another hug. She returned to the kitchen for the rest of the things. As we sat eating biscuits, we told each other our news, Kathleen just listened. The only lie I told was that I was still on the buses. I kept a close eye on the time and too soon, my time was up.

"Well I have to go now, I have a shift to do." I stood up.

"You must come and see me again soon." She gave me another big hug, I hugged her back. She seemed so small and frail.

"Of course I'll come and see you." I felt guilty as we left, I promised myself I would come and see her every week.

"Shall we walk?" Kathleen looked at her watch, "we can be there in ten minutes."

I was feeling better having seen my Gran.

"Yes, we have loads of time." So we walked back to Kathleen's house in the sunshine, but deep in my heart, I was dreading the rest of the day.

Johnny was sitting on the wall at the end of the street and joined us as we went in to Kathleen's house. The kettle went on and I sat there smoking, while Johnny went into the cupboard and took the gun out. I cleaned it, while we finished the tea. Once I had packed it away, I carefully washed my hands, twice. I then lit another cigarette. The desire to just run away, never really left me on any of these jobs.

We sat there making small talk until five to two, every minute seemed like an hour, but at last Johnny looked at the kitchen clock, "Come on, Jonas will be waiting." Johnny picked up the duffle bag and I looked out of the door both ways. We were on our way. We were very close to the back lane and were soon climbing the stairs.

Jonas was in the upstairs room.

"Have you checked both houses have their doors open?" Johnny and I looked at each other.

"I'll go," I said, ran down the stairs and along the back lane, kicking old bricks to the side. I would hate to trip on those, while running flat out. I walked through the house and came out the front. I could see across the road, Kathleen's door was open. By the time I returned, I could see that Jonas was already set up, with the rifle tied in place. He was still washing his hands at the tap with no basin. Johnny was sitting on the floor at the far end of the room. I lit a cigarette and leaned against the wall.

"Phissst" Jonas attracted our attention.

Johnny sprang up and grabbed the duffle bag. I stood where I couldn't be seen from the road. We held our breath whilst one shot rang out. Jonas kicked the bolt action of the rifle and the empty shell fell to the floor. He removed the scope and placed it in his inside pocket. Then he took a brown paper bag out of his pocket and placed the shell into it, and finally peeled off his yellow rubber gloves.

"Don't run, walk, and be at mine at six." He calmly walked down the stairs and was gone.

During this time, only a few seconds, but it felt like a life time, my mouth had dried up, my body couldn't handle the adrenalin. I thought I was going to pass out.

Johnny had split the gun and put the two pieces into the bag.

"Come on." He launched himself down the stairs, I followed as fast as I could, falling down the last six stairs. Johnny didn't look back. I picked myself up and followed, through the back gate and into the house. An old woman was in the hall, we pushed past and out into the street. Kathleen's door was open and we burst in.

"That was quick." The cupboard door was open with the floor boards ready, the bag was flung down and the boards were down on top of it in seconds. We both gave Kathleen a quick peck on the cheek and left by the back door. I wanted to run, but Johnny just put his hands in his pockets and strolled down the back lane.

We jumped onto the first bus that came. It didn't take us home, but it did go into Belfast town Bus Station where we were able to get a bus going over the Albert Bridge. As we passed the end of the street where it had happened, I looked away, but Johnny peered through the window. We jumped off the bus at the depot and soon caught the sixty four, over the bridge. It was only two stops, but it got us on to our side of the river quickly, where we felt safer.

"Are we going for a pint?" "No I'll give you a knock at quarter past five." I needed to talk to Simon. I quickly turned and strode off in the direction of No. 37. I could feel tears welling in my eyes. It took for ever to get the key in to the lock, all field craft ignored, I just blundered into the bedroom and buried my head in the pillows and sobbed.

It was quite some time before I pulled myself together and as I lay on the bed, smoking a cigarette, I decided that that was it. I had had enough; I was going to tell Simon.

I unpacked the phone and sat there for a bit longer, slowly coming to terms with what had happened.

"Hello can I have Simon please." There was a pause.

"Hello." I was aware that he and everyone in the office knew I'd been blubbing. They would have been listening to the loud speaker, on the direct microphone in my flat.

"Do you need to come in?" I shook my head. With a big lump in my throat, I just managed to tell him I was okay.

A cup of tea and a cigarette later I was feeling better. I looked at the clock, it was four thirty and Johnny would be at the club still. I threw my jacket on and made my way around there. As I walked into the club, I could hear the noise, cheering and singing. Johnny was sitting at the main table surrounded by well wishers. He had three pints standing in front of him.

He saw me and jumped to his feet. "There's the boy." Everyone turned to look at me. I was shocked, they all knew what I'd been involved in. A massive cheer went up and people were patting me on the back. Some bloke asked what I wanted to drink. I smiled weakly and replied, "A gin." I went over to Johnny's table, he was sitting there smiling, loving every minute.

"Come on sit down." The gin and bitter lemon was placed in front of me, Johnny carried on telling the story.

"And then he," pointing at me, "went arse over tit, I was off." They roared with laughter.

Johnny then remembered the old lady, in the hall of the house we had run through.

"Then the stupid bastard knocked over the old lady in the hall and I trampled all over her." There was more laughter. I slugged my gin and people patted me on the back, slowly I got used to the feeling of not caring what I did, not caring who got hurt. We carried on drinking, until Johnny patted me on the back. "Come on, best be off." We went for the door, outside there was a taxi waiting for us.

"Back of Divis, mate." When the taxi stopped, Johnny paid. Seven bob on the meter. He just handed over a pound and told the driver to keep the change. A pound was a full day's wage for most people. At the flat, we were forty five minutes late and we didn't care, but Jonas did.

We followed him into his living room, "and you have been drinking, you must be very careful." I was trying to look as sober as I could.

"I hope you told no one?" Jonas looked accusingly at us.

"Not a chance, mum's the word." Johnny jumped in quickly.

Jonas looked out of the window, "We start to look for a new hide from tomorrow."

Johnny sorted that one out in one go. "Not me mate, I'm in church all day tomorrow." Johnny had set his jaw, "not me." He turned to look at me.

"Church." I said weakly.

"Okay, first thing Monday, you must be here at ten." He pushed a roll of notes, tied up with an elastic band in each of our hands. I could see that the outer note was a fiver. I just put it in my pocket.

Jonas shepherded us down the corridor to the door but before he opened it, he turned back to us.

"Here at ten, on Monday." We nodded as we walked past him. I held my breath, I didn't want him to smell the gin on it. As soon as the door closed, Johnny started to count his money, he nearly tripped over as he walked along the concrete corridor to the stairs.

He turned to me beaming, "Fucking two hundred quid." I pulled mine open and counted, forty notes, all fivers. Blood money. I looked at it a while, then rolled it back up and tied the elastic band round and put it back in my pocket.

We walked into town, not really a safe place to be for two young Catholic men but we didn't care, we were invincible that night.

It was early evening and we went into one of those expensive bars, which were priced to keep out the likes of us. A busty blond barmaid tried to ignore us for a while, but Johnny kept his fiver held up and eventually she couldn't find anyone else to serve.

"Two double gin and lemons." The barmaid looked towards the steward who was polishing glasses at the end of the bar. As an after thought, Johnny said, "please." The steward nodded and she served us.

"Ice and lemon?" She asked, Johnny nodded.

"That will be ten and four please." Johnny turned to me, raised an eyebrow and smiled.

I leaned against the bar and lit a cigarette. As the gin sank in, I started to feel more relaxed.

"I fancy a pub crawl." Johnny said. My defences were weakening.

"Yes so do I but not in pubs like this." We were out of our depth, our eyes were the wrong colour. Most people in Ulster could tell Catholics from Protestants. If you didn't know a person, it was wiser to assume the worst.

"No but let's enjoy this one." I lifted my drink.

I saw him before he saw me, maybe it was my training. Just as we were finishing our drinks, Kerry Howell came through the door. Johnny hated him, but I liked him. He was with a friend, who went to the bar, but Kerry went straight into the toilets.

"I'll just have a piss," I said as I left Johnny standing at the bar, scowling at anyone who looked his way. I did not have much time.

"Hi Kerry." He spun round and gave me his easy smile.

"How you doing?" I was glad to see him but wished I had been on my own.

"Look, I'm out with Johnny, so I haven't got long, but do you fancy going for a pint soon?"

"Well you wouldn't believe it, but I'm meeting Jill on Thursday and her buddy is coming along. Do you remember them on the bus that day?"

"Oh yes, I remember them."

"What's the other girl called?"

"Denise, she's nice."   He finished washing his hands. "I'm meeting them at eight in The Blue Bell on Ravenshill Road. Thursday," he patted my arm, "come along."

I left the toilets before Kerry had finished combing his hair and went over to Johnny.

"Come on, let's go."   Johnny led the way. Kerry came out of the toilets but Johnny didn't see him, this suited me fine.

They were glad to see the back of us in the bar, but we didn't care. Johnny knew the safe pubs and we did the rounds. By ten thirty, I had had too much to drink and I caught myself ordering a round in my Liverpool accent. The alarm bells started to ring. I needed to get home before I said something stupid. Last orders had been rung while Johnny was at the bar, so this was the last pint. He laid them on the table and as soon as Johnny turned his back, I knocked my drink over.

"You fucking useless bastard," he shouted.   Some of the drink had gone on Johnny's leg.

"Give me half of yours."   I held my glass out.

"Not a chance."   He held his drink where I couldn't reach. "Not a chance."

I tried to look hurt, "Go on."   This made him drink faster, because of the threat of some one wanting some of his drink.

We got a taxi home.

Chapter 17. Sunday 18th June 1972.   168

BBC News. There are reports coming in of an air crash just outside Staines Middlesex. BEA say there were 118 passengers and crew on board. There are no casualty figures yet…….

I was up early and I caught the nine eighteen to Holywood, getting off at the far end of Palace Barracks. I walked back to the main gate, once the bus had gone. After the normal rigmarole of getting into the camp, I made my way up to the op's room. Simon was not there, so I went back down to the cookhouse and had a massive breakfast. Simon came over with a cup of tea.

"How are you?" I carried on eating. "Was it bad?"

"I'll get used to it." I still had my mouth full.

We talked about who was where and when, while we sat there in the cookhouse. Simon took notes and at the end he said, "Do you want to see anyone?" I knew he meant did I need any help.

"No I'm fine." I slugged my tea and lit a cigarette.

"I need to get back, I don't want Johnny to find me missing." I stood up, looking at my watch and walked out, leaving Simon sitting there. I would have to hurry, if I wanted to catch that eighty six back to Belfast. I didn't buy the Sunday papers on the way home. I didn't want to read anything about the shooting.

Monday 19th June 1972.

The next morning I knocked on Johnny's door at five past nine.

"Come in," Johnny's mother answered.

We got to the Divis Flats five minutes early and the door opened as we got to the door. Jonas had been watching out for us, he missed nothing.

He gave us instructions as to what type of place we were looking for. A disused building, good escape route, near junctions that the army would be patrolling, a mixed terrain, with lots of possible shooting places.

We were sent out and within half an hour, had ended up back on our side of the water.

"That'll do." Johnny was pointing at an old engineering building. It had been closed for many years. We climbed over the gates and had a look around. It had two escape routes. It had loads of windows, most of them smashed. It only gave Jonas a small field of fire, but in a way that was good, because it meant that the army had a poor view of the building. We were happy and went and played pool for the rest of the day.

Tuesday 20th June 1972.

The next day, when we rolled up at Jonas' place, he wasn't ready for us and it took a long time for him to answer the door.

"Where have you been?" He was annoyed that we had got to his door without his seeing us.

"Hey, keep your hair on, we've been working hard," Johnny was straight on the defensive, "and we've found a place." He stuck his jaw out and faced Jonas.

He was happy when he saw the place and even happier when a patrol walked past, while we were there. The patrol ignored us; we studied them carefully.

"Okay, I need the gun. I need to set the...." he used his hands to show he needed to calibrate the sites. This would involve taking the weapon somewhere in the country.

We all caught the bus over the bridge to Kathleen's house and dug the gun out from under the floor boards. While we had a cup of tea, Jonas cleaned the gun and packed the weapon away in the duffle bag. Then he carefully washed his hands. We talked about anything, but the shooting.

Jonas told me to get a taxi so I went over to the pub. There was a public phone in the corner, with taxi numbers written on the wall. I was soon back at Kathleen's house and within minutes, there was a peep of a horn outside.

"We can start work on Monday, just come and see me." Jonas opened the door and looked both ways, then he came back into the kitchen for the duffle bag.

"And don't get into any trouble." He was trying to look stern. Then he was gone.

"Amen, off till next week, I might and go and see my mother." I wanted out for a few days. I also wanted to see Kerry on the Thursday night, without Johnny knowing. I looked on the calendar hanging on Kathleen's wall. Johnny had his hands dug deep into his pockets.

"I could be back on Saturday." I turned to look at Johnny, he was scowling.

"That would be nice," Kathleen said. Johnny was trying to think of reasons why I shouldn't go.

"You'll miss the pool competition on Wednesday."

"Well it'll be easier for you then." I ruffled his hair, he shrugged my hand off.

"I'll book the ticket when I get there," I looked at my watch, "Yes I'll catch the half ten tonight." I thought I'd tease Johnny a bit more. "You can come if you want."

"Fuck off." No sense of humour. I finished my tea, put my jacket on and gave Kathleen a kiss.

"I'll give you a knock when I get back." Johnny didn't even make eye contact.

The bus was coming down the street, as I reached the bus stop. "One to the town, please."

Once in the city and with my pocket full of money, I bought myself a complete new outfit, including a brown suede jacket. Then over to a barber; it was the first time I'd had my hair blow dried.

I told the taxi to drop me off on Mount Pottinger Road, about fifty yards down from the Police Station, I didn't want to be seen getting out of a taxi with all my carrier bags. I quickly slipped into my flat, but still checked all the signs. I could never drop my guard.

I filled the bath right up to the top, no mother to nag me here. Then after a kip on the sofa, I packed my suitcase, all my new gear, tooth brush and all the things I would need from the bathroom, finally my still bulging wallet. I lifted the carpet in the bedroom and rang Simon.

"Simon ,please." I heard him say, "Lt. Adder."

"Hello." Simon sounded chirpy.

"Simon have you got a patrol in my area, I'm coming in for a few nights."

"Hold on a sec." It always feels like a long time, when you can't see what's going on. I just lay there on the bed, while Simon checked the locations of all his mobile patrols.

"No, but I fancy a ride out. I'll come and get you." I guessed that he must have been sick of sitting in the op's room, day after day.

"You're as good as anyone. I'm ready packed."

"I'll get a wagon from MT, give me thirty minutes."

"Pick me up outside Thompson Engineers. I'll be in the gateway." I lay back and went through my mental checklist, it was easy to take your eye off the ball. I wasn't going to do that.

I wanted to know if anyone came into the flat, while I was away, so carefully placed my triggers. I left the kitchen and bedroom lights on too. Then, in good time, I walked down to Thompsons with my suitcase. They had a nice little gateway, in the shadows and I stood and had a cigarette. Simon pulled up.

As I got in the car, I said, "I'm not needed till next week and I'm pissed off just playing pool all the time."

Simon pulled away from the curb. I looked around to see if anyone had seen me.

"I need a return ferry ticket to Liverpool, and then I'll treat you to a pint." Yes, I was getting cocky, you can't order an officer around like that and then offer him a pint, but I did. The pendulum was swinging and he knew how important I was.

He accepted that I was doing a very dangerous job and I needed some slack.

We drove out to the booking office on Corry Road, only a ten minute drive.

"A return Belfast to Liverpool, leaving tonight and coming back on Sunday at ten thirty in the morning."

I gave him a fiver. The booking clerk said, "Four pounds eighty pence and four bob change." He was the same as me, we still hadn't really come to terms with the new money, so I knew what he meant. He gave me the ticket and I sprinted out to the waiting car.

"Fancy a quick pint?" It was still quite early.

"I know a nice pub." As he drove, we covered all the intelligence I had missed and I gave him extra details about Johnny and Jonas.

Without my noticing, Simon had pulled into the car park of a small pub. We strolled in, still deep in conversation and ordered drinks.

I was just finishing the story of the shooting and was explaining the details of the gun. I described Jonas' behaviour afterwards. ", and then he calmly picked up the shell, put it in a paper bag and disappeared." Simon ordered two more drinks.

I told him about my falling down the bottom of the stairs, because I was so nervous.

We ordered scampi and chips and had one more drink before Simon looked at his watch. I was enjoying a cigarette. "So what are you going to do now?" he asked.

"Well I'm coming back to Holywood Barracks for a bit of rest, but I'm going to be in town on Thursday night." I carried on "But tonight, I fancy seeing what this midweek piss up is like." Simon's face changed.

Most of the soldiers in Holywood Barracks were Paras. It was their place. The other units in the camp gave them a wide birth. Other units were allowed to go to the midweek dance, but they never did.

We drove back in silence, the whole atmosphere had changed. I smoked, and Simon had the window wide open. We pulled straight into the camp, there was no fuss getting through the gates with Simon in the car. I took my suitcase up to my room, well the one I had been sleeping in, on and off. All the beds were taken. I walked back to and looked for Simon in the OP's room.

"I need a bed my old bed's been taken." Simon phoned the Sergeants mess, I heard him say quite forcefully, "Get me the duty sergeant." I looked at the incident board and listened to the radio, but I could still hear Simon.

"Yes, a separate room," Simon was on form, "and yes he will want breakfast." There was a pause, then Simon said, "Two days, minimum." There was a long pause, before I heard him say thank you.

Simon looked over at me. I was still listening to the radio and the two radio operators. We had all heard Simon's phone conversation.

"Jenkins take Deery's case to the Sergeants mess, they're expecting him." Jenkins had not joined the army to carry suitcases, I wasn't surprised at has antagonistic behaviour, as he went off. But it wasn't heavy, so I let him carry it. The duty sergeant wasn't expecting a civilian, particularly a long haired civilian, who hadn't shaved and wore old Wellingtons. I didn't care. He showed me to my room, it was large and comfortable, but it had two other beds there, one was being used, but empty. I got my good clothes out and washing gear and stowed the case under the bed, then went to found the showers. When I returned to the room I found a bull of a man, in a Para uniform, getting undressed.

I closed the door and he turned to look at me, with my towel round my waist. He was surprised. "Hi I'm Billy Deery, Military Intelligence." I stuck my hand out. "I'm only here for a few days, that's why they've put me in here." He shook my hand. "Tom White," he replied as he carried on getting undressed. "We've just got back from doing a two day hide and seek mission and I'm clamming for a pint."

"I'm going to have a look in at the midweek dance, over in the mess," I said, he smiled.

"They'll eat you alive." I looked into his face, for a sign that he was joking, but there was none.

"I thought anyone could go." I was sticking to my guns.

"Oh they can, they can, but they don't. The boys are a bit wild." He picked up his towel and left the room. I finished drying my hair and put my new clothes on. Then I packed away my old stuff, into the suitcase. I'd left before Tom came back. I made my way back to Simon's office but he wasn't there, so I asked Jenkins where the NAFFI was.

"Turn left out of here," he pointed to the door, "and keep going left, you can't miss it." He was smiling.

I hadn't needed to ask, as I left the building three girls, all dressed up to the nines, were walking past, I just followed them.

I stood in the queue enjoying being so close up to the three girls, smelling the scent of females and listening to their chatter.

The doorman, still in uniform, asked for our ten pence. He stamped my hand with a blue ink pad, DANCE it said. I was in.

During the day it was just a normal NAFFI canteen, but tonight, with the aid of two spinning mirror balls and a disc jockey, set up in the corner, it had become a dance hall. There was a bar, with roll down shutters. I made my way to the bar and felt as though I had a flashing light on my head. Every eye in the place was following me. I stood in the queue for a drink, the woman behind the bar was doing her best, but she was very slow. The girls in front of me were just finished being served, when I was pushed aside by someone pretty strong. I looked around and saw a thick set man with two mates. The look on the man's face, told me that it would not be worth complaining. I stood and waited till they had been served, but when they left the bar, the next soldier immediately put in his order and the barmaid served him. I decided to go to the back of the queue again. Eventually, I was served and I made my way over to one of the posts and leant against it. Now I understood, why I had been advised to stay away. The room was full of mostly highly charged young men, with just a smattering of very attractive girls. I decided I would finish this pint and go. I was due to meet Kerry in town the next night anyway. Two girls who had been dancing round their handbags to a James Brown song, suddenly picked up their bags and came over to where I was standing. I was wearing my new suede jacket and a new pair of brown Cuban heeled cowboy boots with my new jeans. I liked the outfit, but it wasn't what everyone else was wearing and with the long hair and sideburns, I stood out.

"Hi." She took me by surprise. The taller and slimmer girl opened up the conversation.

"Hi." I felt a bit embarrassed and could feel myself starting to blush. I stood up straight and stopped leaning against the post.

"You're new here?" She turned to the smaller girl, "This is Anne and I'm Maggie." I nearly choked getting out my name. What the hell was I going to say? I hadn't thought for one minute about a cover story, to explain why I was here. "Do you want a drink?" I asked.

"I'll have a brandy and Babycham and Anne likes Rum and black." I made my way to the bar and while the drinks were

174

being poured, I conjured up a reason for being in camp tonight. We sat down at one of the tables. The night was starting to take off, people were starting to dance. I started to relax.

Maggie did most of the talking. "We're from Newtownards; the army put a bus on for us." Anne added that there were ten of them. I looked round the dance floor, the place was filling up. "Some of the girls go to the pub, before they come here, they don't want to look too keen."

I finished my drink, but didn't fancy getting myself one, without offering another one for the girls.

"Do you want another?" Anne declined, she'd hardly touched hers. "I'll have another." Maggie was holding up a near empty glass. I stood in the queue, but this time, didn't have any problems getting served. I made my way back to the table, to find two soldiers chatting up the girls. I put the drink next to Maggie and turned to watch the dance floor. I enjoyed watching people being sociable, so was quite happy sitting there. The body language of the soldier talking to Maggie was clearly stating that she was his.

I bought myself another drink and this time, when I got back to the table, Maggie was on her own. Anne was on the dance floor with the ape-man she had been talking to.

"What do you do?" Maggie was looking at my hair length, she knew I wasn't a soldier.

"I work on the vehicles up at the top of the barracks. I'm a diesel fitter."

Her face lit up, "I'm a trainee hairdresser."

I tried to keep the conversation going, "I've just had my hair cut, but you can do it next time."

She looked at my hair. "Which one?"

The music changed and I fancied a dance. "Want to shake a leg?" I nodded at the floor, it was quite full now. Maggie put her bag in between us and we danced round it. We stayed on the floor for two records and then made our way back to the table. Both the soldiers were sitting with Anne and they made room for us as we sat down. At the end of the day, I was there to relax, in a safe environment. I was not looking for romance, just a few pints and bed on my own. I was quite happy for Maggie to start talking to the soldier boy. They chatted away, whilst I watched the dance floor. I finished my pint and went over for one last pint. It was getting rowdy and the air was filled with testosterone and cheap perfume. Because of the imbalance of male to female, men had started to dance with men, or in groups of girls, with twice as many men as girls.

While I was being served I felt a dig in my ribs, I turned round to see ape man and his mate.

"Them women are with us." I handed over my money to the barmaid.

"No problem," I replied. I picked up my pint and made my way back to the table and put my pint down. I gave Maggie a wink and went to look for the toilets.

The building had been built just after the last war and the toilets reflected this. Large urinals, with brass pipes running down from the cistern and white wall tiles with hair line cracks. The central drain was slightly blocked with cigarette ends, so there was always a small puddle of yellow urine in it. I think I'd just relieved myself, but to be honest I can't remember, when a glass bottle smashed just above my head. The shot of adrenaline that entered my body nearly made me pass out. Any tiredness or tipsiness disappeared in a flash. I turned round to find ape man, with his mate, standing between me and the door. I was in big trouble. Of all the dangers I had been in, of all the people I had mixed with, this was bigger trouble than all of those right now.

"Did you understand me when I told you they were with us?"

I tried to hide the shake in my voice. "Yes."

"So why are you still here?" They slowly started to move towards me.

"I'm just finishing my pint, and then I'm off." My Irish accent was not helping the situation at all.

"Who the fugg are you?" They were now shoulder to shoulder and together formed a two yards wide wall of muscle.

They would have known I didn't work in the camp "I cut the grass round the camp, I've got a special pass." I stalled, looking in my pockets, they moved forward. It was at this point, even though I was a devout atheist, I started making promises to someone I didn't believe in.

One of the toilets flushed and the door opened with a clang of locks, and there stood Tom White, my room mate from over at the mess.

"Billy." He nodded to me and finished doing up his belt. "Are you going to get me that pint?" He walked forward and pulled on my elbow.

As we walked past my two adversaries, he turned, "I expect my junior NCOs to behave better than this."

We walked straight out of the building; my body was in crisis. I was shaking all over and still had shards of glass on my jacket and hair. He was calm, poised and in control. He helped me brush the glass off.

"Come on, you owe me a pint." As we walked to the Sergeant's mess, I was like a puppy, round the feet of his master.

We entered the mess and made our way over to a table, where clearly, the most senior members of the club were sitting.

"Sir," Tom almost stood to attention, as he addressed the Regimental Sergeant Major, "this is Sergeant Billy Deery, Intelligence. Just in for a few days rest."

The old warhorse looked me up and down, well someone had to mix with the locals. He raised his glass as a sign that all was well. Tom jabbed me in the ribs, protocol done with.

I ordered myself a large gin and tonic and asked Tom what he was having. I told him he could have anything he wanted, I owed him big style.

He asked for a large vodka and coke, the bar steward nodded.

The only table not taken was very close to the dart board, but we sat there anyway. I looked round at the club. It was sumptuous, you can't buy your way into a mess, you have to earn it. We sat there with the deep pile carpet, heavily varnished wood and original paintings of war scenes on the wall and told each other stories. His were much more interesting. Mine missed out the last few days.

I didn't hear last orders, but everyone got one more in just after the Regimental Sergeant Major left. My head was spinning, so I didn't order myself one. I don't remember getting to bed.

I woke at eight to find Tom's bed empty. I didn't feel like having any breakfast, so when I'd dressed, I made my way straight over to the OP's room.

It was quiet, giving me plenty of opportunity to read all the incoming reports and follow up the arrests resulting from the information I'd handed to Simon. There were a large number of these arrests and I wondered if links would be made to me, as a result. There was a tap on my shoulder and I turned round to see Simon.

"How's it going?" He filled his cup from the urn of coffee, which stood at the end of the long cluttered counter.

"Bit of a funny head, but I had a good sleep." Simon leaned back on the desk.

"Ellis wants to talk to you, before you shoot off." I pulled a face that said I wasn't too keen.

"What time will he be in?" I asked.

"Oh, about one. He was on the desk last night till four." Simon obviously wanted to see how I felt about that.

"I'm off for some grub and a lie down." I put the files away, "I'll be back at one."

"Have you seen these?" Simon handed me some photographs. At first my eyes couldn't comprehend what I was looking at. There was a black and white photograph, of what appeared to be bits of meat strewn on a floor somewhere, but when I had taken all the information in, I realised that it had been a body, which had been blown up.

"That's the sort of people you're putting away, people who will do anything to get their way." I kept leafing through the pictures. "You've put three known bombers away and one day you might get the bomb makers." He smiled as he said this, "Now go and get that food and I'll see you at one."

I made my way down to the Sergeants Mess and had a coffee and a slice of toast, then made returned to my room. It was empty. I lay down and checked my watch, one and a half hours before my meeting with Ellis. The next time I looked at my watch, it was ten past one.

I leapt up from the bed. Now I've learnt that once you're late, it's not worth hurrying, so I washed my face and strolled in to his office at just gone half past. Ellis was on the phone and Simon was writing a report, so I just hung around.

"Ah Deery," Ellis had seen me, "I'll be there in a minute." He completed filling in the log.

"Let's get a coffee and go to my room."

Simon looked on as we disappeared off, down the corridor.

"Sit down." We sat facing each other across his desk. Simon followed us in and sat to the side.

"So how do you think it's going?" An open question. He wanted me to babble on and so he could see what my frame of mind was.

"Well sir, I seem to be accepted by the men on all levels. I find it a bit strange really, mostly because I don't have a long association with these people. The only reason I can think of is that in times of need, they just use who they can."

I looked at Ellis, he was nodding and this encouraged me to go on. "Also, because I'm partnered with Johnny O'Neil and his father is top dog in East Belfast, I seem to have some extra pull and if you add that to being in a hit squad, that only the big boys know about, it all adds up to a high level of trust, on their part."

Ellis put his hands on the back of his head and stretched. "Yes", he nodded, to give himself time to construct another open question.

Simon handed Ellis a list of the men, who had been lifted, as a result of my information.

"Mmm, good." He had a quick glance at the second page. "Good, well how do you feel about yourself?" I didn't often look down this corridor of life, so it took me a while to formulate my answer.

"Well it can be stressful and I have to watch my drinking, but there's only just over a month left on my assignment." Ellis looked at Simon, the alarm bells were ringing. It was one of their main problems, working hard to get someone in and then having to wrap it up, their time being over.

180

"Well all I can say, at the moment, is well done Deery. We must ensure that you get as much rest as you can." He opened my file, which Simon knew inside out. "I see your mother lives in Liverpool?" He looked over at Simon.

"I think you should get out of Belfast, as much as possible, we don't want you to burn out, do we?" I wondered if this was a hint, that it might be a longer tour than originally planned.

Ellis stood up, to signal the meeting was over. "You're handling this very well, Deery." He stuck his hand out, I'd only had an officer shake my hand once before, the time I beat Lt. Billings in the orienteering final, and that was more like a slap.

"Thank you Sir." I left the office with Simon close on my tail.

"You might get a medal for this."

"I'd deserve it just for last night." I quickly told him the story of the midweek dance.

"Yes, the Paras are a bit of a handful, when they've had a drink, I should have warned you."

"I would have still gone." We walked over to the canteen, because I wanted to line my stomach before I went out that night.

"What are you doing tonight?" Simon asked as we loaded our plates with army food.

"I'm off into Belfast to meet Kerry, a mate of mine from the buses. He's bringing two girls." I smiled, but I wasn't sure that Simon liked the idea. "Don't worry I'll be coming back here to sleep."

"Well just be careful; you don't want to run into anyone who thinks you're away in Liverpool." But I knew the risks.

"No chance, we'll be in Proddie areas all night. I'm meeting them in the Blue Bell at seven thirty." I finished the last of my meal. "Could you organise a lift for me?"

"Okay, be ready at seven fifteen." Simon patted my arm as he left.

I sat and had another cup of tea and read one of the many newspapers on the tables. I felt a friendly slap on the back of my head and looked around to see Brian Fodden, the fat lad who had been seconded at the same time as me, he sat down.

"How's it going?" He looked happy enough, but I was sure he'd put on a bit more weight.

"Fine and yourself?" He bit into his sandwich and answered through a full mouth.

"Great, it gets a bit boring, but it's better than standing in the rain every night." He filled his mouth again. I didn't want to elaborate too much on my side of things, so I just agreed with him.

He went on to tell me of all the incidents he'd been involved in. They made good stories. I just listened and enjoyed his exaggeration of his part in the action.

Eventually, he burned himself out.

"Are you still on the buses?" I didn't want to lie, but I didn't want to tell him what I was really doing.

"It's great on the buses," (not a lie), "I'm off for a few days, so I decided to come into camp." (Again, not a lie.) I looked at my watch, not much time left. I stood up.

"Brian it was nice to see you, but I'm going to have a kip, then get ready for tonight." I patted him on the back and made my way out. I looked around as I left Brian was going for another sandwich.

I made my way back to my room in the Sergeant's Mess. It was empty; I quickly dropped off to sleep, still wearing my clothes.

I was awake in a flash, when the door opened. Tom threw his webbing onto his bed and started to wash his hands.

"I've had a lazy day." I said, still sitting on my bed. I lit a cigarette and lay back.

"Well I've been kicking arse all day," he smiled, "with our two friends from last night."

"I'm on the piss again tonight. Off to meet a friend, who just happens to have a spare girlfriend. She's a nice looking girl."

He wiped his hands on the towel, "I'm happily married."

"I'm not." I replied. The gong went, somewhere down the corridor. We could hear doors opening and people making their way down to tea.

I followed close behind Tom, not quite sure if there would be a meal place for me. I needn't have worried; it was casual, people sitting where they wanted. We had a nice curry, with all the trimmings and Tom got a couple of pints on his mess bill.

After the meal Tom made his way to the bar and started chatting to some of the other members, so I got Tom a pint, then made my way upstairs to get changed.

I sat in the television room, until just before my lift was due and then stood outside having a cigarette.

One of the squad cars rolled up and tooted his horn. I didn't know the man, which was good, as it meant I didn't have to lie or make small talk.

"I'm going to Ravenshill Road, East Belfast, there's a pub called The Blue Bell." We roared off, the guard on the gate, only just got the barrier up in time. The driver didn't ask any questions and I sat in silence. That's how I liked it.

As we got near the pub, I asked the driver to drop me fifty yards or so short of it.

As I got out, I thanked him he nodded, then did a racing start.

The pub was small with a bar and a snug, I looked in both rooms. Kerry and the girls hadn't, arrived so I went back into the bar.

"Can I have a small lemonade please."

"Ice and lemon?"

"Yes please."

"Eleven pence."

"Ta." I sat down, the room was carpeted, it was clean and the heating was on. There were not many in, but those who were knew each other. It was still not eight yet but when you're waiting for someone, it feels like its forever. I wished I had turned up a bit late, but here I was.

Two men came through the door and went to the bar. While they were being served, Kerry popped his head around the door. Life was looking up. He waved at me, to come over to him.

"We're meeting them next door, in the snug." I went back for my drink, the barmaid looked at me, I pointed next door to the snug and she nodded. The prices were a bit more where we were heading, so it was not best practice to change room, half way through a drink.

Kerry was leaning on the bar, waiting to be served, smiling, smart and all poshed up.

"They'll be here soon, what do you want?" he asked, pointing to my drink.

"I'm okay, thanks." I went to find a table in the corner. The same barmaid was working in both rooms, she served Kerry. He came over to the table, still smiling. "How's things?" he asked as he pulled his chair in.

"Oh fine." I started to realise that I would need a cover story about my new job. I could hardly tell him I was a gun carrier.

I asked him about the buses, to give me time to think of something. He babbled on I wasn't really listening though.

I decided to continue the story of being a diesel fitter at the barracks that I'd started with the girls last night.

Kerry carried on talking about the buses; with lots of stories about girls he had chatted up and driving misdemeanours.

Our dates eventually came through the door. I had forgotten what they looked like. Jill was very pretty with long legs and a lot of them showing from beneath her mini skirt. Denise, just as pretty, but like so many girls who wore glasses, you could miss that if you didn't look carefully. They sat down and Kerry immediately got up to get them a drink.

"What are you drinking?"

"A Babycham." Jill was in first, he looked at Denise, "Vodka and lemon please." I was impressed, they chose sophisticated drinks. They also dressed smartly and knew their way around a bar. I decided I was among friends and maybe I should have a little drink, it would help me to relax. I joined Kerry at the bar. He'd already rung the bell, to call the barmaid.

"I'll have a gin and tonic," I said. The barmaid came through.

Kerry gave the barmaid the order and turned to me, "What do you think then?" He asked, pointing at the girls.

"They're nice." I smiled. Kerry gave me a little punch in the ribs. "Remember, Jill's with me." He gave me a look to make sure I was taking him seriously. I didn't want to tell him she was not my type he might have taken it the wrong way.

"Fine, I like the look of Denise." Kerry smiled again and patted my face.

He paid for the drinks and we went back to the table. The girls had obviously been discussing us, because they stopped talking as we approached. We sat down.

"Kerry said you've left the buses." Jill was looking at me, as though I was mad.

"Yes, I started a job at the army barracks out at Holywood." Jill and Denise had a look of incredulity.

"As a diesel fitter." They clearly didn't know what that meant. "I repair engines, its good money." That was all they need to know, it was good money. Kerry backed me up here by nodding.

"Yes, the best paid men at the depot are the mechanics," he added. I tried to play it down, I didn't want them thinking I was rolling in money.

"Hey, I'm only a glorified grease monkey." We chatted for a while and had a few more drinks. I had time to watch Denise. I also caught her looking at me a few times. Kerry did most of the talking, but Jill could hold her own when it came to talking. She was a trainee hairdresser and had some good stories. Once she'd forgotten to rinse a customer's hair after she'd put colour put on. It went over our heads, all the technical details, but we could follow the story and it made the girls laugh. That was good enough for us.

Kerry looked at his watch, "Hey, where are we going next?" Every one except me knew, but they played the game. Each one shrugged their shoulders. I didn't have a clue.

"We could go to Jacksons." Jill was first to drop the name, Denise nodded. I looked at Kerry. It was where they'd gone last time and they had had a good time. We downed our drinks, while Kerry went through to the bar to use the pay-phone to get a taxi.

Kerry joined us outside and told us it would be with us in three minutes. He grabbed Jill and embraced her. Denise and I stood close together, that was good enough for me. I wouldn't make the first move. I had a total fear of rejection.

The cab came quickly and we jumped in, Kerry got in the front, and with the three of us in the back, Denise and I had to sit very close together. I was enjoying the ride, her long legs pressing next to mine; the ride was over too quickly for me. At Jackson's, we paid our seven shillings entry and went down the stairs into the club. At the bottom of the stairs, we paid another shilling to hang our coats in the cloakroom. In the club proper, there were ultraviolet lights, which caught any white clothing making it glow.

"What are you girls drinking?" Kerry held a five pound note in his hand.

Denise was first in, "Brandy and Babycham please." Kerry smiled, that's what he wanted to hear. He looked at Denise, "I'll have the same." Kerry nodded to me to go with him.

The bar was busy, people were pouring in from all over the city, for the late night drinking time.

"We are well in here," Kerry said. He stood with his back to the bar nodding at the girls. I did my normal check of the club, looking for faces from the mug shots. There was no IRA, but I did notice two UVF middle ranking bad boys, who were on a report only list. I started to relax a bit. Kerry was busy paying for the drinks; I leaned over his shoulder, grabbed the two brandy drinks and went over to where the girls had squeezed into a half round table with red velvet seats. I sat down next to Denise and put the drinks down. Kerry came over with our two pints. He sat on the other side, next to Jill.

The girls sipped their drinks and then song Knock Three Times blared from the disco.

"Fancy a dance?" Denise was looking at me.

I nodded and grinned. She held my hand to lead me on to the small dance floor, she had lovely soft hands. Once we had made physical contact, I was not letting go, so we danced holding hands. After a few more songs, we sat down. Kerry and Jill were still on the floor. We sat close, still holding hands. She was giving me the green light. She told me about her job, how she hated being a dental nurse. How time dragged while she was there and how difficult it would be to get to any other work. I watched her closely whilst she talked, admiring her soft white skin. Behind the glasses, she was a very attractive girl. Kerry and Jill returned and Kerry nodded towards the bar.

"Same again girls?" I stood up, finishing my drink. The girls nodded and smiled. I told Kerry I'd get the next round.

At the bar, I ordered the same for them, but got myself a tonic; it looked the same as gin and tonic, but would keep my head in order. The night carried on with more drinks and more dancing. Eventually, although last orders hadn't been called, we knew it was the end, when the disc jockey put on the last waltz. I was holding Denise very close; we weren't really dancing, just swaying to the music. I was enjoying the smell of her perfume too. Outside in the taxi queue, we held hands. Jill turned and whispered in Denise's ear, Kerry winked at me. But it still came as a shock when Denise pulled my head down to her level. "I don't want to go home," she whispered. I tried to make calculations. I couldn't take her back to the barracks and I couldn't be seen going into my flat.

Kerry and Jill jumped into the first taxi, too soon the next one pulled up and we jumped into the back.

"Mount Pottinger Road please." I nuzzled her neck as we drove, I was past caring. Any thought of risk had evaporated from my mind.

I asked the driver to stop well down the road. Most of the street lights were off, their timers had all been taken out. I slipped the driver a pound, well over the top for a tip.

We stood on the corner for a few seconds; I looked up and down the road. There were sentries watching from the Sangers in Mount Pottinger Police Station. A door was open further down Madrid Street, a light was on but there was no one in the doorway. With my key ready, we approached my door. I quickly checked to see if the bit of lollypop stick was still in place, meaning no one had opened the door whilst I'd been away. I skipped inside quickly and reached up to knock the master switch on the fuse box, to the off position. I pulled Denise inside, closed the door and slipped the sneck down. I held Denise in my arms for a while; my heart was beating fast for more than one reason. We went up the stairs in darkness. I led the way, still holding her hand. I flicked the light switch at the top, but no light came on. I tried again a few times, no light. The living room light was just the same.

"Shit, the fuse has gone again, I'll have to tell the landlord tomorrow." Denise didn't seem disappointed; I didn't think she'd planned on having the lights on for long. We sank onto the sofa. She was on top of me and we started kissing. This gave me the best position, to run my hands over her. Stockings were an absolute nightmare to a beginner like me.

Meanwhile, in the op's room, the speaker on the direct line to the microphone in my flat was turned up. Someone had sent for Simon, while the duty officer and all the duty radio operators were listening in.

Needless to say, I got too excited and suffered from a bad case of premature ejaculation, but she never complained.

Eventually, we sneaked into my bed, which felt damp and cold, but it soon warmed up. We went to sleep, enjoying the feel of our naked bodies close together.

The sun woke me up early I just lay there, looking at Denise.

She had very white skin with a few scattered freckles and there was a fuzz of fine blond hair on her arms.

I didn't want to open the curtains, I didn't want anyone looking at the house and knowing people were inside. I slipped out of bed and went to the toilet. I was glad to see, I'd left the curtains closed in the bathroom. I climbed back into bed.

"The electricity is still off," I whispered. She rolled over to face me.

"What's the time?" she said sleepily.

"Just gone six." I wrapped my arms around her and we snuggled up. The feeling of being wanted, was over powering. Lying there, naked, next to a lovely girl just felt so good. No guilt, no hidden agenda and no reason for this moment to end. Slowly, we built up to a return match and afterwards I made tea and toast, which we ate in bed. The bread was stale and the tea had no milk, but we enjoyed it.

"I have to be at work by eight thirty," she said and started to get out of bed. I enjoyed watching, she showed no shame. I lay in bed while Denise had a bath then she dressed in the same clothes as she'd been wearing the previous night.

"Will your parents ask you where you've been?"

"Oh no, I told them I was staying at Jill's, she told her parents, she was staying at mine." She gave a wicked smile. We made a careful and quick exit and I walked her to the bus stop on Albert Bridge Road.

Chapter 19. Friday 23rd June 1972.   190

As soon as she was on the bus, I turned and headed to the bus stop, to get the bus to Holywood. Whilst I sat on the bus, I reminisced about the events of the night before. I had a track record of falling in love too quickly, it may have been something to do with my home life, or Mother Nature had given me a strong bonding mechanism. Either way, I was falling for Denise and it changed everything. Carelessly, I got off the bus directly outside the barracks, instead of going on to the next stop. All my field craft had disappeared in one night. I didn't even look to see who was watching, as I walked in through the gates.

I made myself a coffee from the brew kit on the bench. I had forgotten all about the microphones in the flat and assumed that I was the only one to know about my night with Denise.

One of the radio operators, still on from last night smiled at me, "I think Ellis and Simon will want to talk to you, Casanova." I blushed and lifted my coffee to my mouth, to think about the remark.

"Oh why?" I lit a cigarette.

"You'll find out." He looked at the speakers on the wall. "Oh yes, you'll find out."

"Well tell them I'm in the canteen." I stormed out of the office, embarrassed and angry, and made my way across to the canteen.

Surely the microphones were powered from my electricity supply, so would have been turned off, when I pulled the master switch. I couldn't believe I didn't want to believe, they had listened in.

I loaded my plate with two of everything and ignored a remark from a squaddie.

"Hey, get your hair cut." The squaddie persisted, but my mind was elsewhere.

Whilst eating my breakfast, I ran the whole night through my head. I tried to remember if I'd made any mistakes, whether I'd said anything out of place. I was fairly sure I hadn't.

Simon didn't normally come in the canteen, he mostly ate in the officers mess or had a sandwich in the office. So when he sat down next to me with a cup of tea, I thought something was up.

"You were listening to me last night." I was furious.

"We switched it off, as soon as we established it was you." I was sure he was lying.

"Why did that twat, this morning, call me Casanova."

"He's just putting two and two together." Simon slugged his tea and watched me. "You said you were coming back here after your night out, your mikes were on, and so we could keep a listening post on your flat. And when they first heard voices, they had to be sure your flat wasn't being broken into." It all sounded plausible.

I went onto the defensive. "Well, you would have taken the chance with her, wouldn't you?"

"Oh you did nothing wrong," he was trying to calm me, "a bit risky, but......" He left it at that.

He changed the subject. "When do you get back from Liverpool? What have you told Johnny?"

"I said I'd be back today or tomorrow, there are four ferries so, I said I'd just make my way back about mid-afternoon."

"Okay, I'll catch you later. Try and read some of the bulletin boards before you go, get yourself up to speed." I knew what he meant, just a few days out of the loop and you could be left behind.

I bought a newspaper and sat and relaxed. Later, I made my way up to my room in the Sergeants' mess. Tom wasn't in. I packed my few things in to the small suitcase and left a note on his bed. It just said "Ta, see you soon, Billy D."

I caught the bus back to town and I let myself in my flat. I had to switch the electricity back on. After a cup of tea, I went to the washeteria and I did the lot, sheets, whites and colours.

I expected Johnny to knock on my door at any time, but no. So about seven thirty, I picked up my pool cue and made my way to Johnny's. His mother opened the door.

"He's at the club." She looked at me, a bit curious. "He left about two hours ago."

I walked away in the direction of the club; I was a bit surprised that he hadn't called at mine. He'd passed right by my front door. I walked into the club; Johnny was sitting with his back to the door, watching a game of pool. I made my way over to the bar and bought two pints. Still Johnny hadn't seen me.

"There you go, Bud," I greeted him as I put the pint down if front of him. I stood there slugging on my beer.

"Hey, you're not due back till tomorrow." And that was that, no questions; I was relieved. I felt I should explain though, we were supposed to be buddies. "I caught an earlier ferry, because, well my Mum's got a new boyfriend and I was in the way, you know how it is?" He didn't, his parents were old school and wouldn't even think about splitting up, or looking outside their marriage, but he nodded anyway.

I got my pool cue out, joined the two pieces together and sat down with Johnny.

"Has anything been happening?" Johnny thought for a moment, and then his face lit up.

"The Paras were at both ends of Thomas Street and they started shooting at one another." He laughed. I had read, in one of the reports, that the Paras had been in a gun fight, but that no gunman had been caught.

"Did anyone get hit?" I said hopefully I had a grudge against the Paras now.

"No, the bastards are such bad shots, they missed each other." We both smiled.

We played pool till closing time and like clockwork Johnny started a row with our opponents at the pool table. We were thrown out of the club by the steward.

"Don't come back." The steward looked defiant.

"You're not barring us are you?" Johnny looked at the steward. The steward knew how important Johnny's father was to the community.

"Yes," he said, then paused, he was probably thinking of the consequences, "for three days." We strolled off. As we neared my flat, my head started to get back to business.

"When do we see Jonas again?" We went past a section of troops on patrol, but they let us pass.

"We're not due to see him till Monday he's off getting the gun sorted." Johnny wandered off towards his house.

I unlocked my door and I made my way upstairs, listening as I went. Everywhere was silent. I went into the bedroom and dug the phone out of the floorboards.

"Hi, just tell Simon that all is well." Simon took the phone off the radio operator.

"How did it go?"

"Fine, he was expecting me back tomorrow, I think I'd left it open. We're going to see One Shot Willy on Monday." We both knew what that meant.

"Well, catch up on your mugshots because there are some new men on it, mostly Protestants, but still just as dangerous." He paused, "The new book is under your wardrobe."

"Okay, good night." I was miffed that he had been in the flat and I didn't know about it.

The bed still had the smell of Denise. It was nice.

Chapter 20. Monday 26th June 1972. 195

BBC Radio 4…… The Chancellor Anthony Barber has announced his decision to temporarily float the pound. The news comes only a day after the bank lending rate was increased by 1%...........

We approached Jonas' flat and looked around, before we knocked on his door, but there was no sign of watching eyes. He took a long time to open the door.

"Quick," he said as he closed the door behind us. He'd obviously only just woken up and he must have slept in his clothes. There were empty bottles scattered around the bed.

"What's happening?" Johnny wanted to get on with things.

"We must start work again." Jonas sat down on the bed.

"Well we could start with the warehouses we looked at the other day?" Johnny was leaning on the windowsill.

"Don't stand there," Jonas pointed to the window, "there was some shooting last night, the army are very nervous." Johnny moved away, after a quick look. He could see the temporary army quarters with its steel windows and tin and wire walls.

"Ok, we'll meet at the factory at three o'clock, but before I get there, you must check that the getaway is clear and the gun is in place." He pointed to the duffle bag in the corner. He must have already done all the calibration. Jonas opened another bottle of beer and drank straight from the bottle.

Once outside, we walked along in silence. I carried the duffle bag. I was dreading the day and hoping for a blank. Johnny was hoping for a hit, the money was better.

It was only twelve fifteen, but we made our way over to the factory. There were some houses directly opposite the factory gates, so we sat on a wall and watched the flow of the day. After half an hour, we walked round to the back of the factory. The fence had plenty of holes, which led into back streets. There lots of rows of terrace houses, all with back lanes and alley ways, ideal for getting away.

We walked along to the main road and stood at the bus stop, the number forty two came along, spot on time. We jumped on and went upstairs. The conductor didn't bother coming up to collect the fare. Nobody tried to take money off the son of the union shop steward.

We went to Kathleen Kerry's house; the gun was still under her floor.

"Come in," she walked ahead of us, "do you want a cuppa?"

Johnny looked at the clock. "Just a quick one, we have to be on the other side of town soon."

Kathleen's kettle was always ready filled, she lit the ring under it and it was soon boiling.

Johnny looked at me. "Go over to the pub and order a taxi," he glanced at the clock, "for about fifteen minutes time." I was glad to get out, not that I didn't like the two of them it just made the time pass more quickly. I always liked to be doing something.

With the taxi booked, I returned and went in to the kitchen.

"Okay." I gave the thumbs up to Johnny.

He bent down, opened the low cupboard door and started to lift the floor boards. I sat and drank my tea wand ate a slice of bread and jam. Out came the duffle bag, which still had the badminton racquets sticking out of it.

"We'll clean the gun when we get there." He placed the bag on the floor, between his legs. His knees looked a bit wobbly; I could tell he was getting a bit nervous.

"Have you been to see your Gran lately?" Kathleen was talking to me. I came out of my little daydream.

"No, not for a while, I've been to see my Mother in Liverpool." I finished the last of my tea.

"Oh, how was she?" At that moment the taxi driver knocked on the door and we all jumped up.

"Fine but her new man is a tosser." I was glad we were moving on, I didn't want to have to invent too many lies.

I paid the taxi, while Johnny carried the duffle bag. We walked along the main road and slipped in through the gate, its chain was too loose to stop any determined person. Even though there were many smashed windows, it still took quite a long time to get in.

The factory was quite clean on the inside, just some shards of glass, where the kids had thrown stones through the windows, but it was largely free from debris, which would hinder our quick escape. We wandered around until we found the stairs which best suited our escape. There were two offices, giving us a choice regarding the field of fire. We chose the office nearer to the exit. We quickly stood a chair on the only table, for Jonas to rest on. We took out the three windows that would be in his firing line. We didn't want bits of glass falling outside and giving our position away. I walked down the stairs looking for the best escape route. It was fairly easy, a long concrete floor with high shelving, lead all the way to the back doors. These were double doors like cinema exits, with push bars. Light weight wire had been wound round and round, to stop anyone entering, but I just unwound the wire and left the doors wide open. The back yard was enclosed mainly by a wall, but the last ten yards was fenced. There were bars removed in two places, it would be easy to get out. I popped my head through the gap and had a quick look at the lines of side streets, with back lanes too small for vehicles to go down. The area was Protestant and Catholic mixed, but we didn't intend stopping on this job.

I made my way back across the yard and met Jonas coming towards me. We walked together to the front office.

"Nien , that is not good." Jonas' language got worse when he was excited. He didn't like the set up of the table and chair. He disappeared out of the room, coming back with a heavy metal tripod. I had no idea what it could have been used for, but its height was adjustable and there was a rest on the top. Jonas spent a few minutes getting it set up to the right height, and then he took the gun from Johnny who had been cleaning and oiling it. Jonas inspected the gun, taking a long time to look down the barrel. He slid on the telescopic sights and wrapped a piece of cordage around the barrel of the weapon. Then he cleaned and polished the round, to make sure there were no finger prints on the bullet and snapped it in to the breach. Finally he wiped the gun off and he was happy. He disappeared out of the room, coming back with his hands still wet. He delved into the duffle bag, found the towel which was part of the sports gear. Once his hands were dry, he pulled on the washing up gloves, from his inside his jacket. They were a bit tight, but he was ready.

"Go clean your hands," he looked over his shoulder at us, "get the oil off, they can check it."

"We'll have the fucking gun on us, you stupid git." Johnny didn't like to be told.

"You may have a chance to drop it." I followed his instructions and left the room to wash my hands, it sounded like a good idea to me.

Jonas put his hand up, "Be ready." He went in to shooting position. Johnny stubbed his cigarette out and he moved over to stand behind Jonas.

In cases of real panic, my mouth gets this electric feel. I don't know if it's a taste, or my nerves going ape shit, or what, but at that moment it happened just as the gun went off.

Jonas stood back, removed the sights and peeled the gloves off. He walked calmly out of the door. I was just not ready; I'd been expecting to be sitting around for hours. Now some poor soldier would be lying at the gates, with his brains blown out. I knew Jonas did not miss. I froze. Johnny unfastened the gun from the tripod and split it into two parts, ramming them in to the duffle bag. I still just stood there.

"Get fucking moving." He was gone.

We both ran down the length of the factory floor, out in to the light. Jonas was already climbing through the fence; he turned left and walked away. We sprinted to the fence got through and turned right. The first corner was only twenty yards away. As we got round the corner, Johnny grabbed my jacket.

"Walk," he whispered. I just wanted to keep running, "walk," he repeated, "just keep calm."

Calm he wanted. My heart was pushing blood round my body so fast I thought I was going to pass out. We turned another corner, making the main road at last. An army vehicle shot past the end of the road. Before we'd gone ten yards more, another Land Rover had passed the end of the road. We slowed down even more.

"We need to be off the street." Johnny looked around trying to think of anyone he might know living near.

But we needed to act straight away. Johnny walked to the next front door and knocked. We kept glancing around, to see if any army vehicles were coming. The house door opened slowly, but Johnny just pushed the door open and the old lady behind it, fell backwards. We rushed in. I closed the door behind us. Johnny went straight through the house, looking for anyone else who may be in, but she was alone. I stood in the hall and lit a cigarette and inhaled deeply.

"I've no money." The old lady thought we were robbing her.

"Shut your mouth." Johnny peered through the window, trying to see up and down the street. There was nothing on the street. Johnny came over to the woman and grabbed her shoulders.

"Look, we're being chased by a man with a gun, he's going to shoot us because…..," Johnny stared into the woman's face, then had a quick look round the room, to see if there were any Catholic icons. He decided she was a Protestant "because we're Proddies." He let that sink in. She looked at the both of us, we had brown eyes and the look of Catholics, and we were Catholics, but it had a strange ring of truth. She obviously came to the conclusion, that for her to come to no harm, she'd be better playing along with us.

"Well then, you can stay a while, I'll put the kettle on." She pushed past me and went to the kitchen.

"Can you see a phone anywhere?" I asked Johnny. My brain was starting to function again and I didn't want to be walking around with the gun. I wanted a taxi. We both followed her into the kitchen.

"Have you got a phone? I'd like to phone my Dad or the police." Johnny put on his most innocent face.

"Oh I couldn't afford a phone." I looked around she was right, the place was threadbare. At least we knew that she couldn't ring the police. As she finished making the tea, we could hear the army vehicles flying past. We knew then we could be there sometime.

"So, what school did you go to?" Was she fishing, or just making conversation. I didn't know which, but I could see Johnny flush.

"I went to school in Liverpool." I jumped in quickly, to give Johnny time to think. She poured the tea.

"But you've come back to Belfast then?"

"Yes, I fell out with my Mum and came back here for a job." It didn't matter what I said to the little lady, but Johnny was listening as well, so I had to walk a fine line.

"Do any of your neighbours have a phone?" I really wanted to get out and away. "My sister in Antrim has one and there's one at the end of Saint Thomas Street." Johnny face lit up, he was thinking like me now and wanted to get out as soon as possible.

I took a last drink of my tea, put my cigarette out, and went over to the sink. There was a crusty old bar of carbolic soap on the side of the Belfast sink and the tap was an old brass type coming off mild steel pipe. I turned the tap on, slowed it down to a slow dribble and washed my hands very carefully. Johnny carried on talking to the lady. When I was sure there would be no oil on my hands, I dried them on an old tea towel hanging on the back door.

"Which taxi company should we call?" I asked. Johnny thought for a while.

"Well most won't come in to this area, it's too dangerous, one taxi driver was shot a month ago, just around the corner in Tower Street."

The old lady looked at us, "I used East End Cabs to go to hospital, just a few weeks ago." She went in to the front room to find the number. "Here you go tell them it's for Mrs Agnew, 26 Edwards Street." I left Johnny and the old lady in the kitchen, Johnny was washing his hands.

I went out the back in to an alley, no wider than it needed to be to be able to carry the dustbins down for emptying. At the end a sharp left turn and out on to the street behind Mrs Agnew's. When I got to the phone box the phone was empty. No phone and most of the windows were out. The Catholic club was only a few streets away and I knew the telephone would be working there.

The doorman recognised me as I went in, "Johnny's not in." He trying to be was being helpful.

"I just need to use the phone, do you have a two pence you can let me have?" The doorman peevishly went in to his pocket hoping he did not have one but when he pulled out his small change there was a handful of copper.

"Ta, I'll see you right."

"Hello, could I have a taxi for Mrs Agnew, 26 Edwards Street." The clerk said wait.

"Is that in Ballymacarret?"

"Yes, straight away please." I stood there waiting, taxi companies were very cagy about who they picked up if there were not known customers.

"Okay, the taxi will be there in five minutes." I hung up.

"Tommy I'll square with you next time I'm in, you saved my life then."

He smiled, "Aye, make sure you do."

I quickly made my way back to the back lane trying to judge how many army patrols were running around, but the initial burst had quietened down.

I knew Johnny would be jumpy, so I tapped on the door and let myself in.

"Be here soon." Johnny nodded.

"Well thank you Mrs Agnew we're grateful, we could have been in real trouble there." There was a peep of a horn outside, Johnny did something strange, he bent over and gave the woman a peck on the cheek, and I just nodded.

"The taxi is for Mrs Agnew." The taxi driver was not expecting two young upstarts to get in.

"No you must have misunderstood it's for Mrs Agnew son." The taxi driver did not like this and thought about picking up his radio handset.

Johnny bent over from the back seat "we're just going in to Belfast," he handed over a pound note, "keep the change."

This was four times the fare and greed overran any danger he might have anticipated. We jumped out just out at the top of Divis Road and the taxi driver roared off, he was well outside his comfort zone.

Knocking on Jonas's door we waited, there was no answer. We still had the gun and were getting edgy. This job had not been well planned and we had gone off half cocked, this would not happen again.

"We could go to Kathleen's house or get a bus back over the bridge." I did not want to be caught carrying that gun, and walking the streets with any sort of bag or package was not healthy in Belfast.

"It's five minutes to Kathleen's house we can go through the back streets." It made sense, dump the gun quickly. At that moment Jonas came up the stairs and along the open air walkway.

"We may get paid." Johnny's mind was always on money.

"Why you bring the gun here?" Jonas was not happy, he opened the door and we filed in.

"Where do you want it?" Nothing had been agreed, "You should put the gun somewhere safe." We were being chastised and Johnny did not like this.

"Put it in the woman's house." Jonas suggested.

"You'll have to pay her, it's a big risk." Johnny's was here for the money as much as anything.

"Two pounds." Jonas ventured.

Johnny was always going to double the amount, "I was thinking of five pounds a week."

"What is this?" Jonas turned away.

"Well we could leave it here." A hidden threat but Jonas was making good money, he wanted to keep it simple.

"Okay, three pounds every week, work or no work."

Johnny nodded "and you pay us for today." Jonas gave way.

"You wait outside." He shooed us out of the flat, he obviously did not want us seeing where he kept the money or how much. We stood on the walkway spitting over the edge and smoking and after five minutes he came out and handed two rolls of pound notes and the duffle bag.

"It's two weeks money for the woman." He looked around leaning against the handrail, "we are working in Derry, on Thursday we travel up and come back the next day."

Johnny pick up the bag, "How are we travelling?"

"Get a car, good car, not some shit, and bring your sleeping gear." He spat over the edge and walked in to his flat and closed the door.

We counted our money, "I'm driving" I said.

"No your not, I'll drive" Johnny looked adamant.

"Me' I'll nick a good car, the best, you just watch." He ruffled my hair and walked on. We dropped the gun off at Kathleen's house and Johnny gave her a pound, she did not want it but Johnny forced her to take it.

As soon as I said good bye to Johnny I went upstairs and onto the phone to Simon.

"We go to Derry on Thursday, I'm off to bed" Simon listened.

"Do you need to come in?"

"No I'm fine, I'll keep you posted."

Chapter 21. Thursday 29th June 1972. 205

In the big end room at Holywood barrack , eight men were sitting around the large table at the head of it sat Ellis. He was taking his weekly reports from around the province.

One of the men was reporting.... 'And I've now got two men in Omagh, one is behind the bar in O'Tooles and one delivers milk, his boss is James Blaney commander of 'E coy', they go drinking every afternoon, we've had some good information from these men and currently have twenty one men in Maidstone from them'.

Simon Adder was the last to report 'We have three men in deep now with another eight working in several industrial or good observational positions, our best operator at the moment is on active service with the IRA and he alone has been responsible for over sixty six arrests, it all will eventually go through the legal system' Simon looked up feeling pretty good with himself.

'Well if you could leave your written reports with Corporal Tomas in the main office and I'll see you next week, thank you gentlemen'

We needed to be at Divis Flats for about nine thirty and Johnny knocked on my door at eight, I was ready.

"A quick tea and some toast and were away." Johnny pushed in the door.

"I've no bread." I lamented.

"Well put the kettle on and heat the grill and I'll get a loaf, bloody hell you live above a shop, how hard can it be?" He disappeared out the door, I left the door ajar. The kettle was boiling and the grill glowing red by the time he came back, and I had lit the oven and left the door open to warm the kitchen up.

"What we'll do is go to that petrol station on Ravenshill Road and wait until someone's filled up a nice car, something a bit big, a bit roomy and we'll just take it."

"Just like that." I bit my toast.

"Yes just like that." He opened his jacket and inside his belt, just tucked in like some American hood were two pistols.

"Shit, where did you get those?" He handed me one it was loaded I pointed it over the room, Johnny moved out of the way.

"Hey you idiot they're real bullets." He went to slap me on the head, I ducked. The toast was burning, we made some more.

"They cost me ten quid each, so you owe me a tenner," I looked at him knowing that he was lying, but what could I do, "and a pound for the extra bullets." He put ten bullets on the table, "well you want to practice with it don't ya?"

We ate the toast on its own because I could not be bothered to go down to the shop and get marmalade.

It was exciting to have my own gun, stupid, but exciting.

We left the flat and made our way to the petrol station, it was Johnny's plan and it sounded good. It was only a ten minute walk, traffic was busy, the sun was shining and we were packing a piece.

We arrived at the petrol station and walked past, there was only one man on the till. There were four pumps, the new type where you paid inside after filling up. We walked passed again, carrying our rolled up sleeping bags and a few pieces of clothing wrapped up all together. When we got out of sight Johnny stood and lit a cigarette. "We can't just keep walking by."

"So what do you want to do?" I leaned against the wall.-

Johnny thought for a moment, "I'll get a paper and stand at the bus stop over the road, when I see a car I like which is filling up- we'll move in" he looked at me, "you just stay here out of sight."

He dumped his bag on the floor and went into the shop and came out with a paper. I stayed with the bags and lit a fag, Johnny crossed the road and walked up to the bus stop, I settled in for a long wait.

I just managed to get myself comfortable sitting on the sleeping bags when I saw Johnny sprint across the road and into the garage. I jumped up and left the sleeping bags and started to run towards the garage, but my pistol fell out of my waist band and skidded along the pavement. As I bent down to pick it up I looked up and saw the driver of a bread van, his eyes nearly popping out of his head as he saw the pistol on the floor, I could feel myself getting angry, not at the driver but at myself. I picked the gun up as he slowed down to see what was going on, I slowly took aim at his head, he stood on his accelerator and the van disappeared down the street. I turned back to the garage and as I came round the corner I could see Johnny had the door of a car open, the driver was still in the seat but Johnny had his tie in his hand and was pulling it, the driver was determined not to get out of the car, he was grimly holding onto the steering wheel. I opened the passenger door and put my pistol to his head.

"Shall I let him have it?" I had no intention of pulling the trigger, but I wanted him out of the car quickly.

Johnny gave one last pull and the man let himself be yanked out of the car, he fell to the floor and Johnny stepped over him started the car and pulled out of the petrol station, we turned left.

"Our sleeping bags are back there." I pointed back the way we came.

"What the fuck." Johnny yanked the wheel and the car did a half spin, he then selected third gear and stalled the car, all this in early morning traffic.

"Calm down, calm down." This just made him worse, on the third attempt he managed to pull around, as we went past the petrol station there was no sign of our man with the tie.

I jumped out and loaded the sleeping bag onto the back seat. We parked up round the back of the flats and made our way to Jonas's flat.

"Did you haff any trouble getting the car?" Jonas asked has he climbed into the back seat.

"No, no, and it's full of petrol." Johnny made a weak smile, I lit a cigarette and lay back, I did not want to look at Johnny's bad driving.

We raced through town till Jonas told Johnny to slow down.

I leaned forward and helped Johnny with directions, "just follow the signs for Antrim or the A6." Johnny knew his own patch but had not been out of Belfast that many times.

"Left up there." I kept him on the right road, once we got out of town it was more or less the same road all the way to Derry with a few lefts and rights when we went through Antrim and Randalstown.

We pulled into Derry over the Craigavon Bridge and went left passing the very place the army had put up the barriers stopping anyone crossing the bridge.

I was remembering the day when I heard Johnny say "Does anyone know where we're going?" He pulled over and switched off the engine. We all got out of the car and looked at the river. I lit a cigarette.

"Ve haff to be here at two o'clock." Jonas had the name and address of a contact. Johnny looked at his watch.

"I think we should try a Post Office." He looked at us both.

"Yep, sounds good to me, and we need something to eat." We made our way back into the city and drove passed many army Sangers and armoured vehicles and made our way to the far side of the city.

"I think we should dump this car." We were driving a newly hijacked car almost brand new I felt like we had a Belisha beacon on top of the car, and we were asking to be stopped.

"Not a chance baby, I'm keeping this." Johnny patted the steering wheel.

"Come on it does not make sense, when would we be able to have a wagon like this?" I looked around at Jonas in the back of the car, he just raised his shoulders in a motion of "What do I know."

We came round to the back of the city, there were a lot of burnt out and boarded up buildings. As we drove along I was watching for a post office.

"There's a post office." It was in a row of shops , "I think there's a cafe as well." Johnny pulled into the side.

"Could we just put the car down that side street?" I wanted this car out of sight. Johnny nearly took a bus out. He did not like me giving orders. He parked half on and half off the

208

pavement. I stomped off towards the post office with the bit of paper in my hand.

"Well you're not far, which way is your car facing?" The woman behind the glass was trying to be helpful.

"I'm not in a car." I lied. "Well go along this road about half a mile and bare left then first right and the block is more or less in front of you." I was pleased, we could walk.

"Ta." I went outside and found Johnny and Jonas looking at a cafe window menu.

"Where else are you going to go?" I just walked in and ordered a tea and bacon sandwich, "Yep, plenty of brown sauce, please."

"That'll be five and six, twenty seven and a half pence." He still had not stopped quoting both the new money and the old money, "I'll bring it over when it's ready."

Johnny and Jonas were still reading the menu, which meant I could pick the table and get the best seat.

We sat there and ate in silence, Jonas was not the best talker in the world and nothing came between Johnny and food. I lit a cigarette before Johnny was finished but he did not say anything.

"The block of flats is not far from here, I think we should walk." I looked at them to see how this went down.

"No." Jonas had a plan, he just had not told us, "Ve haff to have the car for a quick get away." He finished his last mouthful and with one gulp finished his coffee.

"I don't want to use that car again, we should get another." I just thought it was a bit to flash, nice but not what we needed.

"He may be right." Johnny started to talk sense.

I looked at my watch it was just coming up to one o'clock, "We can jump start an older car and park it up near the job. That way we're not riding around in a well flagged car."

"He's right, come on lets see what we can get." We stood up and left the cafe. The duffle bag and sleeping bags were still in the boot of the car. We walked down one of the side streets and straight away there was one of the easiest cars to steal, an Austin A5. Johnny levered the side window open and put his arm inside and opened the door. Jonas and I just stood and looked both ways while Johnny did something under the dash board, I wondered where you learned that, it felt like he had taken forever but the car fired and we jumped in. We went round the block to where the other car was parked and loaded our bags into the back. Having no key for the tailgate meant that we passed things over to the back seat.

"Left here," I followed the instruction I had been given, "right down that street." We passed boarded up houses and shops, "and when we get the end we should be able to see the block of flats."

There they were. Johnny parked the car in between two other cars we got out.

"I vill go and see the man." Jonas had his bit of paper in his hand and wandered off. We stood around and watched the people wander by. Jonas was gone for about fifteen minutes. We all got in the car.

"We are not here to shoot a soldier." We were in the front of the car and turned round to listen to Jonas.

"No we do a bad man," we looked at each other, "but we get a special price." Jonas smiles at us.

"How do we find this man?" Johnny had asked what I was thinking. At this Jonas pulled out a bit of paper, along with a massive roll of five pound notes which he stuffed back in his pocket, but not before we had seen it.

"The man always always leaves the house at ten to six, he walks along to the club, same time same place everyday, easy." Jonas smiled at us, we said nothing.

"And we get two hundred pounds each." There was more than six hundred pounds in that lump.

"Let's find the street, and see what's what." Johnny started the car and drove till we saw the first post office.

"I was wondering if you knew this road please." I handed the piece of paper over to the woman across the counter.

"Oh yes, it's on the other side of the water, do you have a car?"

"Well it's a van, I'm delivering some tools." I wondered why I was lying; she may just watch me get in the car.

"Go over the bridge and bear left after five hundred yards bear right up the hill to the top then go right, you can't miss it, it's the old Strabane road."

"Ta." I was gone I walked past the car with Johnny and Jonas in and when I was out of sight of the post office I waved then to come and get me. They did not ask me why I had done that.

We still had over two hours before the target was due to leave his house. The house was in Proddy country and would be dangerous for us to hang around.

"Let's do a drive by and just see how the land lies." We were getting edgy, out of our own territory, so any distraction was helping to pass the time. We drove past the house. It was raised up from the road with a bit of a walkway down to the road. Johnny went down the road and turned round, stalling the car at the junction. People were looking and Johnny got flustered and stalled for the second time, his face went red as he hurriedly tried again pulling out in front of a coal lorry.

"Slow down we need to have a look." Johnny was now nearly out of control. He pulled in almost opposite the house.

"You fucking drive." I did not want to tell him the only thing I could drive was army track vehicles and motorbikes.

"I'm sorry it could have happened to anyone in this piece of shit." I said, pointing at the steering wheel, it calmed him down.

This little bit of time had give Jonas time to study the lie of the land.

"Okay I haff seen what I need." He leaned over and pointed at a track leading up to a field with a hedge around it, "we can put car there, and go quickly." He made a movement with his hand.

"Come on let's find a pub, I need a pint." We drove down our exit road and turned left onto the A5 and found a little pub, and we played darts till just gone five thirty.

As we pulled into the lane and up a slight bank I had gone into some sort of blank, I felt exposed. We were there for all to see, and in these times of vigilantes and bombs people were always on the lookout.

"I don't like this." I said Jonas was putting the gun together.

"It's three minutes to go, what if he's late?" Johnny got out of the car and opened the back tailgate which lifted up leaving a full field of fire.

By now all my functions had closed down, I did not want to be part of what was about to happen. Johnny tapped on the side of the car.

"There he is." I looked and saw this overweight middle aged man he was waving to someone on the other side of the road. At that moment Jonas pulled the trigger. Everything else was happening in slow motion, I won't describe what happened to his head, I will tell you that I burst out crying, I could not see a thing I held my head in my hands and froze.

Johnny slammed the back door and jumped into the car and started it with a roar, he then did a u turn in the muddy field and sped down the track pulling onto the road making the traffic scream to a halt. We passed the body lying on the pavement in a pool of blood, with a woman trying to help, he was beyond help. Johnny drove like a madman down the road to where we pick up the A5. Once we were on the main road heading towards Strabane we travelled at the same speed as the rest of the traffic. Jonas split the gun and pocketed the scope, and then he passed it to me in the front of the car. I bagged the gun with the badminton rackets. I looked in the small glove compartment and found a small folded map of Ireland.

"I think we should get to Omagh and then get the forty four to Belfast; we'll be there in time for the five past seven."

Johnny did not like the sound of that he looked at me with disgust.

"What, the bus?"

"Yes the bus, they will be looking for this car and in another half an hour every Tommy will have the number plate, and who would think a murder squad would be travelling on the bus?" I turned around to see if I could get some support from Jonas. Jonas was nodding his head.

"It could be a good idea." Jonas was coming round to my way of thinking.

"No, it's a bag of piss idea, I'm going back in this." He tapped the steering wheel.

"That okay but drop me in Omagh." I'd made my mind up. We travelled in silence for the next forty minutes. As we pulled into Omagh Johnny had one more go at making us seeing it his way.

"Come on boys, you're not really going to get a bus?" He turned to look at me.

"Yes, for fuck sake, it's madness to carry on in this." I stuck to my guns and Jonas got out of the car with me.

"Well fuck you." He put the car into gear and drove off. Jonas walked over to a bin and dumped his pink rubber gloves.

We did not have to wait long for the bus and we sat at opposite ends of the bus. I put the duffle bag on the rack two seats in front of me, I could keep an eye on it but if they searched the bus I would be clear. The bus was like a slow boat to China, stopping at every village. Having passed two army check points and not been stopped I felt vindicated. I got off one stop before the city centre and walked over the Albert Bridge. I had the duffle bag over my shoulder and was just too emotionally drained too care. As I got up to get off the bus Jonas lipped the words "two o'clock tomorrow, come for your money." I gave a little nod.

I closed the door and made my way up the stairs switching all the lights on as I went. I stood in the lounge and burst out crying.

"Sir." The duty clerk clicked his fingers at one of the officers. He was busy giving orders to men on the radio.

They turned up the speaker that was a direct line to my flat. They could hear me lying on the sofa bawling my eyes out.

"Go and get Mr Adder or Ellis, now." The corporal rushed off.

I brushed of the tears and snot with my one good tea towel and still with big sobs every now and again. I replayed the moment that the head of someone's father, son, brother or uncle fell to the floor. Some how I managed to put the kettle on and light the stove.

They listened as I slowly calmed down.

"We need to lift him tonight." Ellis was looking at Simon, Simon nodded, "We will need some help on this, who trained him?"

"Old Jerry Mackie he's at Chepstow, he's working on a new lad at the moment." Ellis scratched his head and thought, "Okay I want him on a plane in two hours, and I don't care what it takes." Ellis turned and left.

213

Simon turned to the clerk, "I want the phone numbers of Chepstow duty officer and the home number of Sgt. Jerry Mackie and unless there is a nuclear war in the next half hour you do nothing else." He went over to the tea urn and poured himself a cup. He stayed close to the speaker with the direct line, by now I was just sulking on the sofa. Simon was trying to plot the nights work.

"I want a car parked on Mount Pottinger Street, and I want them well hidden."

"Hello Alfa seven seven, Alfa one, over." The radio squawked.

"Alfa, seven seven, go ahead, over."

"Alfa seven seven, move to Location fifty-one, park on side street out of sight, stay mounted, over."

"Alfa seven seven, Rodger, out."

Simon picked up the phone and dialled the land line for Mount Pottinger station, "Hello, duty sergeant." It was an Ulster voice that answered and Simon did not want that.

"Hello this is Lt Adder here Holywood Barracks, who's the duty officer tonight?"

"Its Staff Sgt Edmonds sir, would you like to speak to him?" The RUC policeman loved to disturb army personnel while they were having their break, "I'll go and get him sir." Before Simon had chance to think about it, the phone was down and the RUC policeman was gone.

"Hello." Staff Sgt Edmonds had been enjoying a bit of television.

"Hello this is Lt. Simon Adder, Intelligence."

"Good evening Sir."

"I hope I'm not disturbing you but I need a job doing that I don't want broadcasting all over the place." Edmonds was nodding even though Simon could not see him, his interest was picking up.

"Yes Sir."

"We have someone of interest in a flat directly across the road from your position, and we really don't want any RUC personnel poking their noses in, if you see what I mean?" Edmonds was still nodding his head.

"Yes Sir."

"We will be lifting him quite soon," Edmonds was still nodding "and we would like you, you personally to keep an eye on the flat. Could you just do a quick report and then keep an eye on the flat until we lift, understand?"

Still nodding Edmonds, "Yes Sir, I'll have a quick look and phone you back, what's your direct number Sir?" Edmonds jotted the number down and made his way to the main Sanger which had a good view.

"Out happening lads." Edmonds tried to look casual as the two squaddies tried to dispel the cigarette smoke.

"All quite really Staff." They had been talking rather than looking, but not much was moving, which backed up their story. Edmonds tried to make it look as though he was surveying all the views, but he lingered on the post office and the flat above.

"Okay, I'll be back in a minute." He left the two soldiers scratching their heads over this behaviour as he dashed back to inform Simon.

"Yes Sir, all very quiet, which sometimes means trouble but then again it could just mean its quiet." He did like to cover his back, giving the most possible number of interpretations as possible.

"Well done Staff." Simon knew the value of encouraging someone like Edmonds.

"I think we should be lifting quite soon, so if you could just keep an eye on things, we don't want any crowds, if you know what I mean." Edmonds was nodding again, "and you may want to prepare the men for crowd control?"

"Yes Sir."

"But only deploy if it really gets out of hand." Simon was trying to cover all bases.

"Yes Sir."

"Thank you." Simon hung up.

Edmonds went up to the second floor and into the lounge with the television, "Sammy, get the men ready, I want ten men with shields and full riot in the outside yard now." Sammy jumped up, time passed quicker when something was happening and not a lot happened in this patch, they stood in the yard ready to go, excited.

The outside yard was inside the police station walls, but open to the weather. The RUC officers tried to find out what was happening, the soldiers just shrugged.

Simon picked up the phone and dialled the number for Mack's home.

"Hello." Mack's wife answered the phone.

"Hello Mrs Mackie?"

"Yes who's speaking?"

"It's Lt. Simon Adder, I'm calling from Northern Ireland and was wondering if I could speak to Sergeant Mackie please?"

"Yes, yes I'll go and get him." Simon looked at his watch it was nearly quarter to ten.

"Yes." A strong voice on the end of the line.

"Hello Mack its Simon Adder Intelligence, Belfast."

Mackie carried on drying himself, "How can I help?" They had only crossed paths on the training de-brief for Deery.

"It's Deery, he's been on active service with the IRA for a few months, he's bringing in a rich seam of information and he's as deeply in as anyone can go," Mack's wife put a dressing gown over his shoulders and he threw the towel onto the floor and stood on it, "well he's has been on active duty today up in Londonderry and we think the wheels are coming off, we need your help. "Mack scratched his lower back and looked at the clock on the wall.

"What are you thinking?"

"We need you tonight, I've been onto transport and they can have a plane ready from Brize Norton in an hour."

"It will take me more than that, but I'm on my way, get me a police escort I'll be leaving in ten." Mack put the phone down and padded into the living room, his wife was watching the television.

"Make me a packed lunch and a flask love, I'm on a job, two days tops." His wife would never complain. She had been here before.

Simon turned round to the clerk, "Get onto Chepstow cops, I want flashing lights from Chepstow barracks to Brize Norton now."

The clerk picked up the phone and dialled directory enquiries.

216

Chapter 22. Late Thursday 29th June 1972. 218

BBC news...........and the man shot in a drive-by shooting in Londonderry, has been named as..............

I sat on the sofa feeling, sorry for myself. I didn't want to put the television on; I didn't want to see the news. I'd decided I'd had enough; I was going to tell Simon I wanted out. That made me feel better, yes, that was what I was going to do. As he had said at the very start of all this,

"Just shout and we will have you out."   That had been the deal. Yes, that was the answer. I put the kettle on and ran a bath. I let it fill right to the top, it wasn't my gas bill. The kettle's whistle started blow and I put three sugars into my tea. Yep, I thought, I'll just have a bath, then phone Simon and I'd be out of here.

Across the road, Edmonds watched as I passed the windows.

Mack was driving behind the patrol car, with the lights flashing, making his way to Brize Norton.

Alfa seven seven sat in the back lane, wondering what was going on and Simon was trying to second guess what I was doing.

I'm not one of those people who like to wallow in the bath, so I was in and out, dried and dressed in a quarter of an hour. I looked round the bedroom, as I lifted the floorboards. There wasn't much I needed to pack. I could be ready in ten minutes, at the most. I wondered idly, if I could get the gun back to England, without anyone knowing.

I lifted the phone out of the floorboards, "Get me Simon please."

"It's me."

"I want out."   Simon was ready for this.

"How long will it take you to get ready?" He sounded calm.

"I'm ready now." I was surprised; he was going to be fine. I had thought he might persuade me to hang in there.

"Can you walk over to Mount Pottinger Police Station? I'll have you picked up from there." It sounded good to me; I expected a few more questions though.

"Fine, ten minutes, can you tell them to expect me." I hung up. Well that was easy enough.

Simon picked up the phone, "Could I speak to Staff Sergeant Edmonds please." There was pause, and then Edmonds came through from the main Sanger.

"My man is coming into your place, he's undercover with long hair, with the name of Deery. I want him to be kept out of sight of the RUC if possible. We'll pick him up in under two minutes, do you understand?"

"Oh yes Sir."

"Thank you Staff, you've been very helpful tonight." Simon went over to the radio and picked up the mike, "Hello Alfa seven seven, over."

The radio crackled, "Alfa seven seven, over."

"Alfa seven seven, could you be ready to collect from Location fifty-one ASAP, over." The radio squealed, "Alfa seven seven Roger, out."

I ran down the stairs and slammed the door behind me, I didn't put the trigger on, why should I, I was never going back. I walked straight over the road to the main door of Mount Pottinger Police Station. I was carrying my small suit case, which had the pistol at the bottom and a few of my jeans and tee shirts. Over my shoulder, I had the duffle bag with the rifle. I'd left everything else. The door opened as I got there and I walked inside. There was a Staff Sergeant directly inside, who walked me rapidly through the station, holding my arm as though I was under arrest. We went into the back yard where about ten soldiers were standing around, some had short riot shields leaning against their legs, all had piss pot helmets with visors.

"Okay lads stand down, could relieve the Sangers in about twenty minutes." The soldiers shuffled into the building and the Staff Sergeant opened the back gates and took a quick look out, looking both ways. An unmarked car pulled up, he went over to the car and had a quick word.

"Okay son jump in." He held the door open for me.

"Hello Alfa One, this is Alfa seven seven, we've made the collection and are on our way to Location four, over."

"Alfa One, Rodger out." I recognised Simon's plummy voice.

I didn't talk to the men in the car and they didn't talk to me. Soon we were pulling into the main gate of Holywood Barracks.

Mackie and the police escort made good time through the early evening traffic.

Ellis and Simon sat waiting in room seven. The two men from the car, walked with me up the stairs. I could tell they weren't quite sure of my status.

The duty clerk led me down to room seven and knocked, "Come in." I recognised the clipped tones of Ellis.

I put both my bags in the corner and sat down. Then the emotions took over and I burst out in the most heart felt sobbing. Ellis and Simon just sat there and waited. I cradled my head in my arms, resting on the big solid table. After a few minutes, I sat up and Ellis went over to the bottom drawer of a steel cabinet and pulled out a bottle of Scotch.

"Try this, it'll help." I hated Scotch, but I had a little sip. I rubbed my eyes on the sleeve of my jacket.

"I'm sorry sir." I now took a bigger slug of the Scotch; the first one had felt good.

"It's fine; you've done well Deery, very well. It must have been tough out there." I started to feel sorry for myself again and hung my head and had another little weep. Eventually, I lifted my head and wiped away the last tears running down my face.

"Do you want to tell us about it?" Ellis was warmly sympathetic.

Mackie's plane took off; he was the only passenger.

I lit a cigarette and offered my packet to the two officers, they declined.

"Well Sir, I was okay until today, but we did a job in Derry," They must have already known that would have been our

220

team. "Today I watched as the bullet went through the target's head, I watched him die." I looked at them to see their reaction; neither men were likely to have seen this, not many men do.

"At the end of the day, I don't think I can carry on." I had another slug of the whisky. They both sat there a while in silence.

Simon was first to talk. "You've been an outstanding operator, with by far the best lift rate, we understand how you feel." He had a sip of his whisky, giving himself time to decide on the next sentence. "You're probably very tired, I want you to have a good night's sleep. We'll talk more tomorrow." Another sip, while he watched my face for any signs of resistance.

Ellis leaned over and topped up my glass. "When are you meeting Johnny O'Neil next?"

"The plan was to be at One Shot's house for our wages at two tomorrow." The whisky was starting to take effect, I took another drink.

"Right, I want you and Simon to go to the officer's mess and have a damned good drink. In the mean time I'll get your room at the sergeants mess sorted. We'll look at it all in a fresh light, tomorrow."

"But I want out sir, I have to get out."

He turned round and pulled out a steel petty cash box from the locker and carefully opened it with a small key on his key ring. He peeled two pound notes from the bundle in there. "Go and relax now, have a beer." There was a scraping of chairs, as we stood up.

As Simon and I sat drinking, he told me of some of the funniest cock-ups that had befallen some of his men.

Mackie's plane landed in RAF Aldergrove. The customs men quickly searched through the old man's bag, and then he was picked up by a land rover with two armed guards. Within a few minutes, he was sitting having a cup of tea in room seven, with Ellis.

"It's by good fortune that he finds himself in this spot, he just seemed to hit it off with Tommy O'Neil's boy." He looked at the old man as he fed him information, bringing him up to speed with the local IRA pecking order and the importance of the position I had found myself in.

Mackie just nodded and listened and looked at the list of detainees, who I had located.

"The boy's done well. What's his state of mind at the moment?" he asked Ellis.

"I'm not sure that he's a tower of strength at the best of times, but he was part of an IRA active service squad today and watched a man being shot at quite close quarters. It's unsettled him." Ellis remembered the scotch and poured one each, for him and Mackie.

"And where's he now?" Mackie appreciated the scotch and after taking one large swig, looked longingly at the bottle on Ellis's desk. Ellis missed the sign.

"He's with Simon Adder in the officers' mess; we're putting him up in the Sergeants mess. He's stopped there before, not too many eyebrows were raised."

"Could I go down to the mess and join them?" Mackie's status was very ambiguous and he never wore his full uniform, except on Remembrance Sunday.

"Yes, I'll just have a quick look in the op's room and come down with you." They both stood up.

"Is there anything important happening?" Ellis was talking to a Subaltern, who was manning the phones.

"Not really sir, just a small street fight going down in Newtownards, we're keeping an eye on it." The phone rang and the young officer answered it.

Simon was at the bar, when Ellis and Mackie arrived in the quiet surroundings of the officer's mess. I'd been to the toilet and thrown cold water on my face. I felt a lot better; the drink was doing its job too.

Ellis nudged Simon in the back and he turned round and saw him and Mackie, "I'm getting them in sir, what do you want?"

"A couple of double Scotches, get the good stuff." Mackie had quietly padded over, to where I was sitting, facing the bay window.

"How are you doing son?" I spun around. I felt like a little kid who had got himself into trouble at school and was being picked up by his parents.

My bottom lip nearly gave way again and signalled how much pressure I was under. Mackie wouldn't have missed the brief show of emotion, I knew.

"Mack, what are you doing here?" I sat up in my chair, Mackie sat down beside me.

Lies came easily to him and he told me he'd come over to train some local lads in observational skills, his field, just like he did in Chepstow. We both knew field craft was his field of expertise, but I was happy with the explanation.

Ellis brought our drinks over to the table and went back to stand at the bar with Simon.

"I hear you're doing a great job," he smiled at me, "well done." I felt pleased with myself and started to relax.

"Yes, it's been moving really fast, considering that I was only brought in to observe." I finished my pint off and put the glass in the middle of the table and the new pint on my beer mat.

Mackie took a sip of his drink, "Well I've been told you're the top operator and are well in with the IRA." He looked at me, to see how this was going down and I must admit it was nice to get some recognition from him, for my efforts.

I'm not the sort to brag, so just said that I'd been lucky to be in the right place at the right time.

"You wouldn't pull out now would you, Billy?" Mackie was leaning on me. "Without you, more than sixty really bad men would still be on the streets, some of them gunmen, some of them bomb carriers."

"But it's wearing me down," I said and started to feel sorry for myself again.

"It may take us years to get in again, as far as you have penetrated. We could put a hundred men in and not get where you've got to." Simon and Ellis were still at the bar.

I leaned forward, "Do you know what it's like to be in a viper's nest, all the time, one slip up and you're a piece of meat in a back lane." I looked at Mackie, at his solid face, his dependable face.

I continued putting my case, "Kenya, Borneo, Yemen, yes, I've looked down the barrel in a few places and it's not the same as being on your own, in the damp streets of Belfast, often doing things you just don't want to do." I drained my pint. Mackie said, "We do realise what's being asked of you and you will get the recognition you deserve. Stay there a minute." Mackie got up; he came back with two more drinks.

"Would a few days away help, at least you could have a bit of a rest?" I found myself nodding, which meant I was agreeing to stay on the job, even if only for short while.

"I don't know what excuse I could use, we've already pulled a visit to my mother."

Mackie looked into the middle distance, while he thought, then his face lit up. "Okay, we'll lift young O'Neil and slam him in nick for a while, that should give you a breather. You just tell this Jonas character, that you want to lay low for a while."

It sounded good to me, Mackie made some notes on a pad.

"When do you have to be back at the flat?" Mackie looked at his watch it was getting late, but the officer's mess stayed open until everyone had finished.

"Mack, I ought to get back to my flat, I never know when Johnny's going to call. The last time I saw him; he dropped us at a bus stop and drove off in this stolen car. We have to collect our money from Jonas at two o'clock tomorrow."

I was getting worried that Johnny may knock on my door and find me out. Mackie went over to Ellis and Simon and had a quiet word.

Simon came over and said he would run me back to No.37. I finished my beer and followed Simon, we walked up to the vehicle park.

"It's not a nice feeling killing people for money," I said as we walked. I turned to Simon to see how he took that. He took a few seconds to assemble his argument.

"You have to look at the bigger picture, Deery, try and see past your day to day actions, you must realise how lucky we are to have you on the inside. Apart from the arrests, we've been able to make, think how useful it is for us, having someone in the house of one of the local IRA chiefs."

He stopped walking and turned to me, "don't think for one minute we don't know what it's like being in the lions' den, and that's why we have men ready twenty four hours a day, just waiting to pull you out."

He said that to me without blushing, without any regret, but it made me feel better even though I knew it wasn't true.

Simon drove me back to No. 37, he dropped me off two hundred yards down the road. I walked past the flat just to have a good look, it was clear.

I decided to have a bath the next morning and went straight to bed.

Chapter 23. Friday 30th June 1972. 227

I awoke to the noise of my front door being banged hard. I looked through the landing window to try to see who it was, but they were too close to the door. When I opened it, Johnny pushed past me.

"Get the kettle on," he ordered as he ran up the stairs, "we're going on a trip with my Dad, you'll need your gun." I followed him and we stood in the kitchen while the kettle boiled, I offered a bowl of cornflakes, but he declined.

"We're doing bodyguard duties for my Dad, some big meeting out of town." He grinned excitedly.

"How did you get back?" I wanted to know if he got stopped on his return yesterday.

"I saw the road blocks and went round the long way coming in through Newtownards. I dumped the car in Lily Street; I was running on empty for the last five miles." He smiled, he was pleased with himself.

"Jonas wants us to be at his flat at two o'clock today." I shovelled another spoonful of cereal into my mouth.

"Fuck him, he can wait. Whatever's happening with my Dad it's big and he wants me and you as back up," he had a smug look on his face, "anyway get yourself dressed, we need to be at my Dad's in ten minutes."

I went into the bedroom and thought of phoning in, but decided against it. They may have already heard it on the microphone anyway.

Tommy O'Neil was in the front room, when we pushed the door open, at Johnny's. He was having a cup of tea with Noel Douglas, the menace in the air, was palpable.

"Hey you two, wait outside." Tommy was annoyed with us bursting in. We disappeared outside and stood against the wall and smoked. I was speculating on what could be happening that would get O'Neil and Douglas to go to a meeting. Suddenly a couple of cars pulled up and Johnny's Dad came out with Douglas. They got in the front car, both sitting in the back seat;

we got in the rear car. There wasn't much room for me and Johnny. There were four of us squashed up in the back seat. My gun was digging in me and I tried to move it from my waist belt. I lit a cigarette. My leg went dead, as we headed out of Belfast.

I tried to watch where we going. The last town we went through, before pulling into a farmyard, was Downpatrick, as best as I could tell, it was about two mile south of the town. As we pulled into the yard, I could see five other cars parked up. Men were milling around. We climbed out of the car and stretched our legs. My right leg was still numb. O'Neil and Douglas went into the farmhouse, we stood outside and smoked. I logged faces and names, Johnny went over to talk to some of the other men.

Tommy hadn't told Johnny anything about the meeting, so we were in the dark. I wandered across to where Johnny was standing with three other men, to listen in.

"What's going on?" Johnny drew on his cigarette and looked at the men.

"Nothing's being said, it's really hush hush." One of the men replied. I recognised the man even though the mug shot, I had seen of him was very poor. He was Henry Steele, famous for knee capping with an electric drill, he was also a bomb planter. Next to him, leaning against the wall, was Eric Johns another well known bad boy.

"There's a big load of guns and explosive come into Ireland from some Arab country. I think they're meeting to discuss who'll be paying for it." Johns spoke quietly, but with authority,

"They'll be planning bank raids and the such, then."

We stood around and chatted, I was making mental notes of who told what story, as all this would be used in law courts at a later date. Eventually the top men came out of the farm house, my jaw dropped as I watched the whole top IRA, pour into the yard and shake hands, before each area chief got into his car and disappeared down the track. We jumped into the last car and followed closely, the car with Tommy O'Neil and Noel Douglas. I would have loved to hear what was being said in that car. We didn't take the direct road back to Belfast, but went a longer way round. At least, this time, I'd managed to get a better seat. I smiled to myself as we passed the Holywood Barracks.

They dropped us off round the corner from the O'Neil's house and we walked the rest of the way. It was still only a quarter past one so we still had time to get to Jonas' house to collect our wages, now the excitement of the meeting was over; this was forefront in Johnny's mind.

Forefront of my mind was me needing to tell Simon what was going on. They might have been able to intercept the weapons and explosive.

Forefront of Tommy O'Neil's mind was how he was going to raise eleven thousand pounds, the amount demanded at the meeting, his 'corner', as he called it.

I turned towards my flat. "Where are you going?" The tone of Johnny's voice unsettled me.

"I need the toilet." I'd hoped to get back to mine, for a few minutes.

"Use ours." He opened the back door and nodded to the outside toilet. I went out and sat there for the right amount of time. I didn't know what useful information I might be missing. The kettle had been boiled by the time I got back in.

"Come on, drink up, we need to get going." Johnny nodded at the kitchen clock.

As we walked up the road and over the Albert Bridge, Johnny filled me in, "My Dad needs to raise eleven thousand pounds in the next three weeks, because that hardware has to be paid for."

"What exactly has been brought in?" I was digging.

"All I know is it will blow the army to kingdom come." We turned towards Divis flats, made our way up the concrete stairs and along the walkways. The door opened, as we got to it. A smell of stale beer greeted us.

"All okay?" Jonas asked.

"Fine, fine." Johnny held out his hand; he wanted to get out of the flat as quickly as possible, as did I.

"We may be working elsewhere for a few weeks. "Johnny said as he opened up the roll of money and counted it. I just put mine in my pocket, not bothering to count it.

"Okay, okay. I will find the next job and have it ready, but remember," he held up his finger, "no work, no money." We had a pocket full of money, what did we care? Johnny patted him on the shoulder. "Okay, get yourself some beer, we'll be back." As we walked back down the steps, we were high spirits, pockets full of money and in the heart of what was happening.

We went to down to the local pub and had a game of pool, no, correction, we had a few games of pool. He won the first three games, I won the last game. We got a taxi home, Johnny paid.

"I'll see you tomorrow." Even though I was drunk, the last thing I did, as I put my key in the keyhole, was to look and see if the trigger was there. The trigger was a matchstick placed in between the door and the door frame. When the door was opened, the matchstick would fall. That night, the matchstick was on the ground. I opened the door and went inside. It is amazing how fast you sober up, when you're in danger. The door closed with a click, I crouched down in the corner of the stairwell and listened. The only thing I could hear was my heartbeat. I didn't have my pistol, it was under my bed. There was a deathly silence. I realised I needed a piss, but I sat there, crouched, all my senses on full alert. I reckoned that I had a chance of getting out and running over the road into the Mount Pottinger Police Station. In theory, my guards were waiting twenty four hours a day to help me. Or I could run to Johnny's house, we could raise a few hands, come back to the flat and beat the shit out of whoever was up there. Or I could flag down a taxi and be in the safety of the army barracks, in less than fifteen minutes.

The sweat was pouring out of me, I was trying to breathe quietly, it sounded like I had walked up a mountain, puffing and blowing.

"Billy?" I nearly jumped a mile.

"Billy?" When someone's whispering loud, you still can't be quite sure who's whispering.

"Billy?"

Bump, bump my heart was thrashing, it made hearing hard.

"It's Simon." He popped his head round the banister.

"For fuck sake." My whole body relaxed so much I found I couldn't move out of my position at the bottom of the stairs.

"You'd better come and help me, I'm stuck." I just sat there, until he came down and lifted me straight.

We did the report by torch light. I was exhausted and it made it much more difficult, but we couldn't have the light on, there were still many vigilantes and they stayed out all night.

"Yes, that's him." I pointed to one of the last faces, I'd been given to identify, a small time crook-cum-trouble maker.

They had more men to lift, off the streets, meaning more time in the law courts for me in the future, behind screens of course.

Simon let himself out, I eased myself into bed.

Another twenty men fingered. That made another twenty reasons, why I should carry on.

Chapter 24. Monday 3rd July 1972.   233

BBC Ulster radio

A man was shot in an armed robbery of a petrol station this morning, Hospital sources say he is comfortable. Police are asking for any witnesses to come forward..................

Johnny and I swaggered into Jenson's, we'd been told to be there by Tommy O'Neil. Johnny set the table up for a quick game of pool, I ordered two pints. I turned to look around the bar once my eyes were accustomed to the light. The people of the night were there, these men would not be seen walking the streets. Some were new, but most were hardened IRA operators and had gone underground. Tommy was holding court on the big end table.

We finished our game of pool, which I won as quickly as I could; I wanted to sit at Tommy's table and find out what the plan was.

"Okay men," Tommy opened the meeting, "we have to raise eleven thousand pounds in the next few weeks. This will set us up with guns and all the bullets we could need," Some men gasped at the amount of money, "and then we can kick the army out of Ulster and get a united Ireland." There was a little cheer from the men sitting around. Tommy carried on, "So I need ideas. I'm thinking banks, I'm thinking payroll snatches and possibly big shops, at the end of the day." Tommy stopped talking and looked around.

"Thompson & Jackson's have one of the biggest wage bags round here." This idea came from someone not on file, I didn't recognise him.

"There is the bus depot." This was Johnny's idea.

"And there's Edwards Engineering, they have nearly twelve hundred men." The men were thinking of big employers and shouting out the names.

"Okay, okay," Tommy held his hands up and everyone stopped talking. "We need to concentrate on two or three places we could hit." Tommy pointed at one of the men, "Billy go and check all the outlying banks, I'm interested in banks with old fashioned security, you know the type, but the bigger the better." Tommy then turned to the Fox brothers, "I want to know everything about Edwards Engineering that must be a big wage bill." He then gave some other men smaller tasks.

Tommy picked up his half of beer, finished it off and nodded at me and Johnny to join him outside. We jumped up and followed him out of the back door.

During our walk back to Johnny's house, Tommy told us that he wanted us to go and see one of Johnny's cousins, who worked in Thompson & Jackson's. He had an office job, he would know about the wage delivery and he may even work on filling wage packets.

Tommy handed Johnny a piece of paper. On it was written his cousin's name, Cuthbert, and an address.

"He won't get home until five at the earliest, but catch him before he gets to the house; he's a right mummy's boy."

In the house, Tommy rummaged through the drawers and found a few black and white photos. "That's him last year, at Elsie and Tom's wedding."

Johnny looked at the photos, nodding his head. "I remember him; he's a little smart arse. He gets the forty four from right outside the gates of Thompson & Jackson's on Sydenham Road, at six minutes past five." Johnny was pleased with himself for remembering the details of the bus timetable.

"Well I want you to go and get him, bring him back here. We'll have a word to the good." Tommy handed the photo over. "I'll get you a driver for this afternoon."

We went to the Catholic Club for a few games of pool, my mind wasn't on the job and Johnny beat me six three. On the way back from the club, I told Johnny I needed to pop into my flat for the bog. I said I'd meet him at his place.

Once inside my bedroom, I lifted up the carpet and reported to Simon.

"Yes, that's eleven thousand pounds just from East Belfast, so God only knows how much money they'll be getting from all the regions together." Simon was taking notes, this was dynamite.

"Okay, keep me informed." I replaced the carpet and made my way over to the O'Neil's. There was a Transit van sitting outside Johnny's house. I pushed open the unlocked door to the house, in the back kitchen Tommy, Johnny and a stranger were sat having a cup of tea. I helped myself to a cup, whilst Tommy introduced the man as Jacky, he was the van driver.

I didn't recognise him. He may have been from outside the Belfast area.

Tommy was keen to talk to me in private and nodded in the direction of the front door, I followed him out.

"No talking in front of Jacky," he nodded towards the kitchen, "all he knows, is that I want to talk to some boy, okay. Let's keep it that way." He patted my back, as we went back into the kitchen.

We planned the lift. It made sense to pick Cuthbert up as he got off the bus, not while he was waiting for the bus. It was decided that I would travel on the bus and sit close to him.

They dropped me off on Sydenham Road at quarter to five. The bus stop windows were smashed and it was drizzling rain. All the manual workers had gone, they finished at four thirty. The frenzied rush was now over, just the office workers were still at work and they would come out at five. No mad rush with this lot, young girls in mini skirts, older women who had qualifications and could get good jobs in the warm and men who had other skills, purchasers, draftsmen, accountants. These were the jobs that started at eight thirty in the morning and not some cold, ungodly hour. They wore clean clothes, their hands were manicured and they read broadsheet newspapers. I stood, there totally out of place, at the front of the queue.

Cuthbert was not in the queue. I looked at my watch, three minutes past five. I could see the bus coming; it turned round in the turning circle and pulled up at the stop.

The two busmen were not from the Short Strand depot, so they didn't know me. I jumped on the back step and glanced over my shoulder. Cuthbert was running for the bus, he caught it just in time good.

"Eight pence to town," he said. I held onto my ticket and kept an eye on Cuthbert all the way. The bus made its way into Belfast. It was a works special, and didn't pick up, so the conductor had gone upstairs for a smoke and to read his paper. A glance out of the back window, told me the Transit van was following.

Cuthbert looked out of the window most of the time. I watched carefully for the bus stop where he would get off, my heart was racing. Right on cue, Cuthbert stood up and I followed and as the bus slowed down, we both alighted. He was a slight man, so if it came to a fight, we shouldn't have much trouble. He walked towards where the van had pulled up. Johnny stood, leaning against the van. I was right behind our target.

Johnny stepped out into his way, "Cuthbert, hiya." He was startled; he stopped dead in his tracks.

"My da wants a word with you." Cuthbert turned away, unsure. "Don't worry, you're okay, it's just a quick word." I was standing close by, he faced Johnny again.

"My tea will be ready, my mother is expecting me." Cuthbert cast around for reasons why he shouldn't get go with us. Johnny opened his jacket and there, silhouetted against his shirt, was the pistol.

"You'll be fine, come on get in the van, just a word with my da." Cuthbert's body sagged, his head went down and he paused for a few seconds. Then with a slow nod of the head, he climbed into the van.

We didn't talk on the way back. When we had Cuthbert in the house, Tommy gave me a five pound note, "Give that to Jacky, tell him thanks." I went outside and handed over the money.

For the next two hours, Cuthbert was questioned very closely about the wage delivery. It couldn't have been better, Cuthbert always helped on payday. Thousands of pay-packets to be filled, it needed a lot of hands.

After a while, Cuthbert started to relax and confessed that he'd thought about robbing the wage bill many times. Tommy helped, by telling him he'd get his cut, bingo.

It was unbelievable how slap dash the wage collection was. Thompson & Jackson's used one of their own vans to transport the money, no fancy expensive security here; they were even too tight to pay for the wage packets to be filled by the bank. The pay office manager and four men, armed with pickaxe handles, plus a driver, drove over to Belfast's main bank and in front of everyone in the High Street, loaded the money then drove back to the docks.

"And you say they always cross the Albert or The Queen Elisabeth Bridge?" Cuthbert nodded and smiled, he was getting into this, his dream.

"Right Cuthbert, get a taxi home and tell your mother you had to do two hour's overtime at short notice. Tell her you were on double time." Tommy handed Cuthbert a pound note. "There's a taxi office over on the corner with Albert Bridge Road. What do you do on Saturdays?" Cuthbert was a bit lost with this question.

"What do you mean?"

"I want to talk to you on Saturdays without your mother knowing." Tommy didn't like anyone being cute.

Cuthbert couldn't think of anything that would interfere with him talking to Tommy. "I just walk the dog and sometimes...."

Tommy stopped him. "That's fine, you be here at ten on Saturday and we'll wrap this up." Tommy leaned towards the boy, "but remember this, sonny," he used his index finger as a threat, "don't even think of telling anyone about this little chat, do you understand?"

Cuthbert had already started to nod. "I don't need to tell you, nobody double crosses me." The hairs stood up on the back of my neck and the threat wasn't even directed at me.

Cuthbert stood up and looked around, we looked at him, hard and quietly threatening, but Tommy eased the mood. "It'll be fine and you'll get a good cut." He patted Cuthbert on the back, as he led him down the hall to the front door.

Tommy came into the kitchen smiling; he wasn't a man you saw smiling much.

"Sounds too good to be true." Johnny said.

"Well, if what the boy said is true and it could be, we may be onto a winner here." At that moment we heard a light tap on the front door, we waited a few seconds, then Johnny went to the front.

I heard Johnny say, "Come in, we're in the back." The kitchen door opened and Danny Steele came into the kitchen, he clocked me straight away.

"We did a petrol station today, here's the money." He had a small bag of cash, which he poured onto the kitchen table.

Tommy looked at the money and took a small black book out of his inside pocket. "How much have you kept for yourself?"

"Nothing, nothing, not a penny." Danny was lying of course, Danny always lied. Tommy looked at the money on the table, picked up two five pound notes and gave them to Danny.

"Well done, who did the job with you?" Tommy had the book open and licked the end of his pencil.

"Jenny Edwards kept watch and me and her brother, Sam did the work." He smiled and looked for approval, Tommy nodded, and we stood stony faced. I for one would not be forgiving him for stealing my T.V. and toaster. Tommy wrote the details down in his book and counted the money.

"Put your name here." Tommy pointed to the bottom of the page and Danny signed.

Tommy walked him to the front door and we relaxed.

Tommy sat down and drank the dregs from his cup of tea. "One hundred and eleven pounds down, just ten thousand eight hundred and eighty nine to go, but it's only day one." He smiled again. It had been a good day; I had a lot to tell Simon.

Tommy picked up a lone pound note from the table that had not been put in the pile. "Get yourself a drink boys." He handed the pound to Johnny. We didn't need telling twice and slammed the door, as we left for the Catholic club.

That night, Johnny and I'd been playing for beers, against all comers, we hadn't lost one game. I lay on my bed and told Simon all the details I could remember. I was beginning to feel detached from the army, beginning to feel as though I had a foot in both camps. I went to sleep thinking of Denise.

The heads of department sat in room seven, along with Simon and Ellis. They had gathered for their weekly meeting and had been discussing the information, which had been pouring in from all their sources. My close contact with the O'Neil's, gave a certain amount of extra weight to my report. They were considering the whispers and snippets, coming in from all over the province.

"There have been two petrol station robberies and a night club in Derry was done over last night, but the word on the street is, the IRA needs cash and a lot of it. They're starting to raise cash in America as well as Ireland but this all takes time and time is a commodity they do not have." Ellis looked over his glasses at the men in the meeting.

"Well sir, we have to decide whether we take the position of warning all cash run businesses, or just let it run its course." A young officer from logistics had put his finger right on the button.

"If we warn everyone, or anyone and it gets back to the IRA, they will know we have insiders. It could set us back months, even years." Ellis looked around for dissenters. "No, what I propose is that we keep a watchful eye, try and find the reason for the need for so much cash, and nip it in the bud at that end."

"But sir, if the IRA were to get more powerful weapons, more sophisticated explosives and timers, our lads would be sitting ducks." The young officer was spot on, again.

"All the more reason we find out what they are up to." Ellis was now pointing his finger to add weight to his words. "No, we have to keep listening and watching, we have to sift all information, no matter how insignificant, for a hint of what this

money is going to be used for." All the listeners were silent, as Ellis drove home the message. "Go back to your districts and brief your men, nothing over the phones, nothing written down." Ellis hammered the desk to emphasize his point. "They need money, they need a lot of money, and what is it for? We'll meet again, a week today."

I woke up wanting to see Denise, I also wanted to get off the daily grind of IRA work, but we needed to see Jonas about our money.

I went round to Johnny's house, his mother let me in. She shouted up the stairs, "Hey John, Billy's here, get your'sel up."

"Tell him to get to fuck, I'm lying in."

I shouted up the stairs, "I'll go and get your wages from Jonas and see when he wants us next."

"Okay, but don't fucking run off with my bit." His bedroom door slammed then opened. "And tell him we're busy for a few weeks." His door slammed again.

I walked round to the bus stop and thought about the day ahead. It would be too early to knock on Jonas' door, without any warning. I jumped on a bus, which was the direct bus to the area where my Gran lived. This had a couple of advantages; one it killed more time and it gave me a better alibi.

My Gran opened the door and beamed "Well hello son, come in, do you want a cup of tea?" I followed her in. She turned and gave me a big wet kiss and not having her false teeth in, made it much worse. She kept running in and out of the kitchen, while the kettle boiled, giving me news about the family.

"And your Uncle Sam's had his leg broken in a car accident; he's the one who lives over Anderson Town." She brought the tea in on a tray with a small plate of chocolate fingers, all laid out neatly in a straight row,

"And Helen, one of June's daughters, is pregnant and she's only sixteen." She carried on talking as she poured tea. I went off into a little day dream, wondering how I could get in touch with Denise. I knew where she worked, so I could just sit outside of her dentists' surgery and wait for her to come out. I knew where she lived, so I could just wait at her bus stop, for her to come home.

"Did you hear what I said?" My Gran brought me back to life with that question, my eyes started to focus and I nodded. "So what do you think?" she asked. I did a quick re-run of what she had been saying, I must have heard, but not really registered anything.

"Aye it's a funny old world we live in." My response was the first thing I could think of that let her think I'd been taking it all in, without meaning anything. I now listened properly, as she filled me in with loads more small time family tittle-tattle. When she had run out, I filled her in with what I had been doing. Not a lot of it was true; I could hardly tell her the truth.

"Well I better get going; I start work in an hour." I stood up, my family duties done.

"Look after yourself." She fussed over me and I gave her a kiss and wiped my mouth, as I turned away from her, it was like kissing half a pound of tripe. But I felt good that I'd visited her. I decided to walk the short distance back into town. I was still trying to kill time.

There is something nasty about the concrete stairs and walkways around the Divis Flats, but the sun was shining and I was about to pick up a good wage.

I knocked on Jonas' door and stood back, so Jonas could see me easily. He opened the door and walked away down the hall, I followed him.

"Where haff you been?" He had been drinking and his accent was more guttural than usual.

"We've been put on some other jobs for Johnny's dad and we have to work with him for a few weeks." I watched how he took this. He gave a grunt of dissatisfaction.

"I could find a new team." He said as he lifted his beer bottle to his lips. This time he watched for my reaction.

"Come on, it's only two weeks and we don't want to overdo things." He rubbed his thumb and fingers together, the international sign for money.

"Aye, well talking about money, I've come for our bit." I made the money sign with my fingers. He shook his head then took another swig from the bottle.

"Johnny muss come here for his money." He wasn't going to be happy about that.

"Hell man, you can give me his." But he kept shaking his head. He disappeared into the bedroom and returned with a wad of pound and five pound notes. He carefully counted them out into my hand.

"No weekly wage when you not work." He meant he wouldn't pay the seven pounds a week retainer, while we weren't at his beck and call. This was fair enough, as far as I was concerned.

I left Jonas' flat and made my way down the stairs. I had a pocket full of money and time to spare. Denise didn't finish work for a few hours, so I went into Belfast City and bought myself some new clothes and had a hair cut. It had grown quite long. Then I was walking past a city centre shoe shop and there in the window was pair of platform boots, in soft brown leather. I went in hoping that they had them in my size. I went crimson with embarrassment, when I took my left shoe off, to try the boot on. My big toe was poking through the sock. By the time I'd finished shopping, I had a brand new look. I made my way to the dentists and sat on a bench, where I could see the door. It was still only quarter past four and I wasn't certain what time she finished. I pondered whether to go in or just continue sitting outside.

I decided that I would go in; she might not be working, or she might be working late.

I went up the stairs and opened the door. The bell above my head rang, as I walked in the door. The waiting room had a hatch, with frosted glass, which slid back for the receptionist to talk to me.

"Oh hi, I've just moved back to Belfast and need to register with a dentist." The woman, who was framed in the hatchway, looked me up and down like she was deciding whether or not she should register me. I could hear the dentist's drill grinding away and I imagined someone sitting there gripping the arm rests, with the drill slowly turning in his mouth.

"Fill this in." She handed me a form. I bent down slightly to get a better look into the surgery, but I was too tall.

I filled the form in and handed it back. "We could give you a check up on Wednesday at nine fifteen." She looked at me.

"Fine." This had got out of hand, I only wanted to find out if Denise was in. The receptionist wrote the time of my appointment on a small card and handed it to me. I took the card.

The surgery door opened, as I was picking up my shopping bags and a young girl came out and ran over to where her mother was sitting. As the door slowly closed behind her, I had a quick glimpse in the surgery. Yes, she was there.

On my card was the name and address of the dentist with the opening times, '8.30 till 5.30'.

I made my way downstairs, about five doors down on the other side of the road, was a cafe. I decided that was an ideal place to wait for Denise and went in. Once I'd bought my tea and a scone, I picked up a newspaper from one of the tables. Sitting behind the dirty net curtain, I was well placed to keep an eye on the dentist's door, whilst catching up with the news.

The lady who had given me the appointment card came out first, then Denise wearing a short skirt and equally short coat. I jumped up, picked up my bags and ran out. Denise was walking purposefully towards the bus stop. I looked at my watch, I knew her bus and I knew the times it ran. She had about five minutes, before the forty nine was due.

I wanted to see the lie of the land. Did she still want to see me, had anything changed? I caught her up, just as she arrived at the bus stop.

I walked up behind her and said, "Hi." She looked round.

"Hi? Is that all you can say? I've a good mind to slap you." This took me by surprise.

"What have I done?" I put my innocent face on, but to be truthful, I didn't really know what I'd done.

"What have I done?" She mimicked me. "I'll tell you what you've done, you've," she paused to look round at the other people at the bus stop. She lowered her voice and came a little closer, "you've…." There was a little tremble in her lip.

By then, she didn't need to say anymore. I dropped my bags on the pavement and grabbed her and kissed her. I was smitten. She was soft, she was petite, she smelled gorgeous, just as a young woman should smell and she was with me. I held her so tightly, her feet came off the ground and she was on tiptoes. I heard her bus come and go, but that was irrelevant.

Eventually, we parted. "Are you coming home with me?"

She thought for a moment, "My Dad's in hospital and my Mother'll be visiting him all night, let's find a phone." We both stood in the phone box, as she made the call. "Hello Jennifer, it's Denise here, yes I'm fine, how's yourself?" There was a little pause while Jennifer told Denise, how she'd won thirty three pounds on the bingo. "Lovely, look could you pop round to my mother's house and tell her I've bumped into Jill McIntire and I'll be stopping round her house tonight." Denise nodded. "I'll love you for ever, see you tomorrow." The pips started to go, indicating more money was needed, but she put the phone down and turned to me and gave me a big kiss. There was tapping on the window.

"Hey come on you two, people need to use that phone." An old man was anxiously waiting.

We made our way down the street to the taxi office above the cafe.

"Where you going?"

"Mount Pottinger Road." The fat lady behind the desk, looked me up and down, then gave Denise the once over.

"Seven, where are you?" She spoke into the microphone.

"Just dropped off at Bell Street." The speaker was on too loud, we could hear everything.

"Job at the office to cross the river," she looked up at me and said, "he'll be downstairs in two minutes, it's a red Cortina."

We sat in the back seat, holding hands and I directed him to about fifty yards past my flat. I gave him a four bob tip, he didn't say thank you.

"Could you get a pint of milk from the shop?" I asked Denise. I did need milk, but my main thought, was to quickly check the flat over and cover the microphone up, so we weren't overheard. I just had enough time, before I heard her slam the front door and come running up the stairs. It was only six, but we went straight to bed.

I heard someone knock on the door at about seven thirty, but wild horses would not drag me from that warm bed. Johnny knocked on the door, on the way home from the club, but quickly gave up. His car roared all the way down the street He wanted his money from Jonas, but he was well aware of the police station across the road, with soldiers on watch continuously.

We kept waking up all through the night and enjoying each other.

Wednesday 5th July 1972.

The next morning after a bath, Denise wandered around the flat in just her knickers and bra. I made toast and two big mugs of tea. We sat on the sofa, I said, "I could get a few days off work." She still thought I worked at Holywood Barracks, as a diesel fitter. Then I remembered the wage snatch job. That would be time consuming and Jonas would need some day's work from me too, "but that wouldn't be for a week or two, because Edward's still away."

She said, "Well why don't we go for a drink on Saturday?" That gave us both, something to look forward to.

"Okay, I'll meet you in the Blue Bell, what's a good time for you?" I asked.

"Eight"

"Fine." She went into the bedroom, quickly got dressed and gave me a peck on the cheek. We both went down to the door. I had a quick look out before she left. I watched her, as she made her way up the road to the bus stop. I went back to bed and slept until I heard the knocking on the door.

"Did you get my money?" Johnny asked, as he pushed past me up the stairs.

"No, he wouldn't give me yours."

"Useless bastards, both of you, now I'll have to go over to see the little toad." He made his way into the kitchen and put the kettle on. I noticed that Denise had left her scarf on the arm of the sofa. I quickly folded it up and took it into the bedroom.

Johnny shouted above the din of the kettle, beginning to boil "Do you have a motorbike licence?"

"Yes." I carried on dressing. There was a pause.

I shouted through "are you any good as a pillion?"

"Do you think I'm useless?"

246

Johnny carried on "Well my Dad thinks we need to follow the wage run on a bike, he says it would be nippier in traffic and less likely to be spotted." Johnny had finished making the tea and we sat drinking it in the living room.

"Okay, we'll get a bike, we'll get something fast." I reckoned that this would be a good idea, for getting around for other jobs. The army don't pull motorbikes over, to look for bombs and we could easily carry the rifle in the duffle bag, with the badminton racquets sticking out.

We discussed the merits of buying a bike and having insurance. Then if we did get stopped, we'd have one less thing to worry about.

We finished the tea off and went to get a bus over the river to see Jonas. He took for ever to answer the door.

"Why didn't you give him the money?" Johnny was confrontational right from the start.

"You muss come for your own money." Jonas was defiant, but he had the money rolled up ready and Johnny calmed down after he'd got it.

We wanted to get out as quickly as possible, as ever, the place stank of beer.

"We're working for my Dad for two weeks, so we'll come and see you, two Mondays from now." Jonas lifted his bottle of beer to his mouth and took a long swig.

"Yus that's fine." We made our way out.

There were two motor bike shops down on Castlereagh Road, so we got a bus back over the bridge and made our way to the first one. They sold all sorts of second hand cars, bikes and lawn mowers, anything which had an engine. The second motor bike shop had a good selection of new and second hand bikes. Mostly scooters, but over at the back of the showroom, was a Honda 175. It was a light weight two seater, with a price tag of £65 and it had three month's road tax. It would be fast enough even with two of us on it. With two second-hand, open faced helmets, a light weight pair of gauntlets and twelve month's insurance, we were on the road for £74.

I sat on the bike with the documents in my back pocket, while the salesman explained the gears. Johnny sat on the wall, while I had a trial run down the road. My face went red, when I stalled the bike at the first junction. I nearly dropped the bike in my hurry to get the thing going again. I went down a quiet street, just off Castlereagh Road and stopped and started it a few times. I quickly got used to the clutch.

Now I felt I could ride with a pillion passenger and went back to pick up Johnny.

"Where the fuck have you been?" He was always so impatient.

"Just get on." He jumped on the back and we headed out of town. I jumped a red light, but we made it safely on to the open road and then enjoyed an hour or so just riding round. As I started to make my way back to Belfast, I realised I had to fill her up, so stopped at Newtownards. Arriving back in Belfast, we passed Holywood Barrack on the way.

We dismounted outside my flat.

"There you go, I enjoyed that," Johnny's face was beaming, "but I want some gloves too, the wind gets in every corner." He was rubbing his hands. We went round to Johnny's house to show his father and mother, she wasn't pleased.

"Oh shut up mother, we'll be alright." Tommy walked round and poked and kicked the bike, as though he knew what he was looking for, but it only had four thousand miles on the clock and the tyres looked brand new.

"Do we have any gloves?" Johnny asked his dad.

"No, but that Steele lad sells all sorts of things, he's always peddling things like that." Johnny ran off and came back with a pair of black leather gauntlets, which came almost up to his elbow.

"I told him I'd buy him a pint, when I saw him in the club." Johnny wouldn't pay for anything he didn't have to.

For the rest of the day we rode around, dropping in on Kathleen Kerry, to give her the storage money from Jonas, for keeping the gun and dropping in on one of Johnny's cousins, who he hadn't seen for quite a while, just because we could.

By the end of the day we had used nearly the full tank of petrol.

"We could park it opposite the police station, nobody'll try to pinch it, right outside a cop shop, with twenty four hour a day surveillance." I had been wondering where we should park it, but

Johnny was right. We were nearly legal, so why not reap the benefit of the Sangers. The whole of next day was spent riding around. First, we checked out the routes, that the wage collection van might take, but after that we went for a ride round the coast, crossed over into Ireland from Ulster. We got back in time for the midweek pool match, but we played badly, but then again, neither of us cared.

Chapter 26. Thursday 6th July 1972.   251

I arrived at the O'Neil's house at eight sharp. Tommy let
me in and I followed him into the kitchen, but as he passed the
foot of the stairs, he shouted up,
"Hey, get your arse out of bed, we've work to do."
Mrs O'Neil was making toast and had two large kippers in
a frying pan. She quickly buttered more slices of toast and put the
loaded plate on the kitchen table. The kippers were flipped onto
plates, she put before Tommy. She sat down and started to tuck
into the other one.
"Dip some toast in the frying pan; the juice is lovely on
bread." Mrs O'Neil pointed to the pan. I grabbed a couple of
slices of toast and began to mop up the oils in the frying pan.
Johnny came into the kitchen, just as I wiped up the last of it and
Tommy picked up the last bit of toast.
"Greedy gits." Tommy looked up at his son and pausing,
before he finished off the last bit of bread toast he said, "You
could get your self up in time. You'll expect your mother to make
you some now, I suppose." But his mother was enjoying her
kipper too much and had no intention of getting up. I had my cup
of tea and a last bit of toast, so leaned there against the cupboard
and enjoyed the scene.
After breakfast, we discussed where we were going, to
watch the money being loaded.
Tommy wanted us to follow the minibus from the docks, to
the bank. He planned standing in the High Street, at a bus stop
and watch from there. Cuthbert had told us what time the minibus
left and what time it arrived back, so we knew that they must go
more or less direct to and from the bank.
Tommy set off to walk into town. We got on the bike and
went out to the docks. It wasn't long before the minibus passed
us. With the driver, there were five men sitting in the back,
relaxed and smoking. We stayed one or two cars behind, easily
keeping up and not losing sight of it.

They went the most direct route and were soon stopping outside the bank, parking on double yellow lines. Two men went into the bank and after a few minutes the other men jumped out, with their pick axe handles. The first two men came out of the bank, carrying four big black cases, one in each hand and threw them into the bus. Everyone then jumped back in the bus and they were off. The whole thing had taken about three minutes, maybe less. We followed to the end of Donegal Quay and turned right, then straight over the Queen Elizabeth Bridge. They were back in Thompson & Jackson's, ten minutes after leaving the bank.

We returned to Johnny's house, Tommy was sitting in the kitchen, busy with some union paperwork. It was strange that he led this double life, but it was all the same to him, he was looking after his people.

We told Tommy what he already suspected, that the minibus went straight back to the docks and into Thompson & Jackson's after the bank.

They must have been doing it for years and had no thought of wage snatches, so no thought of security.

We didn't have much to do till following week and Tommy wanted us out of the house, he had lots to organise, so we went for a bike ride, our new passion.

That night Johnny and I went into Belfast and ended up in a pub, over in the Market area. I got the feeling people were starting to talk about us both, because we didn't have to put our hands in our pockets all night.

I overheard someone in the corridor, say, "Couple of hit men, that's what I've heard."

"No, No put your money away, this one's on me." All night, old men were patting us on the back as they brought more pints over, "there you go son."

My biggest problem was getting rid of the stuff. Not being much of a drinker, meant I still couldn't hold much and even with my best efforts, I was very soon falling over drunk. I don't remember getting home. I don't remember anything, really.

I stayed in bed for most of the next day and apart from a short report to Simon, it was just a wasted day.

That night, I went to the Blue Bell, to see Denise. I was still recovering from the night before's drinking and not very good company. We went back to No.37 early and after an hour together in bed, I walked her round to the taxi office. I arranged to meet her on Saturday.

Next day, Johnny and I went out on the bike, we even had a day in Dublin. We didn't stay all that long it was more about the bike ride really. The week passed slowly and apart from losing again at pool, at the Wednesday night match, not much happened. At the back of my mind, was what was going to happen on the Friday morning.

Tommy had been working hard on the logistics of the wage snatch, telling as few people as possible, but raising the right sort of muscle.

On the Thursday, Tommy told us to be upstairs in Jenson's that night and we weren't to drink.

So by seven, I was following Johnny up the stairs into the function room. It was dark and musky smelling and obviously hadn't been used as a function room for quite a while. We were first to arrive and got seats near Tommy. Then in ones and twos, the other men came in and found themselves a seat.

I looked at the men assembled. Each and every one of them should have come with a health warning. It was like a 'who's who' of the hard men. I logged each and every one, listening very carefully for their names, in the cases where they didn't appear in the mug shot book.

"Okay," Tommy started the meeting, "Jacky, have you got the wagons sorted?"

Jacky Woods nodded. "Yup, they'll stop anything believe me."

Tommy made a tick, on his bit of paper.

"Seamus, have you got the guns?"

"I've got three sawn off shot guns, a Thompson machine gun with a full mag that sometimes jams and five hand pistols, plus five pick axe handles." Seamus smiled nervously, he never wanted to let Tommy down, he knew the consequences. Tommy smiled.

"Okay, listen in carefully." Tommy told each man what his job would be and gave them instructions, to cover any anything else that might happen.

The plan was to hit them, just after they came over the Queens Bridge, where the road narrowed under the railway bridge. The big wagon would ram them head on, whilst another wagon would ram them from behind. Anyone who offered any resistance would be very quickly overpowered.

"We leave nothing behind, fire the wagons and lift any one who's hurt," Tommy leaned forward and lowered his voice, "and I'll tell you this," the menace in his voice was chilling, "if anyone breathes a word". He drew his hand across his neck; it was enough of a hint. Most men there knew the score, but Tommy just wanted them to make sure they knew.

My heart was pounding as we made our way out, but others were laughing and joking, probably to ease their own worries, or maybe they weren't worried. I was worried about their attitude, as well as Tommy's threat.

Johnny and I went down stairs and had a couple of games of pool, which meant we had a couple of pints as well.

My mind wasn't on the game, my mind was how much should I tell Simon. If the army decided to stop the raid, there would be blood spilt and it could be my blood. I could have decided not to tell Simon the time of the raid, and then there would be hell to pay from Simon. Or, I could tell them later that I'd been kept in the dark, and say I hadn't been part of the raid. I sat thinking, trying to decide.

"Hey, it's your shot." I came back to earth, with Johnny nudging me with his cue.

"Okay, okay." I took a slug of my beer just to show him that I wasn't to be hurried. I missed an easy shot.

Whilst Johnny had his turn, I thought of another option. I could go missing and not go on the raid, but I decided against this. I almost certainly would wake up dead one morning, or at least have my knee caps drilled with a Black and Decker. No, my mind was not on the game of pool.

"Make that your last you two," Tommy warned us as he left.

I walked home with Johnny, his mother made sandwiches in the back kitchen.

"Fancy a quick bike ride?" I needed to get some fresh air.

"Not me." Johnny shook his head. I jumped up and left, before Johnny changed his mind. It would take a long bike ride, just to clear my head.

I stopped on the way out of Belfast, to fill up and then just followed my nose, not really caring where I was going. After about an hour and a half, I realised I coming back into Belfast through Holywood. I decided I would go in and see Simon.

I pulled into the main gate and the Para came from behind his sandbag wall. I pulled my helmet off, so he could see my full head.

"I'm here to see Lt. Adder, Intelligence, or Major Ellis." I handed him my driving licence and he disappeared into the gatehouse. After a while, he came back, handed over my licence and lifted the gate.

Simon met me downstairs, we stayed outside; I was still very wound up and felt better outside.

Simon listened whilst I told him of all my fears. We sat down on one of the walls.

"Listen, Billy, what you're involved in, has gone right to the top; The Secretary of State and all the top brass are following this." He watched my face. "And it's come down from above, that we need you where you are at present. We're watching all the ports and we're aware that there is a big load of armaments coming in from somewhere in the Middle East." Simon took his cigarettes out and offered me one, "the money the IRA get tomorrow will fund more action, but it's small beer. It costs the Government seven million pounds a week, to keep the army here, then there's the cost in lives lost. We're losing lads every day as well as civilians getting killed or maimed." He sat quietly for a while and let me digest this information. "If we could shorten this conflict by a week, a month, or maybe a year, think of that?" I sat there taking all this in. He needed to build me back up more, "I'm sure there's a medal in this for you." I kept eye contact with him trying to evaluate, what he was saying. "Ellis and the top brass, they know what you're doing; they know what you're going through." He paused, "If it all goes tits up, remember this, you're only following orders. You'll be pulled out of there so quickly. Your tracks will be covered, you'll be the hero. One last thing, how many men would it have taken, to get someone in as far as you?" I took the last drag out of my cigarette and threw it on the ground.

"Okay, I need a good night's sleep now." Simon patted me on the back, which was as much as he could do.

I wandered down to the food hall and filled my plate, ignoring the four Para's giving me grief, making remarks about the length of my hair. I couldn't finish the meal.

On the way back, I filled the tank to the top; I didn't want to run out tomorrow. Although I was in bed by ten, I didn't fall asleep until well after two.

Friday 7th July 1972.

The next morning, I was wide awake at five thirty. I lay there for a few minutes, but started to fret, so I got up and had a bath. I couldn't finish the toast I'd made, I just chain smoked, as I drank my tea. I rode round to the O'Neil's house and stood the bike outside. I checked again that my pistol was in my pocket. The front door was open, the kitchen was full. I stood in the corner, while Tommy gave his final orders.

"Then on Sunday morning, we all meet upstairs, in Jenson's and I'll have your shares. It's a thousand each for soldiers and two thousand for commanders and that's the way it is."

Tommy looked round to see if anyone was going to disagree. No one said anything. A thousand pounds was more than they could ever save.

Johnny climbed onto the back of the bike and the rest got into the removal van, to be dropped off at their respective places. Tommy's job was now done and he went to the bus depot; he had a meeting with the bus management. He would have an alibi.

As we rode to the docks, it was our job was to find out which vehicle they were using and run round and tell the each of the drivers.

We put our scarves around our faces as we stood on the side of the road waiting. Every minute felt like an hour, but eventually the short minibus bus came along, the same one they had used last week. We let them pass rode to where the ram vehicle was sitting and told Jacky Woods what they were driving. He gave Johnny the thumbs up, but stayed in his cab. I wondered what people thought of a driver sat high up in an earth moving truck, wearing a helmet. We drove on and told the next lorry, which was a flat-back, still with its load of coal; it had just been stolen that morning; then we were off to the bank on the High Street. They'd loaded up the money and were shutting the back doors, as we rode past. We turned right at the end of the road, the trucks followed. I was trying to stay just far enough ahead, so I could keep an eye on everything. The minibus turned off, exactly as we had expected.

I raced ahead even more. As I passed the coal lorry I beeped the horn to warn the driver the bus was coming. Then I went under the bridge and beeped Jacky Woods sat in the earth moving lorry. I pulled over to the side of the road, Johnny leapt off the bike and I stood the bike on its stand.

As the bus came down the road it moved out to pass a car parked under the bridge and at that moment Jacky pulled out and with he heavy truck and drove straight into the bus full on. The bus had nowhere to go. The back of the bus lifted up, the driver shot halfway through the windscreen.

That would have been enough but the coal lorry sped up behind and rammed into the back of it, surely anyone in that bus would have had all the fight knocked out of them.

I followed Johnny under the bridge. All the windows in the bus were out, steam pouring out of the front, the driver half in half out covered in blood. Four of the men, who until now had been sitting in the back of the removal lorry, now ran over. One was carrying the old Tommy gun and the rest had sawn off shot guns or pistols.

One of the men in the bus had started to get up; he would have been better off staying down. The first man on to the bus, who was carrying a shot gun just fired straight at the head of the stunned guard, bits of the guards head had gone out of the smashed window.

"Stay down." The gunman was wasting his breath; everyone else had been knocked unconscious or was in no position to get up.

There were four big, heavy, black, padlocked boxes. The men quickly got them out of the bus and across the road into the removals van. Then every one jumped into the back of the van, including Johnny, which took me by surprise. I couldn't leave that way my bike was still on the other side of the bridge. It was registered to me at my address and I'd only covered up the number plate with a piece of cardboard and black sticky tape.

I turned and ran back, past the carnage under the bridge. People were starting to come out of near by offices. I still had a scarf on my face and still wore my helmet. I pulled the pistol out of my waist band. I had no intention of letting anyone stop me get away.

I jumped onto the bike and kick started first time. I didn't want to ride under the bridge, the gap was too small and I'd be vulnerable to someone stopping me and pulling me off my bike. I knew the area well and decided to go the opposite way down, into the dock area. Then I left the docks by the Dee Street exit and made my way back home, my part was done.

I now needed to get rid of the bike. The doorbell rang, as I went in the shop.

"Hello my friend." Sid, the shop owner was behind the till as usual. I was good business to him; I paid good rent, kept quiet and didn't cause him too much trouble with the flat.

"Hi Sid," I closed the door, "Could I put my motor bike in your back yard, I'm worried someone'll try to pinch it."

"Sure, sure. Anything to help, I'll open the back gate now."

He yelled through to his wife, "Mallika, come and watch the shop." His wife came out smiling and Sid went through to the back.

I had to rev the bike quite hard, to mount the back step and the exhaust made a scraping sound, as I pushed it hard to get it over the sill. Sid had to move his dustbin and I nearly dropped the bike, but we managed to get the bike inside. Sid didn't say anything when he watched me remove the cardboard, off the number plate.

"I don't use it that much, so it might be here for a while." Sid closed the back gate and bolted it. I never saw that bike again.

I let myself in to the flat and hid the gun under the floorboards, beside the phone. I then stripped all my clothes off and got dressed in a fresh set. To get rid of the clothes, I got a brown paper carrier bag, from the kitchen, which was big enough for the helmet and the clothes.

I left the flat and turned straight down the back lane. There were dustbins outside most of the back gates, but I chose to go a bit further and crossed over the street, into the next alley. The first couple of dustbins were full, but the third one had loads of room. When I got back to No.37, I put the kettle on. While that boiled, I scrubbed my hands making sure I got under the nails, I didn't want any trace of gun oil on me.

It was still only twelve fifteen. I put the radio on and sat on the sofa, waiting for the twelve thirty news. There was a quick mention in the news that a man had been shot in the dockland part of Belfast, but no mention was made of the wage snatch. By half past two, I'd had enough of waiting and decided to go round to Johnny's house. There was no answer there, so I wandered along to the bus stop and caught the bus to Holywood.

Ellis and Simon listened carefully, making notes of who was on the raid, asking questions every now and again. To talk it through did help me come to terms with what I'd been involved in and also somehow getting the nod of approval.

I didn't stay long I thought I might be missed. If Johnny came by, I wouldn't have an excuse to be out of the flat, so after the meeting, I left and went back to No.37.

Just before the six o'clock news, there was a knock on the door and a quick look out of the top window, told me it was Johnny. He followed me up the stairs.

"Where the fuck did you go to." He didn't sound too angry though, just one of his normal greetings.

"I wasn't leaving the bike there, I had to get rid of it and you fugging left me on my own." I sat down in the lounge,

Johnny threw a paper bag onto the table, he was smiling from ear to ear.

"Well I wasn't letting that money go off with them thieving bastards." He pointed to the bag, "Go on have a look." I hadn't really taken much notice of the bag. "Go on," he persisted.

I opened the bag it was half full of bundles of pound notes, still with the bands around each bundle. I looked at Johnny, he grinned and nodded.

"Six grand each." He took the bag off me and poured the money over my head.

"Six fucking grand." I sat there, amazed. "There was nearly a quarter of a million pounds in them boxes, a quarter of a million." While I sat there in a puddle of money, Johnny told me what had happened after he'd left me to dispose of the bike.

"Well after the removals van was torched and them lot disappeared, Seamus Docherty and me took the boxes back to his house and counted the money." He beamed at me, "We couldn't believe how much money there was and guess who turned up."

I just sat there, how could I have known? "Noel Douglas himself," he announced.

"I'd fucking turn up as well, if you were giving me sacks full of money." This appeared to go over Johnny's head, either that, or he just chose to ignore it.

Johnny said, "Well I'm happy with six fucking grand, for less than two day's work." I looked at Johnny, he looked very pleased but I wasn't sure he had thought of the consequences, if we got caught.

"Let's just hope no one talks." I said as I stacked the bundles of money in neat piles. "Every one of those men will be dying to tell someone about today and when they do, that person will tell some else and the next thing you know, we'll all be banged up."

Johnny nodded; he'd started to see where I was coming from.

"They won't talk, no." He thought about it a bit longer. "No, they won't talk, my Dad'll see to that." But Johnny still had a worried look on his face.

I wanted to get out. "Come on, let's go into town and have a ball." I looked at Johnny. He thought about it for a few seconds, and then his face broke into a smile.

"Why not?" He jumped up, "I'll go and get ready."

He disappeared down the stairs, leaving me to find a place to hide the cash. Eventually, I just put it under the floorboards, with the direct phone line. If someone was looking that hard, I was in big trouble anyway, but just in case, I left ten pound notes on the table in the lounge. If anyone did burgle the flat, they might be happy with that, after all it amounted to half a week's wage.

I jumped in the bath and dressed in some of my new clothes, made my way to Johnny's house. I was surprised to find him ready, not that he'd done much, just changed his jeans.

We walked over the Albert Bridge, being careful. You always had to be careful in places which Catholics and Protestants both used. It had been a way of life, even before the troubles.

I don't remember getting home, what I do remember is saying, "Never again."

When my head did get sorted, I couldn't get rid of the feeling, that I'd said something stupid.

I met Denise on the following Saturday night and we
repeated the pattern set on our last date. A few drinks, then back
to my place early. I think we were starting to fall in love at this
point, I know I was. I loved her easy smile and smooth white skin
and the passion. We lay in bed, until just after eleven and then
walked her round to the taxi office. The taxi came too soon for
me, but she had to be home. I gave her two pounds to cover the
fare and kissed her goodnight.

"I'll see you on Thursday."

The taxi roared off, I was left there watching it go.

On Sunday morning, Johnny knocked on the door. I was
daydreaming about Denise and almost jumped through the roof,
even though I had been expecting a knock.

"Are you not ready yet?" Johnny was carrying a small,
cheap suitcase.

"What's in the bag?" I pointed at the case.

"It's the money for the boys." He held it up. "My Dad
didn't want to be carrying it around, so we're taking it. You'd
better hurry up."

We entered the upstairs room of Jenson's and there was a
little cheer. Tommy was leaning on the back wall. Johnny walked
over and handed the suitcase to him.

Tommy stood up, "Before I give out the money, I want to
repeat," he leaned on the suitcase, everyone's eyes were on it. "I
don't want to hear of people throwing money around, shooting
their mouths off, or any boasting. Remember if the boys," he
nodded in the direction of the police station, "get to hear of this,
we could all go down for a long time." He sat down and opened
the suitcase. Inside were brown paper bags, with names on them.

"There's a bit of a bonus in each one, Jacky," he said as
Jacky went over and collected his parcel.

One by one, they collected their money, most of them
quickly looking inside, but closing the bag quickly. Counting the
notes, I assumed, would come later, in private.

There was a good atmosphere in the room after that, everyone laughing and joking, before drifting off downstairs to have a pint. Some slipped away home.

"Come on, anyone. Play for a tenner?" Johnny was up for some real pool, to the death.

For most of the afternoon, we played pool.

"Double or nothing" we both called out, we didn't care. It started at ten pounds, but we'd won a couple with double or nothing, straight off and soon we were playing for eighty pounds.

The drink began to kick in, we'd been there for over four hours. The pub was full now of regular Sunday afternoon drinkers.

Over in the corner, a couple of friends of Danny Steele were watching, but we didn't have a game with them.

A hundred and sixty pounds sat on the table, the money always had to be on the table, it was part of the game. Whether it was for a pint or ten bob, it had to sit there as the reward.

The game was cagey, safe from the start. Pocket blocking, leaving the man up on the top cushion, it was part of the game. It was also much harder, because everyone was watching by then, everyone knew that a month's wages sat on the table and egos were going to get damaged.

Every shot was discussed, options, options, and options.

Old men, who played dominoes for two pence a point, started to go quiet. Top pool players, who played for clubs or pubs through the whole of Belfast sat and watched.

"Just lay that ball over the pocket," Johnny whispered in my ear.

The beer was clouding my judgment. "But I could wrap this up, if I run down there and pot that, and then I'll be on the black."

"No, lay up," Johnny insisted. My hands were sweating. The pub had gone very quiet.

"Where the fuck has this sort of money come from?" The pub was so quiet every one heard the question.

"It's the wage snatch money," said a voice from the corner.

Johnny, like a viper was over and punched the man, one blow and he went down, he was wise to go down. I would've gone down just as easily, because everyone knew who his Dad was. Everyone knew it was not worth standing up to Johnny, the price was too high.

"Come on, play." Johnny pointed at our opponents.

But it was not the game that was important now. No, what was important by then was everyone knowing where the money had come from.

Anyone, who would like to stitch Johnny, or his father or indeed me, now had that little bit of information they needed. We played out the game and we won, but we had lost.

Johnny hands were trembling as he collected up the pile of pound notes, we were out of there.

It was drizzling as we left.

I said, "Maybe we should tell your Dad." Johnny spun on his heels. "What? That we just won at pool, don't be daft."

"No, what really happened." We stood head to head.

Johnny knew that we'd done wrong. Johnny knew that apart from putting an advert on page one of the Belfast Gazette, we couldn't have done much worse. We walked back to his house in silence.

I tried again, "I think your dad has to know."

"No, it's nowt to do with him." Johnny was getting mad, his quick temper ready to blow.

"When do we go and see Jonas then?" Johnny didn't want to think about this either, I could see him building up a head of steam.

"Look we'll talk about it tomorrow." I patted him on the shoulder. He was happier to leave things for a while.

"Aye, see you tomorrow." He went into his house,

I continued on to No. 37. On the way back I decided that I was not stopping in that house that night.

Up in my bedroom, I quickly lifted the carpet.

"Get me Simon Adder please." I waited, it seemed like forever.

"What's up?" It was Simon. I quickly told him what had happened in Jenson's. About the pool game and the remarks and Johnny punching someone.

"So?" Simon wanted to find out how I felt about it.

"Well, I think people will be talking." I made it a bit clearer, "I think they'll be talking to the police, or someone who might want a piece of all this money." There was one of Simon's little silences.

"The RUC are involved in this, you won't be able to save me from them." Silence again. I continued, "I need to know, if you've heard anything from the police?"

"Just the normal intelligence coming in," Simon was being guarded, "but I'm monitoring it all, they don't seem to be getting anywhere." I heard Simon shuffling some papers, "They've got a lot of men on the job. What could you expect?"

I'd heard enough. "Okay, but I want you to come and get me if things turn sour; I'm not sitting in jail for years waiting for you lot to get me out."

"All right, phone in later today, I'll have a full update."

I put the phone down and took out all of the money and the pistol, from the hole in the floorboards. Then I got my suitcase from the top of the wardrobe and quickly packed the few clothes I had. I threw all the money and the pistol, into the suitcase as well.

It was still only five thirty in the evening, as I strolled along to the taxi office.

"Hi, I'm going to Newtownards, my Gran's ill. But I don't want to stay at her house it stinks, so I was wondering do you know any bed and breakfast places there?"

The taxi driver smiled, "Sure I know few, I used to live there." We set off.

"So what's wrong with her?" The taxi driver was just trying to be friendly.

"I think it's a heart attack, but I'm not sure. It sounds like she might not last long." It took twenty five minutes, but eventually we pulled up in front of a pub. The driver jumped out and disappeared. I sat and waited.

"Come in kid." The driver was tapping on the door, I followed him inside. There was a strong smell of beer and dust, men sitting quietly nursing their drinks. The landlady was behind the bar.

"It's thirteen shillings a night."

"That's fine." What else could I say?

"And one and six for breakfast." She was trying to earn a bit more, once she'd seen how easily I had taken the price.

266

"Fine." I started to get some money out.

"And if you want the room to yourself, it's another two bob." She was on a roll, a good little bonus.

"Fine." The taxi driver was beaming and the landlady too.I paid her for three nights.

She looked at the taxi driver, "What you having Billy?"

"Just a double." She turned to Billy, and gave him a look, but she gave him a double, anyway, but out of the cheap whisky optic.

As she led the way up the back stairs, I gave her the story about my Gran to explain myself being there.

"So I don't think she'll last long, the dear old thing." She showed me the room. It had two beds. A double and a single, with a wardrobe, because of the shape of the room was half in front of the window.

"You must be in by closing time and breakfast isn't till nine, we don't get up too early and no lady visitors." She stood there watching, to see if I accepted these late instructions.

We both went down stairs; Billy was just finishing his whisky. I gave him a ten bob tip.

"Do you want another?" I offered Billy a drink.

"No, no, well okay then, just a double." I also bought the landlady one and got myself a pint of shandy. They exchanged glances at my choice of drinks.

Billy had one more before he left, explaining that he'd got a long night ahead of him.

I sat in the early evening, reading the local paper and finishing off my drink. Later, I went upstairs and had a look round the bedroom. I needed somewhere to hide the money and the gun. The wardrobe looked good, at first glance, but it was full with someone else's clothes and sheets and blankets.

Under the double bed was thick with dust and there were some pieces of fishing tackle. The dust told me that no one went there very often. Under the single divan, were Wellingtons, waterproofs, long johns and fishing reels. I eventually went for putting the stuff under the corner of the mattress of the double bed. I laid the money and the gun as flat as possible, and then lay down on them to flatten them even more; I had a little sleep too.

I awoke not feeling very refreshed, groggy really. I washed my face in the tiny basin. Then I placed the suitcase on the double bed, so it would be the first thing seen as anyone came into the room. I took a matchstick and put it in the fold of the lid. If anyone opened the suitcase, the match would fall on to the bed and I would know when I returned. I left a five pound note on the top of the suitcase and memorised the exact position, just one more sign. Then I had a final look around the room, and tried to memorise how everything was placed.

I went down stairs, the bar was busy. There were people playing all sorts of instruments, banjo, fiddle, guitar and whistles and some singing. I bought myself a pint and managed to find a seat. The night rolled on and the singing got louder and the songs became more rebellious. Last orders came and went, the beer continued to be pulled, the songs got louder, and it was a great night. As the crowd started to thin out, I made my way upstairs. As soon as I entered the room, I knew someone had been in. The fiver was still there but was nowhere near where I had placed it. The match stick had fallen out and was lying on the bed. Someone had been in my suitcase. I quickly lifted the mattress up and saw the money and pistol were still in the same place. Then I looked round the bedroom, most things had moved, just a little bit here and a little bit there, but someone had been through this room. I sat and considered the implications, should I carry the money with me, it was fairly bulky, or leave it where it was. I fell asleep, still not sure what to do.

The next morning, when I awoke, it was still too early to get breakfast. I thought I'd have a nice lie-in. I put the radio on, to listen to the morning news.

BBC, Radio Ulster.

Over twenty men have been arrested in dawn raids throughout the province. The RUC stated that most or all the men involved in the wage snatch, which is believed to have netted the raiders over half a million pounds, have now been rounded up. The raids started at four in the morning and have been going on all morning. Chief Inspector Thompson of the RUC went on to say........

268

I shot up in bed, my heart went into overdrive. I leapt out and got dressed. There was no sound of the landlady, or anyone else about. I made the bed; I didn't want anyone else touching it. I quietly went downstairs and went to open the front door, but it was bolted, a strong iron bar was across it and there was a big brass padlock. I stuck my head into the bar; a strong smell of stale beer hit me. As I made my way back up the stairs, the landlady came out of one of the other bedrooms, wearing a dirty old dressing gown.

"It's too early for breakfast," she said, when she saw me.

"No, its okay, but I need to get to the hospital, to see if my Gran's alright.

She padded down in front of me, carrying a large bunch of keys.

"Well, breakfast will be over before you get back."

"I'll be okay; I'm not sure when I'll get back anyway."
She slammed the door behind me. I walked down to John Street and waited for the bus back to Belfast. It seemed to take forever. I got off a stop early, so I could come in along Madrid Street. It gave me the longest view of my front door. I walked straight past, on the other side of the road. Everything seemed normal and I could just see that my drop trigger was still in place.

I made my way round to Johnny's house and knocked on what was left of the door.

Mrs O'Neil opened the door, she had clearly been crying. I could see the door had been smashed in.

"They've taken Tommy and Johnny." I followed her into the kitchen.

"When did that happen?"

"Four o'clock this morning." She started to weep again; I waited for her to calm down.

"They searched the house, they turned the place upside down, and all of Tommy's union papers have been taken. They even turned the bed, right over." There was a bit more sobbing, "I think they broke Johnny's arm."

I put the kettle on and listened, as she continued with her story.

"The house was full of the dirty army bastards, beating her family half to death and dragging them off, to God knew where. Have they not been to your place?" Her eyes narrowed.

"I don't know, I stayed at my Gran's house last night, slept on the couch." It was the first thing that came into my head, "I might not go home now, I might just stay with Gran for a while." I tried to be calm her, "They may let them go, you know they've no proof."

"They don't need proof; they'll be locked up in Long Kesh. I'll never see them again." She started to cry again, I touched her shoulder, but she shrugged me off.

I needed to get out of there. I needed to talk to Simon. I now wasn't too sure that Simon had been telling me the truth, or that I had the protection that he claimed.

"Well I'm off now and I'll try and find out what I can."

She didn't look up. The front door didn't close properly as I left.

I decided to go over and see Jonas, after I'd phoned Simon. I hadn't let him know where I was and I thought he would be worried. There was a line of four telephone boxes on Chichester Street and I had three two bob pieces in my pocket.

"Hello." The pips went and I pushed the money in.

"Hello, Holywood Barracks," a young girl answered.

"Hello, could you please put me through to Intelligence on extension 3232?"

"Who's calling?"

"Billy Deery."

"One moment please." I heard buttons being pressed.

"Hello, Intel." The speaker was obviously eating breakfast.

"It's Billy Deery, can you get me Simon Adder."

I could hear the buzz of conversation in the office, "Lt. Adder, it's Deery, he's in a pay box."

"Where are you?" Simon sounded a bit flustered.

"I'm in the middle of Belfast, I stayed out last night." I looked round to make sure no one was listening, "look have they done my place?"

"No, I called them off."

"What, are you mad? If I don't get lifted, I'm a goner. You either pull me out, or you lift me." I was fuming. Simon muttered something, I just hoped that now he realised his mistake.

I continued, "I've got a few things to do, but I'll be back at the flat in four or five hours. Remember, you either pull me or lift me."

"Fine, be careful." He replied. I hung up.

I made my way to Divis Flats and knocked on Jonas' door. I could see he was drunk, as soon as he opened the door.

"Everyone's been lifted," I told him. He looked unconcerned; his wages came from another source and as for the men, he could have another team set up, in a few days.

"Did you get followed here?"

"No, do you think I'm stupid?" Actually, I hadn't even bothered to look once.

Jonas said "They want us to do a bomb disposal shooting, double money." He watched my face, to see my interest. It was all about money with Jonas.

He looked at me and said, "I need the gun." He took another pull at the bottle of beer. I wanted to stall. I needed to find out if Johnny was getting out.

"No way, we'll be ready in two days, then we'll be up and running as a team." I looked at him defiantly.

"Okay two days, then I go for the gun myself." I was out of there as quick as I could. I made my way back into the bus station and caught the bus to Newtownards.

Back in the pub, the landlady, asked how my Gran was.

"Not too good, I've been with her all day, she wants me to go back to Belfast and not hang around here." I watched to see how this went down.

"Well, I can't give you a refund." She pointed to the beer pump and I shook my head.

"No thanks, I think I'll just pack up and go." I went to my room, the triggers were still in place, so the first look round they'd had last night was enough.

I peeled back the mattress, the money and gun were still there.

I caught the bus, with a few minutes to spare and put the suitcase under my seat. I needed a safe place for the money. I wondered whether I could I trust Sid the shopkeeper, but decided not. I couldn't take it home to No 37; they'd be searching that place in a few hours. I got off the bus in the town centre, still not sure what to do with the money. Eventually I decided that the warehouse where Jonas had left the gun on that very first day was as good a place as any. I strolled over, but before I went through the fence, I had a good look round to check that no one was watching.

The window had been boarded up again, but the board soon came off and I clambered in. The rickety old stepladders were still at the far end of the warehouse, there was one more rung missing, but it did the job. I hid the money and the gun and made my way back to No. 37.

I phoned to tell Simon I was back.

I made a cup of tea and watched the news on the television. Then, I started to think if there was anything else, I didn't want them to find. I hid the mugshot book under the floorboards. Finally, I poured the half pint of milk away, I didn't want the smell of sour milk hanging around, when I returned. I made two slices of toast with the last of the bread.

My eyes kept closing, so I went off to bed. I kept my clothes on though; I didn't want to be dragged out in the buff.

When they did eventually arrive, it was just after three in the morning and as I was led out, the vigilantes were there to see it. Women came out onto the streets and banged anything that would make a noise, dust bin lids, pots and pans.

"Leave the lad alone, he's not done anything." They put on a good show, but then they always did.

I was taken out in hand cuffs and stuffed into the back of a grey Land Rover, soldiers stood around at the ready.

Chapter 28. Sunday 9th July 1972.   274

They took me to Crumlin Road Jail. The corridors were half lit and no one was there to see me being signed in. Eventually, I was placed in a cell, on the second floor of 'B' wing.

Simon came in the room, with two cups of tea and sat on the edge of my bed.

He handed me a cigarette and said, "So what happens now?" I lit the cigarette and stood leaning against the wall.

"Well what have you done with all the others?" I wanted to know how near any trouble might be.

Simon thought about it for a while, "They're spread all over the province, in police stations, some in Long Kesh and one in Holywood Barracks." I thought for a minute.

"Has any one been released?"

"Yes, most of them, because the RUC just lifted anyone, who could have been involved and they all had alibis."

"So in theory, you could just question me for a day and then release me?" I didn't want to stay here, I'd just needed to be seen to be lifted.

"Yes, OK, you're calling the shots. We've released Tommy O'Neil already. He had an alibi, but we still have Johnny."

I looked quizzically at him, "Why?"

"He had three hundred pounds in his pocket and no way of explaining it." We both went silent.

I threw my cigarette into the bucket in the corner, "Ok, leave me in here for a day, then release me, I'll make the rest up."

Simon stood up, we had a plan and he was happy with it. I sat in the cell all the next day, only being let out for meals.

I was taken into the mess hall, when all the other inmates were coming out. This was so I couldn't communicate with any one. But it made sure I was seen.

Monday 10th July 1972.

The next morning I was released and went straight round to see Jonas.

I told him why I hadn't been to collect the gun.

"We must work, we have a job." He kept looking at his watch, he was clearly in a hurry.

"Okay, just tell me where and when." I needed to stay in the loop.

"It vill be more difficult, they want a bomb disposal, that's what they want." He shrugged and nodded his head.

This was something I was not happy with, it made it too personal, too selective and it made me realise I'd had enough.

"Can you have the gun by tomorrow?" Jonas asked.

"Of course."

"We set it for tomorrow, a package, a phone call." Jonas made a pistol with his hand, "Poof."

I kept a straight face, this was not the time or the place, but it was soon approaching.

I walked home, it's just one of those things, walking helps me think.

At my front door, I got out the key, but of course it didn't work, the door had been repaired and a new lock fitted. I went round to see Sid.

"Hi Sid, my key doesn't work." He finished giving change to an old lady, a regular and opened the till. He took out a key. "This is the second time my friend, are you a bad lad?'

"No, no, there's someone who looks like me and they keep lifting me." I put my best innocent look on, "Any way, how much did it cost? I'll pay you."

The receipt was right in front of him. He picked it up and showed me. It was almost half a week's rent. I got a pint of milk out of the crate and picked up a loaf.

"What's the damage altogether?"

He nodded his head as he added it up. "Two pounds twenty one."

I paid up and he smiled, we were friends again.

The lock had been put on badly and was stiff, but eventually the door opened. I made my way upstairs, expecting chaos. All the cupboard doors were open and the sofa cushions were on the floor, but they hadn't really done much and most important, the carpet was still down in the bedroom. I made a cup of tea and got on the phone to Simon.

Simon had been waiting for my call and picked up the phone immediately.

"I've been to see Jonas, we start work again tomorrow. Simon, he wants to shoot a bomb disposal, it's all planned. I'm not happy. I can't justify this; we have to stop this now. I think you should just lift the man. Cut and run."

Simon took his time answering me, "Those higher up the ladder decide. They know what's going on, right up to the Secretary for State, this is big beer. I wouldn't be surprised if the Prime Minister knew that this was going on."

I was starting to feel trapped. I hadn't been in control of what was happening, but a least until this point, I felt I had a get out clause. My batteries had just run out.

"Alright, alright I get the message." I hung up without saying good bye. The phone didn't take incoming calls, so Simon couldn't ring me back.

I quickly tidied the flat, and then went round to the chip shop.

On the way back, I called at Johnny's house. I didn't go in. Johnny was still banged up and Tommy was at a meeting.

I talked to Johnny's mother on the doorstep.

"I thought I'd just let you know that I was out, no evidence against me and my Gran covered my arse, with a few lies about me cutting the grass all day."

The next morning I knocked on Jonas' door, bright and early. He was dressed and ready to go and seemed unusually sober. He made two cups of tea; I looked out of his window, which overlooked a small army station across the road. They'd taken over an old builder's yard, which had an arch door entrance and on each side of the gate, they'd put big steel Sangers, with camouflage netting strewn over.

Jonas handed me my tea. "So where is Johnny?"

"Still inside I think, he had money on him when they called." I took a slug of my tea, it was still very hot. "My grandmother gave me an alibi; she said I was cutting her grass all day." I looked at him to see how he accepted my explanation.

"Well, we don't have time to get someone else in. Will you be able to get the gun on your own?"

"Sure." I wondered if Kathleen Kerry would be in, if she was, I could still carry the gun on my own.

As we finished our tea Jonas, went over the plan.

He was to meet me at the junction, where the attack would take place. I had to be there, with the gun, no later than two thirty.

I checked his wall clock with my watch and left. I had quite a few things to do before two thirty. First, I went round to Kathleen's house.

As she answered the door, she asked where Johnny was. She popped her head out of the door and looked both ways and waved me in. "He's in nick, he got lifted." I went through to the kitchen.

"Do you want a cuppa?" She started to put the big kettle on the stove.

"No, I've just had one thanks, but I need the gun." I opened up the cupboard and lifted the floorboards. The bag inside was damp.

"Go on then I'll have one." The gun's metal was showing a bit of rust, if Jonas saw that, he'd go mad. I planned on cleaning it, while I drank my tea. While Kathleen made the tea, I told her about the hold up and how we'd been arrested. All the while, I cleaned the gun and oiled it. When I thought it was good enough for the Sergeant Major to inspect, I split it into two and packed it away carefully, putting the two badminton racquets on top.

"I'd better be going, time's a bit short." I gave her a peck on the cheek. I'd never done this before, but I knew I'd never see her again.

I was in one of those situations, where I had to take big risks, today. I had to carry everything myself.

I caught a number seven bus, only three stops, but I was in a hurry and the bag was quite heavy. Four pence well spent. From there, I walked over the Albert Bridge and made my way to the warehouse, where the money and pistol were stored.

The duffle bag was getting full, what with the money rammed in, as well as the gun and racquets and a tee shirt and shorts on top. I threw away the old towel. I checked the pistol. It

277

was a little dry, so I gave it quick oil. I decided to leave by climbing over the wall; it was further away from prying eyes.

My throat was feeling very dry, so I made my way to Victoria Square and had a coffee in the Wimpey Bar, on the corner. Sitting there, I wondered if I should call Denise. I'd have loved to have heard her voice. I decided against it, quickly finished the coffee and walked over to the bus station.

Whilst I walked, I considered my options. I could have just do a runner, and been in Liverpool before anyone realised that I was gone. Or I could have got myself into Ireland and holed up somewhere in the south. But I didn't think I could leave Jonas, to do his dirty work.

I still had an hour before I was to meet Jonas. I still had an hour to disappear. I was wet through with sweat and took my jacket off.

The number fourteen to Lisburn and Omagh pulled onto the stand, it was the bus I needed to catch, to get to where Jonas would be waiting. I decided to walk, to give me more time to think.

Jonas was where he said he would be, standing at the bus stop. It was a good place to meet; nobody would look twice at someone waiting at a bus stop. I walked passed him, he followed me.

"Pisstt. Hey." I looked round, he was in the doorway of some shops that had been closed down and boarded up. He pushed the door and I followed him in. It was dark and damp. We carried on through the building, past some old shelves that had fallen down. The back door had already been broken open; we went through, into the back yard. There was barbed wire on angle irons on the top of the back wall, with a set of wooden ladders leaning against it. I climbed up the ladders, with the duffle bag still on my shoulder. There, I could see that beyond the back wall, only a yard and a half away, there was another wall and beyond that there was waste land open at the far end. The barbed wire had been cut and hung down on both sides of the wall. A good exit then. We went back into the shop and upstairs. Litter and debris lay all over the place, making it hazardous. The stairs were quite clear. We stood looking out the window.

"The car bomb will be planted in half an hour," he pointed across the road, "then a phone call, with the code word."

I got the gun out, making sure that Jonas didn't see what else was in the bag. He inspected the gun and gave it a clean and oil. I cleared a path across the room, to make sure nothing got in our way, if we had to leave fast.

Jonas made his platform for the gun. There was no furniture, but plenty of scraps of wood. Using a piece of twine, he made a tepee out of four lengths of wood and stood it near the window. Then he carefully tied the gun to one of the pieces of wood. Finally, his hand washing routine. I was trying to keep myself busy, checking the exit, looking over the wall again and removing anything in the way. Eventually, we couldn't find anything else that needed doing and we settled down, me with the bag close to me, chain smoking. Jonas was just watching the view from the window..

Suddenly, I saw him tense up Jonas. I went over to look through the dirty glass, with him.

About two hundred and fifty yards up the road, an old van had been parked, and a man was walking away.

"It's a long way away." I said. I was looking for reasons for Jonas to fail.

"Not for me," he smiled. I'd never noticed before, his teeth were black, some of them were missing.

Jonas now had his angle. He picked up an old shoe lying on the floor and pressed it against the small window, which would be directly in the line to the van. It gave way on the second attempt, now he had a clear line of sight. I went back and sat down and gave myself a good talking to.

Why had I let Simon push me into this? I could've just done my duty on the buses, put my reports in, found myself a girl and had a good time. Why didn't they just lift Jonas, when we'd found him, job done, pin the medal on me and move on. How did they push me into all sorts of things I didn't want to be doing? Why didn't I just stand up and leave, I had money. I did not want to be there.

Jonas suddenly raised his arm, I stood up. I watched over his shoulder, the Army had arrived. One of the pigs had blocked the road, no further than fifty yards from us, soldiers deploying, guns pointing. At the far end, I could see the blue flashing light of the bomb disposal Land Rover. The officer was putting on his body armour and face mask. I stood behind Jonas, my heart was thumping, and I was nearly passing out with the amount of adrenalin running through my veins.

Slowly the officer moved forward towards the van. Jonas was watching it all through the telescopic sights.

The officer spoke into to a recording device, bending down to look under the van.

A shot rang out.

Suddenly Jonas slumped to the floor. The top part of his head was missing. I still had my pistol wrapped up in my jacket. I turned away, nearly fainting. Then my breakfast and the coffee I'd just drunk, shot out of my mouth. I fell on to the floor, I could hardly breathe.

I waited, sure that the army would crash through the door and run up the stairs. No sound, nothing.

Somehow I managed to pull myself to my feet and threw my jacket over the head of Jonas. There was blood all over the wall and window. Through the hole in the pane of glass, I could see the army were still facing the bomb. They had heard nothing and were completely unaware of what had happened in the room.

I untied the rifle from the makeshift tripod and split it in two. Then I rammed it into the duffle bag and put the pistol in on top, easier to get at in a hurry. Then, slowly and carefully, I picked my way across to the ladders in the back yard.

The jump from one wall to another was a bit tricky. Falling then, would have been bad news. I threw the bag down and then dropped to the ground myself. I lit a cigarette, as I walk across the waste ground to the road.

There was no going back now, but I didn't care. I had such a feeling of release. A massive weight had been lifted off my shoulders. I'd done my bit, now I was off. But I didn't know if Denise would come with me.

I walked sharply down the road, wanting to put as much distance between me and Jonas' dead body, as I could.

Slowly, I formulated a plan. No one at this time would be looking for me. Even if someone found the body, it would take a long time to identify it. By then, it was ten minutes to four. I knew Denise would be finishing work at five thirty, so I had to get a move on.

"Could I have a taxi please?" I had found a telephone that worked, even though the box had most of its windows kicked out and it stank of urine.

"Yes, I'm on the junction of Ethel Street and Lisburn Road. I'm a bit late for badminton, so as soon as you can. I've got a duffle bag." The taxi must have been close, because I'd only just lit another cigarette, when he arrived.

I jumped in. "Hi, I'm late for team practice," I pointed at the bag on the back seat, "Could you just drop me near the Ballygowan Road motor bike shops, the court's just round the back." The fare was sixty five pence, I gave him eighty and waited for my change. I didn't want to attract attention by giving big tips.

I'd decided, as soon as I walked into the bike shop, which the bike I wanted. It was middle sized and had a rack on the back to carry my bags.

"Can I help you?" I liked the young lad who came over, no shirt and tie here. He was just wearing a pair of jeans and a sweater.

"Yes, I've been saving up for a year now and saw this bike last week." I pointed at a BSA.

"Ah the Roadster, a lovely bike, it's in perfect nick with only one old gentleman owner." He pointed a few things out to me, but I wasn't interested.

"How quickly could I have the bike on the road?" I tried not to look at my watch.

"I think I could have it ready by tomorrow."

"I'll give you an extra two quid, if you had it all done by five fifteen." I held his gaze.

"That'd be fifty one pounds then, have you got that?" He looked me up and down.

"Sure, cash, get the bike ready and do the paperwork." I started to get the money out.

"And do you want a helmet, it's better to have one." He lifted the bike off the stand and together, we pushed it over to the door of the office.

'No, but I'll take a jacket."

I tried a few jackets on, while he filled in the paperwork and found the keys, "I'll have these gloves too and this scarf and this jacket."

"Okay that's fifty six pounds and ninety five pence," he beamed at me, it had made his week.

He gave me a rubber bungee and we fixed the duffle bag on to the panniers. I could see the handle of the pistol in the top of the bag, but he didn't seem to notice it.

I stalled it twice, before I got it going. I knew I didn't have much time, so went straight round, to where Denise would be coming out of work. I was a few minutes early of course, so had a good look over the bike, while I waited. It still had half a tank of petrol.

"Hi," I called to her as she came out onto the pavement, but she didn't hear. "HEY, Denise." She looked round and her eyes focused on me, she ran across the road.

"Come on, I'll give you a lift home," I beamed.

"When did you get this?" she said, looking at the bike. I didn't directly answer her question, but told her I'd bought with my last pay. "Come on, get on, I'll go slowly." I got on, but she had quite a hard time getting on, with high heels. With her short skirt, she was flashing her stocking tops, to anyone who was looking.

I took the long way round to her house. A few times she tried to talk to me, but I needed to keep my eyes on the road.

Eventually I stopped the bike, in a lay-by. She got off too and I stood the bike in the stand and put my arms around her. After a quick kiss, I pulled back.

"I'm leaving here, I've have got to get out." I watched her face; she was confused and looked hurt.

"Where are you going?" "I'm going to England, anywhere really, I just have to get away from here." A tear was welling up in her eyes.

"I want you to come, but I'm leaving tonight. You can come later, or you can come now. I've got money, plenty of money, but I've lost my job and I want out of this place, so I'm off." I gave her time to think, but my heart was pounding.

"I'll go and pack," she said. I nearly did a somersault. I kissed her on the lips.

"Don't bring too much, we have to travel light. I'll meet you here in an hour." I kissed her again. She walked off in the direction of her house and as I rode past her, I shouted, "Wear jeans and some warm clothes." Then I sped off.

I still had one more thing to do.

I made my way round to The Divis Flats and parked the bike right outside the army depot. I thought no one would touch a bike, right in the front of the army Sangers. From there, I went up to Jonas' front door. I didn't know if he had strong locks, or any other nasty surprise waiting. I launched myself at the door; it gave way, with just one push. It flew open and I quickly closed it behind me. I could smell the stale beer immediately.

I took the pistol out of the duffle bag and stuffed it into my belt, then started to search the flat. It didn't take long. In the back edge of his dirty mattress, there was a slit.

I was so pumped up, I ripped it open easily, to reveal rolls of notes, each with an elastic band round. Some of them were rolls of fivers. There were some rolls of foreign money too, which I threw on the floor. Then I had to get rid of some of the stuff in my duffle bag, to make room for the notes.

Nobody was around, when I returned to the bike.

Denise was already standing in the lay-by, as I pulled in. It was me who was late. Her small brown case just fitted on the rack and I fastened it with the bungee, she hung the duffle bag over her shoulder.

I'd no plan where we should go, I just followed my nose, why should I worry, I had my girl, I had cash to keep us for a couple of years and I had my life.

Chapter 29. 10th July 1972.   285

BBC Radio 4   The Secretary of State for Northern Ireland, Mr William Whitelaw has been in secret talks with the IRA, he announced today in Parliament………

The evening, Tuesday 11th July 1972

I rode out of hell that night. Eventually, we found ourselves going south towards the border. I was heading to Dublin, for the ferry to Holyhead.

We went over the border at about eight thirty and filled up the tank at Dundalk. Then it was time to look for a bed. We continued on the Dublin Road, for another twenty minutes, and then pulled in to Dunleer. On the main road was a pub. I parked around the back and we went in. with Denise.

It was a typical local pub and quite full. Everyone in there, watched as we put down our bags.

"Can I have a pint of that," I asked and pointed at one of the pumps, "and a gin and tonic please?"

"Is she old enough?" The grumpy barmaid said, nodding towards Denise.

Denise was quick to answer for herself, "I'm nineteen." I wanted to get a bed in the pub, so I kept my head down.

She pulled the pint and poured the drink, "That's forty seven pence."

"Get yourself one too." I said and smile weakly.

"Sixty seven pence, then." I think it helped.

We sat down with our drinks; I made sure plenty could see the badminton rackets sticking out of the duffle bag. Anyone carrying badminton rackets can't be all that bad and anyone using a duffle bag, in that day and age, must be old school. I didn't like to think what they would say, if they knew it contained a sniper's rifle, a pistol and a small fortune in cash.

We kept ourselves to ourselves, for the first drink, just letting people see we were no threat. I let Denise go up for the next round. Women in this part of the world didn't do that, unless they had no man to get them.

I overheard Denise charming the man behind the bar, "Yes, Billy's playing for Ulster in Dublin tomorrow afternoon, but he's up against one of your best players." She handed over the pound note, "and get your self one and your wife." He smiled and thanked her. "We need two rooms for tonight, have you got any?"

I think, because we had asked for two rooms, which meant there was going to be no funny business, as well as twice the profit, the woman jumped in quickly.

"We have rooms, one pound per room and that includes breakfast." Denise looked round to me and I nodded.

"Well that would be great, such a nice pub." Denise played it to perfection.

We took our bags up stairs and were shown to our rooms.

I pulled my bed away from the wall, to reveal a small built in cupboard. It was a struggle to open the door, which was stuck with paint, but that suited me.

Clearly, it hadn't been opened many times in the last year or so. Inside the cupboard were old newspapers and a great deal of dust, perfect.

I stacked the rolls and bundles of money and lay the two parts of the rifle on the cupboard floor and closed the door. I then pushed the bed back into place. I placed the duffle bag on the bed, with just a bit of the pillow over the string handle. Anyone lifting the bag wouldn't be able to replace it in exactly the same position.

Denise tapped on my door and we went down stairs for more drinks.

It was a good night, a few musicians played in the corner and the pub was full. We went to bed after last orders. The landlady knocked on my door to say goodnight as I was just dropping off. I grunted in reply. Then I heard her knock on Denise's door and she replied, "Goodnight." The landlady went to bed happy.

We ate breakfast at one of the tables in the pub. I left the black pudding, but Denise ate the lot. The room had a smell of stale beer, which put me off my appetite.

I slipped the landlady a ten bob note on the way out and told her if we played in the South again, I'd drop in.

We took the Dublin Road and rode slowly, stopping off in lay-bys, now and then, for a cigarette. I didn't really give much thought to the mess I'd left behind.

We made our way to Dublin city centre and easily found a parking space, down a side street off O'Connell Street. I went and bought a full set of clothes and some towels and washing gear. Then we went to Woolworth's and bought a small suitcase, just big enough to fit the rifle in diagonally. I enjoyed putting my old Donkey jacket in the bin. After lunch, in a café overlooking the Liffey, we got back on the bike and rode down to the docks.

I went to enquire about sailings; there were four each day. I booked our tickets for two adults and a bike.

The sun was shining, as we sat on the pier, watching the ferry unload. Later, getting the bike up the ramp was a bit tricky, but I soon had it tied to a stanchion, with the ropes provided by the sailors.

The crossing was calm and we both had a holiday feeling. I'd deliberately booked to Holyhead, rather than Liverpool. It would have been too hard, not to call in on my mother, if I had booked to Liverpool. Also, though I didn't know whether the Army would be looking for me, one of the first places they would look would be my mother's.

It was getting dusk as we offloaded; I stayed at the back, not wanting to be caught in the rush. We still didn't have a plan, just getting away from Belfast was enough.

The A55 was the easiest way out of Holyhead, so we took that, until we saw a sign 'Rhyl 3 miles'. It was a holiday town; there'd be lots of accommodation.

That night, we stayed in a small bed and breakfast and the next morning had a lie-in. Over the greasy eggs and cheap bacon, we talked about what we wanted to do. Denise still didn't know what I was running away from. I think she thought I just wanted to be out of the Troubles.

"Do you know anyone we could stay with?" she asked. There was my mother of course, but I knew we wouldn't be welcomed there, well not for more than a cup of tea anyway.

"I don't fancy my mother's house." I said.

We had the whole of Britain to choose from, we were spoilt for choice really. Denise talked about the life we could live in London and then about other places, she'd heard of. I listened, but I also pondered over telling her who I was and whether I should go back to my own accent. Not that, by then, I knew what my real accent was. I'd been talking with an Ulster twang for so long; I thought I might never get rid of it.

"I once saw pictures of Cornwall in a magazine, lovely seaside pictures." Her eyes glazed over, as she spoke of sunny coastal towns, nestling at the end of rivers.

"Okay, that'll do me. We can get jobs, find a place to live and settle down." She grabbed my hand over the table and held it tight.

"Oh can we?" A small tear ran down her face, which she quickly rubbed away, leaving a smear in her makeup. But she still looked beautiful.

We left the rest of the breakfast and packed up the bike. It rained most of the day, so we only got as far as Bristol. We stopped at a small hotel, and then carried on the next day. The weather was much better, but the roads to Cornwall were hard work.

It didn't take us long to get settled. We had ended up in a fishing town called Looe.

Denise got a job in the second week. She just happened to be in the right place at the right time and the dentist was a randy old sod. He knew the value of a nice looking girl, who would be there passing the equipment over.

We rented an attic room, with its own cooker and sink, but a shared bathroom. I was used to sharing coming from the army, but Denise didn't like the lack of privacy.

I eventually got a job on the quayside, lifting fish and generally labouring. Strange thing, I used my own national insurance number and no one ever came looking for me.

Denise left me in the February. It had been nice for the first few months, but we started arguing about little things and then she just upped and left. I came back from work on a bitterly cold day and found her stuff gone. I think I was relieved.

I carried on working at the quay for a few months, drinking heavily and generally making a fool of myself. It was time to go back.

Chapter 30. Spring 1973.   291

I packed away most of the little things you buy to make life easier for yourself; an electric toaster, towels, a bedside rug and took them down to my landlady. I paid my rent for the next month, in lieu of notice and gave her a box of left over food.

"I need to travel light," I explained. And on a cold, damp day, I loaded up the bike.

Over the first few months, I had paid all the cash into the bank. The bank clerks always gave me strange looks as I paid in thousands of pounds in Ulster notes, but I went to different branches, sometimes driving all day, to find a different bank. I always used the same excuse, if they questioned me.

"My Granny died and this is what she left me."   The bank clerks usually cautioned me to invest the money wisely and not spend it willy-nilly.

When I went to say goodbye to my boss, an old sea dog, he said he'd be sad to see me go. He'd been good to me, always cutting me some slack when I'd slept in late and giving me a little cash bonus, when things were going well.

With my suitcase strapped on the back, I got on my bike and made my way up to Wales.

I'd been planning it for a while, so I knew the route and the address where I was going. Late that evening, I knocked on the front door of Jerry Mackie's house. His wife opened the door, a strong smell of kippers wafted out.

"Oh it's you, you'd better come in." I lugged the suitcase into the hall and waited. Jerry came out of the kitchen, wiping his mouth on a tea towel.

"Good to see you boy."   He led me into the living room, we sat down.

We sat in silence for a while, just looking at each other, the clock ticking on the wall.

"How's it been?"   He'd understood the pressures, more than anyone. I burst out crying. He sat and waited. I tried to talk, but went into another round of sobbing.

He handed me a shot of whisky, then sat and waited some more.

"I couldn't take any more," I said quietly. More whisky, more crying.

"I've read the reports son and you did well, very well." He let that sink in, it made me feel better.

I lit a cigarette and told him the whole story. He sat there listening, nodding and filling my glass up as the story unfolded.

I finished, by telling him that the rifle and pistol were in the bags in the hall. We got them out and he inspected them, with a soldier's eye.

"It did the job." He lay the gun on the floor, "I'm going to have to tell the authorities, son." I'd known all along, that's why I had gone there.

"Can I stay here tonight? You can hand me in tomorrow." I was tired and I didn't fancy a night in the cells, after the long ride up. He considered it for a while and called through to his wife.

"Jenny, can you make the back bedroom up?" Jenny came through wiping her hands.

"Yes dear." Off she went and made the bed up.

Mack hid the guns. I didn't care about them. They'd been a burden and a memory, a memory that I didn't want.

That night, we went down into Chepstow and had a few drinks. It seemed like an age, since we'd done this on the night before embarkation.

One month later.

The Army's idea of justice can be very strange. I was sent back to Germany and made to stand trial. It was a general court-martial, so I had my civvy brief. He was young lawyer, fresh from the bar. He'd been sent out to practice and he was just practicing, not that it would have made much difference.

I pleaded guilty to 'absent without leave'.

There was no mention of anything else.

My lawyer made a good job of mitigation, I almost believed him myself.

One hundred and eighty six days, I was given. I don't know how they came up with this figure. Nearly six months, but I was out after a hundred and twenty four days. It was a piece of cake.

I went back to building bridges and digging mines up, that's what I do. But everyone who knows you've done a bit in military prison, give you a bit of respect.

It took me years to remember to always speak with the same accent. Suddenly, I'd realise I'd switched from Ulster to Liverpool and back. I stick with my Liverpool accent now. When men started reminiscing about Northern Ireland, I always just listen.

I never got my tour medal and I never asked for it.

BBC News Ulster.

There have been two explosions in London today, and the decomposing body of a man was found in a fire today, in West Belfast. The Chief Fire Officer, Ken Oldham said 'It's very unlikely we will ever know his identity. He could have been lying there for up to a year............